The Invisible Woman

The Wronged Women's Co-operative: Book 2

T E SCOTT

To anyone who feels invisible, and to those that make sure that they are seen.

Prologue

The room was dark, far too warm, and it smelled of wet feet. The young woman in the balaclava pulled out her phone and turned on the torch setting. A beam of light cut through the air, causing her to wince. She just had to hope that no one was watching.

The balaclava was ridiculous, of course. It made her feel like she should be robbing a bank or perhaps beating up someone who was a 'narc', whatever that meant. But it fulfilled the purpose of hiding her face while keeping her hair out of her eyes in a very convenient way. Funny that the beauty bloggers never mentioned it as a life hack.

A line of worry appeared between the woman's eyebrows. It was all a little too easy. She had snuck in through the back door, managing to pop the lock with a credit card, just as she'd been taught. The night was foggy with a light drizzle that would disguise any signs of her footprints in the back garden. All too perfect.

Perhaps there was a booby trap? It seemed a little farfetched, but then she knew just the kind of devious mind that she was dealing with. She scanned the floor of the kitchen and the walls with her phone, taking care not to shine it directly out of the windows.

She tried not to touch any of the surfaces. Partly because,

despite her latex gloves, she knew that any touch could leave fibres that would give away her presence to any forensic investigator that examined the scene. But also because there was a reek of mould about the place and she didn't want to go anywhere near it.

The kitchen sink was slathered with congealed grease that had hardened into a kind of waxy coating. Steady, the woman thought, now would be a really bad time to puke. Taking a deep breath (through her mouth and not her nose) she began a methodical search of the cupboards.

Nothing there. She had wasted ten minutes of her precious time and she still didn't have the smallest bit of evidence to show for it.

Creeping as quietly as she could, she moved into the hallway. Some old prints were dissolving on the walls. She recognised one of them as The Gleaners, a painting that her granny had also had a print of. Maybe they gave them out to working-class people or something? She stared at the painted women, bent over, toiling at their harvest. There was a moral there somehow, but she wasn't at all sure she liked it. The painting was slightly squint and she reached up to straighten it, then paused. Was there a reason it was like that?

She put her phone down on the floor so that it was shining upwards – next time bring a proper torch, she thought – and carefully lifted the print from its nail. When she turned it over she had to bite her lip to stop a gasp of triumph.

A Polaroid picture with two familiar faces on it. Jackpot. She put the painting back on the wall and secured the photograph in a plastic bag, being careful not to smudge any possible fingerprints. Then she moved into the living room.

The sofa was so damp that it had developed its own ecosystem. It had been brown leather once upon a time but now it was turning a lovely shade of mildew green. She checked her gloves were on securely then forced herself to search down the sides of the sofa cushions. She found a few coins and a football trading card. It was still shiny and not mouldy, so she put it in one of her plastic bags, just in case it might be important.

Still no sign of the main object of her search. There was a tiny WC at the front of the house, and she really didn't want to go in there, but she did.

Would her sense of smell ever recover, she thought as she unscrewed the flush section and lifted the top of the toilet cistern.

"There you are!"

There were two knives in the cistern. Huh. She had only expected one. The woman paused for a second, then pulled the plastic bag out of her pocket. The knives only just fit inside and she didn't want to put them in her bag in case they poked through the thin plastic. Safety first, she thought, remembering her primary school teachers. Never run with scissors probably also applied to eight-inch breadknives.

Time to get out. At least the cottage was small enough that she didn't have to bother with an upstairs. She checked that she had all her plastic bags, then turned off her phone and made her way out through the front door.

"Don't move!"

Two men came out of the shadows, emerging from the fog like something out of a horror movie. The woman let out an unfortunate squeal. Superheroes never squealed, she thought in annoyance.

"Put the weapon down and lie on the floor, face down."

"It isn't what you think."

"Sure it isn't. Just do what you're told, okay?"

She put down the bag with the knives, very slowly and carefully. Then she lay down next to it. Seconds later she felt someone twist her arms roughly and snap a pair of handcuffs around her wrists.

"Stay down until we tell you to move. Can you confirm your identity?"

"Alice Paterson."

"Miss Paterson you are under arrest. Constable, read the woman her rights."

Alice twisted her neck so she could look up at the men. "All right. But after that, you better give my Auntie Bernie a call. She's going to be seriously mad at you."

Chapter 1: Mary

"A training exercise?" Constable Walker's eyes were nearly popping out of their sockets. Mary watched him in fascination. She had never actually seen that happen before. Was it something to do with blood pressure?

"I mean, what was she in training for, the apocalypse? She looked like something out of The Terminator."

Mary wondered if she should speak. Up until now, she had felt it was probably better to let Walker get his rant over with. After all, nothing she could say would make things better. She opened her mouth, then realised that he was still talking and closed it with a snap.

"Your blooming training exercise has ruined my weekend. First, we get a call to the old cottage up by Hillside farm to say that someone has broken in and we need to get up there right away."

"We had permission to be there," Mary said, not willing to let this one go.

"Yes, you already said. One of Bernadette Paterson's many cousins has bought the place and is going to turn it into a 'hot yoga retreat space', whatever that means. But, of course, we didn't know that at the time."

"An honest mistake," Mary said, with a small smile that was not returned.

"A costly mistake, given that two police cars attended the scene complete with four officers who could have been doing other jobs. And what do those police officers find when they get there? A young woman dressed for a night of housebreaking, wielding a knife and fleeing the crime scene."

"Well, that might have been what it looked like, but actually it was a Wronged Women's Co-operative training exercise. WWC for short. Alice was only doing what we had asked her to."

"She was carrying knives. I mean, that at least could earn her a caution."

Mary shook her head. "They were breadknives. And they came from Annie McGillivray's drawers so they're probably fifty years old. I don't think they could kill anyone. Unless maybe they died from tetanus."

"That's not the point!" Walker said, his usually calm voice threatening to turn into a yell.

"I know. We really are very sorry. But I checked the legislation. If you're carrying the knife for work purposes – which our training session would come under – then that is a legitimate defence according to subsection 5c of the Carrying of Knives Act from 1993."

Walker groaned. "You've been on the government website again, haven't you?"

"I just like to know where I stand," Mary said primly.

"Look, clearly there was no intent for Alice to use the knives,

10

so we can't charge her. But this whole thing is a bloody embarrassment all around."

"I know," Mary kept her eyes looking downwards. She was starting to find the conversation a little wearing. She wondered if the kids had brushed their teeth for the babysitter or if they had just pretended to, like they usually did.

"And what the hell is this?" Walker had picked up a plastic pocket with something inside that had been lying on the table.

Oh dear. Mary had been hoping he hadn't noticed the photograph. "It's Liz and Bernie when they went on Slaggy Fiona's hen night in Blackpool. We had placed some fake clues for Alice to find and that was one of them."

"Slaggy Fiona?"

"It's an affectionate nickname."

"Sure. And is there a reason they are wearing t-shirts saying 'Baps Out!'"

"You probably don't want to know, but Slaggy Fiona works in the bakers and –"

Walker held up his hand. "You're right. I don't want to know. And don't tell me about the hand gesture that Bernie's making either, thank you very much."

"We really didn't mean to cause you any trouble," Mary said, trying her best to look apologetic.

"I'll bet. I don't know how I'm going to explain all this to the new Inspector."

"Is it not Macleod anymore?" Mary had liked DI Macleod. He had always struck her as a bit of a sweetheart.

"No, he was just here with the Major Incident Team when they were in town. Now we've been sent a permanent Inspector. Dianna Shearing. That was her in the foyer when you came in."

Mary remembered a young white woman in a trouser suit with her blond hair in a tight bun. A very pretty woman with shiny hair that flicked out nicely at the bottom.

"She's quite young for an Inspector isn't she?" Mary asked.

"Just a year older than me. She's a brilliant officer, one of my tutors at police college."

"Ah right." Mary tried to ignore the smile on Walker's face when he talked about his colleague. It was hardly her business anyway.

Walker sat back in his seat and rubbed his eyes.

"Tired?" Mary asked.

"Of course I am. This shift was meant to finish two hours ago but I've been cleaning up this mess, haven't I?"

"You weren't up late gaming then?"

Walker gave her a tiny smile. "Well, I might have been on a couple of quests. Downed a few tankards of mead in a tavern. Nothing serious, you know."

"I heard that there's a new expansion pack for Fantasy Realms due out this week," Mary said.

"I did too. Might see you online."

"Sunday night, hopefully, as long as the kids get away to their dad's okay."

And that was it. As close as the two of them could get to a relationship, given Mary's complicated personal life and Walker's demanding job, was fighting demons together on their laptops. In separate houses. To be fair though, she had had considerably less fun with all of her real boyfriends, so maybe there was something to be said for whatever platonic weirdness she and the police officer had opted for.

"You're going to release Alice, then?" Mary asked.

"Aye, with a warning. And you can pass that on to the rest of the WWC as well."

"Noted."

"I'll show you out."

The police station was always a bit of a disappointment to Mary. It looked more like council offices than a hotbed of criminal takedowns and investigative prowess. On the telly, there would have been a couple of daringly dressed prostitutes in reception and maybe even a wealthy landowner come to report a devious robbery. Not a man in a scruffy suit who was complaining about someone stealing his bins. It even had pot plants, although she was pretty sure they were plastic.

"Did you just stroke that plant?" Walker asked as they walked into the reception area.

"Just checking," Mary said with a shrug.

"Of course you were."

A young female officer at the front desk turned to Walker. "Did you hear the news? It's definitely human remains out at the B307. They've sent forensics out already."

Mary raised her eyebrows.

"Just give me a minute," Walker said, pushing Mary none-too-subtly towards the door.

"A deceased male, so they're saying."

"Confidential information should not be shared with everyone in the building," Walker hissed. The young Constable blushed red in mortification.

"Sorry."

"Don't worry," Mary said. "I'm a professional."

Walker's face had turned expressionless. He pointed at Mary. "That's it. You. Out!"

She took the hint and hurried out of the reception to the car park. Waiting there were Bernie and Liz, leaning on a wall in a more PG version of the Polaroid the police officer had found.

"You were in there for ages. Constable Walker giving you a thorough interview was he?" Liz asked, with an eyebrow waggle worthy of a sixties sitcom.

"We're just friends," Mary said automatically. "Any sign of Alice?"

"Not yet," Bernie sniffed. "Police harassment it is."

"Hmmn," Mary said, not wanting to contradict Bernie. She could be pretty fierce when she wanted to be. "Tell you what though, something interesting is going on in the station."

"Oh yes?" Bernie pushed herself off the wall.

"They've found a body in the woods."

Liz and Bernie glanced at each other with a look that Mary couldn't understand.

"Do you know whereabouts exactly?"

Mary frowned, trying to remember. "I think they said off the B307."

Liz was already nodding.

"The old military road," Bernie replied. "Bloody hell, you know what that means? The witch is back."

Chapter 2: Bernie

"Sorry, did you say a witch?" Mary looked confused, but Bernie knew that Liz could tell exactly what she was thinking. Had it been twenty years since the last time?

"I forget sometimes that you're new," Bernie explained. "The witch on the hill. We better go somewhere so we can explain."

"Pub?" Liz asked, "There's the Captain's Arms just around the corner."

"Shouldn't we wait for Alice," Mary reminded them. "I mean, it was kind of our fault she got arrested in the first place."

"They can't charge her with anything," Bernie said, rather impatiently. "They'll have to let her go. Didn't Walker tell you that? Or were you too busy making moon eyes at him?"

"I certainly was not," Mary replied with a little too much force.

"Anyway," Liz said, putting a hand on Mary's shoulder. "I'm sure Constable Walker is much too sensible to waste his time with Alice. She can come to the pub when she gets out."

"I'll text her," Bernie said, pulling out her phone. "She won't mind."

Meet at pub on corner when you get bail. Lol.

"Sorted," she said. "Let's get a drink."

When they got to the Captain's Arms, Liz bought a round of drinks and Bernie made a mental note to reimburse her from the WWC funds. Her friend was currently 'between jobs' and although she was too proud to mention it, Bernie was pretty sure that money must be tight. The WWC paid reasonably well, but not on the same level as the high-powered financial position that Liz had left recently.

Mary cupped her hands around her half pint of cider as if it was a cup of tea. "So go on, tell me what the hell's going on. What was all that about a witch in the woods?"

"She's called the witch on the hill," Bernie said, fidgeting in her chair. It was a little too comfortable, one of those squashy armchair types. She preferred to be more upright. "It's an old legend, the kind that no one really knows how it got started. I think there was an actual woman that was hanged as a witch a few centuries ago, and from then on people said it was haunted."

"The bigger kids used to scare us with it at school," Liz explained. "They'd say if we did something naughty the witch on the hill would come and get us when we slept. That sort of thing."

"They still say it," Bernie said. "Ewan came home all upset the other week because someone had said I looked like the witch on the hill. I told him there were worse things to be called!"

Liz coughed. "Anyway, the legend says that there was a witch who lived on the hill up behind the town on the old military road and she was burned at the stake. Her ghost or spectral presence or whatever comes back every few years to get her revenge."

"All right, I get the story. In fact, I'm pretty sure I've seen the movie," Mary said. "But how does that connect to real life bones?"

"The bones were found twenty years ago, is that right Liz?"

Liz nodded. "In two thousand and something. We were students at the time, so I don't remember much about it. They never identified them, did they?"

"No. A man's bones. People reckoned it must have been some poor homeless guy that had wandered off on a cold night and froze to death."

Mary shuddered. Honestly, Bernie thought, the woman was completely melodramatic.

"And people blamed the witch?" Mary asked.

"Not exactly. I mean, we might be country bumpkins but we're not stupid. It was just weird that the bones had been found near where she was supposed to be killed, so some of the kids took the story and ran with it."

Liz wiped the condensation off her wine glass. "The police couldn't find out anything about the killing, so that just made the tabloids worse. They started to say that people were worshipping Satan nearby and the man was murdered because of that. It all got a bit out of hand."

"I never knew there were witches in Invergryff," Mary said. "It's kind of exciting."

"You're all a bunch of witches if you ask me," a voice said from behind them. Bernie turned around to see her niece standing with her hands on her hips. "Leaving me in that police station while you're all off drinking and having fun. Witches, the lot of you."

"Ah wheesht," Bernie said, pulling out a chair. "We bought you one of those non-alcoholic seltzers that you like."

"And a packet of prawn cocktail crisps," Mary added.

"All right then," Alice said, sitting down with a grumpy expression. "At least let me know if I passed the training session."

"What, getting arrested and annoying half the local police force? Yeah, I'd say you passed with flying colours," Bernie said with a grin.

Chapter 3: Liz

Liz was enjoying her glass of white wine a little too much. She had cut back on booze at home when she had given up her job as it was 'non-essential', but that was something she was starting to regret. Dave had already put his foot down about his Saturday nights with the boys, and she was beginning to see his point. Even though she was unemployed, she needed a little treat every so often. Perhaps Bernie would even let her claim the round on expenses.

"No one really believes in the witch, do they?" Mary asked.

"My mum always said it was nonsense," Liz said, swallowing the last of the liquid in her glass. "Mind you, that was because she said they had proper witches in Nigeria. Servants of the god Esu that take animal form and steal people's souls. They actually still lynch people over there if they think they're dabbling in witchcraft. British witches in funny hats with warts on their noses never seemed half as scary."

Bernie coughed to let her know she had strayed from the subject at hand.

"Anyway," her friend said, "because they never identified the body, the local people said it was something to do with the witch. Satanic sacrifices, that kind of thing."

"They said that when I was a kid," Alice added. She was on her second packet of crisps and seemed to have got over her huff at being led away in handcuffs. "At school people used to say if you stayed out until midnight on Halloween the witch would come down from the hill and steal away children. Parents used it as a reason to get us to bed early."

"And now they've found another body," Mary said, her brows furrowed. Liz wondered what she was thinking. In the last few months, Mary Plunkett had gone from clueless admin assistant to fully-fledged member of the WWC investigative team. Liz had learned not to underestimate her.

"The problem is," Mary said after a few moments thought, "twenty years between killings doesn't make it seem very likely that they are connected. And it makes investigating it tricky. Twenty years is a long time, will anyone even remember anything about the last body?"

"If only we still had Annie," Bernie said. "I bet she would have told us all about it."

Liz reached out and squeezed her friend's hand. They all missed Annie McGillivray, the woman who had been kind enough to leave her house to fund the WWC in the first place. But they couldn't feel too sad for the loss of a person that had lived life to the full, and then some.

"At least we have the internet," Mary said, pulling out her phone. "Let's see what comes up."

"Try searching for 'witch on the hill' and 'unidentified body' for starters," Bernie said. "Oh, and you better add Invergryff as well; we don't want any of those Nigerian horrors that Liz was mentioning."

Liz thought back to the tales from her mother about the skinwalkers. Not to mention the poor souls murdered by the mob just in case they might be witches. "No, you really don't."

Mary tapped away at her phone screen for a few moments.

"All right, I only have a couple of news articles from when the body was discovered in 2004, then a few more when the tabloids went with the witch angle. Which do you want?"

"We should be working chronologically, I think," Liz said, the accountant in her showing.

"Was the internet even around back then?" Alice asked. Liz was reminded, not for the first time, that girl was from a different generation than she was. Sometimes, it felt like a different planet.

Mary laughed. "Yes, the internet existed then. Mind you, the Gazette has all the old editions archived anyway, so it's easy enough to get newspaper articles. Here we go, the headline from 2004 is: Police investigate body found in local woodland. Right next to a photograph of Britney Spears, for some reason."

The others crowded around to read the article on the phone.

Renfrewshire police have launched an investigation after a man's body was found on Wednesday in woodland near the B307. The death is currently being treated as suspicious.

Detective Superintendent Johnathan Marr said: "We are looking for anyone who might have information regarding the identity of the person in question. If anyone saw anything suspicious or knows about any criminal activity, we encourage them to report it to their local station."

"Doesn't tell us much, does it?" Liz said.

Bernie tilted her head to one side. "Johnathan Marr? Where do I know that name from?"

"If he was a Superintendent twenty years ago then he is probably retired by now," Alice pointed out.

"That's it!" Bernie said, nearly spilling her gin and slim-line tonic in excitement. "He's in the home. Early onset dementia, poor soul. Mind you, I might be able to get something out of him."

"Should you be doing that, if he's as far gone as you say?" Liz asked. Bernie gave her a look that would scare off a wild tiger.

"I think I know where to draw the line."

"There's no mention of the witch in that article," Liz asked quickly to change the subject. "When did she become connected with the body?"

"Not sure. Here's an article a week later when the police put out the photofit of the man."

Mary held up the picture to show the others. It showed a very generic drawing of a white man with a thin face.

"Well, that could be anyone," Bernie said. "No wonder they never found him."

"That's when the stories about the witch start up," Mary said, showing them the lurid headlines that came up on the internet search. "I guess because the papers never had anything else to go on, there were no suspects, no arrests… they were desperate for something to write about so they chose the witch."

"Or maybe there was something in it, after all," Alice said. They all looked at her.

"What? I'm not saying that the witch killed anyone, but it might be connected. Someone could be using the legend of the witch to disguise the real reasons for burying the bodies there."

"And what is that real reason?" Bernie asked.

"No idea."

"Were there ever any rumours about who the body might be?" Mary asked. "You know, unofficially?"

Bernie shook her head. "I remember one of the local councillors going on about the body, how it was indicative of how much the area had gone downhill. That people of 'different sorts' were coming here. You know, the usual doom and gloom stuff."

Liz couldn't help but bristle at the 'different sorts' bit. "It was racism then?"

Bernie shrugged. "I'm not sure, just the usual fear of outsiders I think. There was a rumour that the unidentified man might have been a migrant worker. Eastern European, over to pick fruit or something. People thought that that might be why they were never identified."

"And what about this latest body," Mary said. "I mean, could it have been from the same time? And they only found it now."

Liz took another sip of her wine. It really was very good. "I'm not sure. I think the police made a pretty thorough search at the time, so it would be unlikely they could miss a second body. They had the dogs out and everything. I guess it's possible until we hear any more details."

Bernie tapped her thumbnail against her glass. "Right, Mary you're on research duty on the old case. I'm going to noise up the Superintendent, see what he remembers. Liz, you're still busy on the Pearson case, aren't you?"

"Up to my neck in files," Liz said, with some regret. She would much rather be on the mystery bodies and possible witch case than a bog standard investigation into fraud.

"Maybe you can help after," Bernie said. "Alice and I can see what we can find out about this latest body."

"So I guess we're taking on the case then?" Mary asked. Three heads turned to look at her. "Of course we are, I was just checking."

"Well, when you think about it, it is the ultimate wronged woman case, isn't it?" Alice said.

"Is it?" Liz asked.

"I'd say so. The poor witch. Probably just the old-timey version of a feminist and now she's being blamed for people being killed centuries after she's been burned at the stake. Harsh."

Bernie grinned and raised her glass. "All right then, let's make a toast. To the witch and clearing her reputation."

They all clanked their glasses together.

"To the witch!"

Chapter 4: Walker

Constable Walker put away his phone where he had been cramming in a little bit of studying and got out of the car.

"Forensics are done!" Inspector Dianna Shearing called out from halfway down the slope. "Get yourself down here and take a look."

Walker was already pulling on his overshoes and plastic overalls. He might not have skipped out of the office as soon as the call came in like the Inspector, but he was just as excited. An unidentified body was the most interesting thing to happen in the area since they closed the Sam Jones murder case last month. Since then it had been the usual uninspiring business of illegal parking and – in one notable incidence – theft of giant rabbits.

Now there was a body found in suspicious circumstances and although it wasn't officially a murder case yet, no one at the station had any doubts this would turn out to be a suspicious death and burial of remains. Again.

It was a weird one, that was for sure. Walker didn't know much about the previous body – it had been found long before he joined the force – but he knew it had never been identified. Was it just a coincidence that this new body had been dumped here? Or was there some sort of serial killer using the area as their own personal graveyard?

"Come look at this," Dianna said, peering into the grass.

"What is it?" They had set up floodlights, but it was pretty dark up on the hill. The crime scene was a little patch of light in the darkness of the countryside.

"No footprints, obviously, but there's a well-worn path here. We need to check with the farmer where this goes."

"Could just be animal tracks," Walker said, looking at the gap in the bushes. Dianna just shrugged, keeping her eyes on the ground. The earth had been turned over in a rough ten foot square where the body had been found. Tomorrow morning they would send out as many constables and specials as they could find to do a fingertip search of the area. It was a long shot, given that it had been raining solidly for weeks, but you never knew what evidence might be lurking just out of sight.

It was a local dog walker that had found the body, as they so often did. Get a cat, Walker often thought when he saw the shocked face of a member of the public with a very smug looking pup running about around their legs. Poor Mrs Cottrell hadn't expected her little Westie to turn up with a piece of bloodstained clothing, that was for sure. She was on Constable Walker's list of people to interview, once she had calmed down and given the dog a bath.

The slope was slippery and Walker had to tense his legs to stop from rolling down it. That would be very embarrassing.

"You need to work on your glutes more," Dianna said, noticing his pained expression.

Walker just grunted and tried to shift into a more comfortable position. Unlike a lot of his fellow police officers, he didn't particularly enjoy the gym. Instead, he went twice a week just to keep in shape for work and was always happy when it was time to go home to his gaming PC and put his feet up. Dianna had always been one of those strange people that enjoyed the idea of working out. They were very different people, which was probably why they were such good friends.

"How long do you think he was in the ground?"

"Pathologist wouldn't say officially, of course, not before he's done his tests. But he reckoned between six months and a year."

Walker raised his eyebrows. "Not killed at the time of the other body then."

"No. We can't rule out a connection, though. I asked around and there are not that many people still working here from 2004. I'll get on the phone to the higher-ups and find out who was working the cases then, but it might take a while to get in touch with people, especially if they've retired."

"I'll ask the locals," Walker said, "this is a small town and people have good memories."

"Good at keeping secrets too, I'll bet. Someone in Invergryff must have known what happened back then."

"Yeah, they don't like talking to the police here."

"Who does?" Dianna kicked at a stone on the path. "In that way it's no different from the housing estates of Leith. Just fewer gangsters in SUVs and a few more sheep."

Walker laughed. "Tell me what you really think about the place."

Dianna rewarded him with a grin. "Come on, you must feel the same? I know you're dying to get back to city life."

"I was at first. But it kind of grows on you."

"You're seeing someone!" Dianna looked up at him with glee. "Come on, spill! You must be seeing someone to be happy in a place like this."

"Not at all," Walker said, a little too loudly. "I just like it here."

"Sure you do." Dianna pulled off her gloves and went back into professional Inspector mode. "Right, it goes without saying I want you on my team for this. Pity you've not passed your Sergeant's exams yet."

"Yeah," Walker shrugged like it didn't really matter, even though it did. "I'm booked in for another go on Friday."

"I'm sure you'll smash it. But up until then, I need a couple of Sergeants. It might be that they send in an MIT and take the case off me, but up until then, I'm going to take the lead. That all right with you?"

"Of course. Can I suggest Neil Michelson for one of the Sergeants? He's a solid guy."

"Perfect, and I'll ask if I can bring in Suzie O'Connor from Glasgow. She worked on that case where they found remains in a garden in Easterhouse, so she might have some good info."

"Did you work that one?"

"Nah, it was back when I was still at the college. Before I split up with Ricky."

"No chance of you getting back together?" Walker asked. He had liked Ricky, been to the pub with him a few times. Very laidback compared to Dianna's almost hyperactive energy levels.

"We're still friends. Well, as much as you can be with an ex. But while he's in London and I'm up here, there's not much point is there? Sometimes you can have all the feels in the world, but the practicalities don't add up."

"I get that," Walker said, his mind flashing to his regular games nights with a certain Mrs Plunkett. "Believe me, I get that."

Chapter 5: Mary

Mary had been promoted to Head Researcher of the Wronged Women's Co-operative. Well, the position wasn't exactly official, but Bernie had said 'find out everything you can about the other body' and Mary had awarded herself the title.

When she got home after the pub, she decided to take the initiative and get to work while the kids were out. Her mum had been good enough to take them for the day and was going to drop them off at bedtime. Mary opened up a new document on her laptop and started typing up what she knew about the 2004 body. It wasn't much.

When she did another internet search on her laptop, most of the results were just linking to the initial article she had found on her phone. But she did manage to find a follow up article a year later in the local paper.

Missing man still unidentified.

The article seemed to be mainly a piece berating the underfunded local police force, but it did include a nice summary of the facts. Mary noted down the date that the body was discovered: 4th of April, 2004, which she hadn't seen in the first article. There was also a brief comment by Superintendent Marr:

Our inquiries are ongoing in the matter of the human remains discovered near the B307. We are concentrating our investigations around the sighting of a white van on the 26th of March. If any member of the public has any information regarding this vehicle or anything else, we urge them to get in touch.

A white van? Mary snorted. No wonder the police hadn't found anything if that was their best clue. She wondered if Walker might give her any pointers on the case. Of course, officially he wouldn't be allowed, but maybe unofficially...

Better to work it out herself, she thought. After all, she could hardly consider herself a proper private investigator if she ran to a police officer every time she got stuck. Mary dove back into the search results. There was another article that she had glossed over at first, seeing as it seemed to be from some dodgy website, not an official newspaper. But the word 'witch' caught her eye and she clicked on the link.

Police cover up satanic links in local mystery. Read on to find out what really happened to the witch on the hill.

Her interest peaked, Mary settled in to read the article.

In April 2004 a body was found, naked and buried in the soft earth of a farmer's field. What the police didn't mention at the time was that the hill under which the body was found is the notorious haunted site of the witch on the hill.

It is, of course, not the fault of the police that they did not understand the significance of the find. The identity of the dead man has never been revealed, and this might suggest that he was brought in for a purely sacrificial purpose. The witch always swore that she would have her revenge, and might this not be a part of it?

It is my intention to have an exorcism conducted of the site. Yours truly will do what the police cannot: protect the people of the town from the spectre on the hill that wishes them nothing but pain and death.

Interesting, if a little unhinged. Mary noted that the article appeared on a website that seemed to be solely written by an 'S Morecombe'. The articles petered off around ten years ago, but there was always a chance he or she was still around. She made a note to chase it up.

"Mum, we're home!"

The front door banged open as her brood flooded in. Mary closed down the laptop and went to hug the kids.

"How was granny's house?"

"Amazing," Vikki said, already reaching for the telly remote. "She made banana bread and taught us how to knit!"

"Of course she did," Mary said. "Did she get you to learn Japanese and how to stop climate change too?"

"What?"

"Never mind."

Mary's mum came in the door, carrying a half-asleep Lauren in her arms. Mary took her daughter and lay her down on the sofa. She was pleased to see that her mum's hair was sticking up on one side and she looked slightly flustered.

"I hear you've been baking," Mary said.

"Aye. I've brought you half the loaf. They ate the other half. Peter tried to put his in the toaster and set it on fire, so that was a wee adventure for us."

Mary stifled a smile. The kids were normally perfect for their grandparents, so it was a bit of a relief to hear that they had been wee monsters for her mother like they often were at home.

"Are the kids still going up to Matt's over the bank holiday?" Mary's mother asked, even though she knew the answer.

"Yes. He's picking them up tomorrow. They'll be gone for four days."

"You won't know what to do with yourself."

Mary thought of the ninety-six blissful child-free hours she had coming up. "I'm sure I'll manage."

"You'd be welcome at the bingo with me and Auntie Val, you know. Why don't you come along, you might even meet someone special."

"At the bingo?" Mary laughed. "I'm not looking to date a seventy-year-old woman. Actually, I'm not looking to date anyone."

"Ach, you're a catch! Someone would be lucky to have you."

Mary gave her mum a hug. She had been worried about telling her about her marriage breakdown, but instead of urging her to go running back to Matt, her mother had embraced Mary's new single status by trying to set her up with half the town. Mary wasn't too sure which one was worse.

"I've got enough to keep me going with work at the moment," Mary said.

"Ah, your little detective agency. I remember you had one of those when you were at school. You even made wee badges."

Mary's smile became rather more fixed. "Yes, well, this is a private investigation firm. An actual paid position, which is kind of important at the moment."

"Well, if Matt could see clear to paying you what he owes…"

"He's doing what he can." Mary hadn't told her mother quite how bad her ex-husband's debt situation was. She was worried the woman might drive up to Aberdeen and batter him herself if she knew what he'd done with the kids' savings. Still, he was managing a few hundred pounds a month at the moment, with promises that she would get more in time. He was trying. Sort of.

"Anyway," Mary continued, "it's nice for me to have my own money. And I enjoy the job."

"You used to be a scientist," her mother said, not taking the hint.

"Sure. And I can use the same skills here. Honestly, mum, it's the best thing I've ever done."

Her mother wrinkled her nose. "If you say so."

"I do."

Chapter 6: Bernie

Bernie had cut her hours at the care home to two days a week, now that the WWC was making good money. Eventually, she would have to make the decision whether or not to leave for good, but that could wait for a few more months. Finn's work was busy at the moment, but that might not always be the case. Especially if he didn't get a handle on his drinking.

At least at the home it was always so busy that she didn't have to think about the problems in her marriage. She had only popped in quickly after the pub to see if she could visit former Superintendent Marr, but within five minutes she had changed two beds and removed a thermometer for Mr Sharp from a place he should never have put it.

Finally, she managed to escape to the East wing where the Superintendent lived in a sheltered accommodation flat with his wife. Bernie had only visited them a couple of times previously, as Mrs Marr managed nearly all of her husband's care.

"Thanks for letting me in," Bernie said as the woman showed her into the small living area. Mrs Marr was a petite lady, like a little bird, with thin blond hair and hands that never stopped fidgeting. If one word was used to describe her it would be 'anxious'.

"I didn't realise Johnny was due a check-up," she said.

"Oh no, it's not an official visit," Bernie said. "I wanted to ask him about a police matter."

"Well now, he will be pleased," Mrs Marr said, offering her a little smile. "Although you know that his memory is…" The hands made an expressive shrugging movement.

"I know."

The man in question shuffled through from the kitchen with a plate of digestives. For anyone not used to dementia, he might seem like a tragic case. But Bernie could tell that Marr was actually doing better than most early-onset patients. He put the plate down on the coffee table and went over to stand at the window.

"He likes to watch the birds," Mrs Marr said. "Will you take a seat Johnny?"

"All right missus," the Superintendent said and Bernie was struck by how strong his voice still was. She could imagine him giving orders in the station and every person stopping to listen to him.

"Hello, Johnny, my name is Bernie Paterson, do you remember me?"

"Nurse," he said and reached out for a biscuit.

"That's right. But I'm not here as a nurse today. I'd like to talk to you about your time in the force, if that's all right with you."

"Thirty-seven years on the force," Marr said.

"That's right, dear," his wife beamed at Bernie. This was clearly one of the Superintendent's good days.

"I wanted to ask about a case from 2004. A body that was found near the road up by the witch's hill."

"Bloody witch. Told that reporter not to write about it, and he still did."

"What reporter?"

"Stan Morecombe. English bugger over from Norwich way. Always looking for a story where there wasn't one."

As the Superintendent was getting more agitated, his legs were jittering in the chair. Mrs Marr's mouth turned down at the corners and she went to get up. Bernie put her hand on the woman's arm to stop her. She wanted Marr to keep talking.

"What did Morecombe write about the witch?"

"Said that the body was being used for some satanic nonsense. Got some priest to come up and do an exorcism! Bloody waste of time. Victim was most likely some homeless itinerant, wandered off the road and died of exposure. No matter what Paul Lee said."

"Paul Lee?"

The Superintendent ignored her and stared out of the window.

"Paul Lee owned the Chinese takeaway down in the town centre," Mrs Marr whispered. "I think he's got a little mixed up."

"Anything else you remember, Superintendent? About the body on the witch's hill?"

He kept looking out the window, and Bernie thought the interview was finished when he said one more thing.

"What did she do with the bones though? I always wondered."

"What bones?" Bernie asked, but the man's head had drooped down to his chest and he had gone to sleep.

Chapter 7: Liz

Like the others, Liz would have loved to get started on the case of the newly discovered body. Unfortunately, she had been tasked with covering the WWC's current paid job, the investigation into the local MP, Hugh Pearson.

She couldn't argue with the assignment. Given that she had recently worked in the finance industry, she seemed like the perfect person to investigate the man's dodgy dealing with the planning office. It was just so interminably boring.

If only he was having affairs, like most of the other MPs seemed to. Or maybe some sort of fetish scandal. Rubber and high heels would be nice. But no, the WWC had been asked to investigate why he had been involved in the recent planning application for a golf course. Liz had never played golf and didn't ever intend to.

Dave had threatened to join a golf club once, but she had seen it for what it was: an excuse to spend more time with the boys in the club bar rather than a brisk walk outdoors.

Her phone rang. It was Iona from New Dawn Home Management, their client in the Pearson case. It was unusual to have a business for a client, but Liz was learning that in the private investigation world, there was no such thing as a typical case.

"Hello, Liz Okoro speaking."

"Hi Liz, it's Iona here, just looking for an update from you."

Liz bit back a sigh. They had told Iona that it would take at least a week to research Pearson's stock holdings and business interests, but that didn't appear to have sunk in.

"We're still in our initial research phase," Liz explained. "We need to see if there are any irregularities in this project, and in any others that Pearson has been involved in."

"The irregularities are there, otherwise we wouldn't have been in contact."

"Of course," Liz said in a soothing voice. She was glad Bernie wasn't the one taking the call. She had less patience when dealing with awkward clients. "It's just that we need to have clear evidence. From what you have sent me we have little hints of wrongdoing, but nothing we could directly accuse him of. If you give me a little more time I will find it."

"All right. I'll call in a few days for an update."

I'm sure you will, Liz thought, clicking the hang-up button. Just as soon as she got off the phone with Iona, it rang again.

"Just had an interesting chat with the Superintendent," Bernie said before Liz could even say hello. Her friend was never one for small talk.

"He wasn't as bad as you'd thought then?"

"I think I caught him on a good day. His wife was a little nervous about me speaking to him, but I think it actually did him good, get his mind working properly for a little while anyway."

Liz grimaced. Like many nurses, Bernie's bedside manner seemed to be to jolly everyone along, whether they wanted to comply or not. Oddly enough, it often seemed to work quite well.

"He came up with a few names. There was a reporter, Stan Morecombe who wrote about the body, and the Superintendent didn't seem to like him very much. He also mentioned someone called 'Paul Lee', but his wife seemed to think it might be the wrong name. I've asked Alice to look at Paul Lee, not that there's going to be anything there. The thing is, Marr is three years past his dementia diagnosis, so he's hit and miss with names and dates. I still think there's more he can tell us though."

"Right," Liz said, her eyes straying to the time on her laptop. She would never get these blooming files finished at this rate.

"What we need to do is make a list of the players involved with each of the bodies. One for this new body and one for 2004. Then we can work through them one at a time. Fancy setting up a spreadsheet?"

Liz sighed. "Bernie, you know I'd love to, but maybe you should get Mary onto that. I've got all the business records for Pearson still to go through. Iona just called to moan about how long it's taking. It's doing my head in actually."

Bernie went quiet for a moment, never a good sign.

"You're right," Bernie said eventually, and Liz felt her

43

shoulders relax. "The Pearson case is the one we're actually getting paid for, so it needs to stay your priority. Send me a list of anything that you can delegate to me or one of the others and I'll get right on it."

"Thanks, Bernie, you're a star."

"I know. Speak soon."

Chapter 8: Walker

Even though it was a Sunday morning, there wasn't a spare seat in the room for Dianna's nine o'clock briefing. She was still the Senior Investigating Officer, at least until foul play was confirmed and they sent in the Major Investigation Team, so everyone was enjoying the chance to investigate before the plain-clothes guys turned up.

Walker nodded hello to Sergeant Neil Michelson who had come in on his day off and looked a little worse for wear. Neil raised his coffee cup towards him and mouthed the word 'rough'. There was also a tall woman with jet black hair sitting at the front that Walker didn't recognise and he thought that might be the Sergeant from Glasgow that Dianna had mentioned. Everyone else was a uniformed regular just like him.

"Morning everyone," Dianna said, stepping in front of the smartboard. "For those of you who don't know me, I'm Dianna Shearing and I'm your SIO on this case. I'm not giving a full briefing right now, because we've not had any of the lab results back, but I'll tell you what we've got so far."

"All right, let's start with what we know, and work towards what we don't. On Saturday evening Mrs Yvette Cottrell discovered human remains in a farmer's field near the west side of the B307. Or more rightly, her west highland terrier did. She called the police straight away, but given that we already had two teams engaged in a suspected burglary, we didn't get out to the site until after eight pm."

The bloody WWC, Walker thought, keeping his face straight. I should clap the lot of them in jail.

"Very quickly, Constable Mackenzie who was first to arrive on the scene, realised that we were in fact dealing with human remains and put the call out to forensics and senior officers. Good work, Stevie."

Stevie Mackenzie, a new lad who looked like he was barely out of high school, flushed with pride.

"I arrived at quarter past nine. The pathologist has confirmed we're looking at a male deceased who has been buried for at least six months, but other than that we'll have to wait for the lab work. Forensics removed the body by eleven, but it was felt best to wait for daylight to do the full search of the area. That is what I want Sergeant O'Connor to organise just now. You'll need everyone you can get, Suzie, so look your wellies out." The girl with the black hair nodded.

Dianna took a deep breath. "I realise I've only been here for five minutes, but it strikes me that this is a good opportunity for us all to earn some brownie points with HQ. At some point they will probably take SIO off me, but until then I want us all to show them just how good a job uniform can do at this sort of thing. And we don't want any sloppiness, otherwise you know that they'll crucify us for it. Walker is going to help me with local knowledge, but I know that he hasn't been here all that long. Who is the longest serving officer in the station?"

Stevie raised his hand. "It's Sergeant Bob Daniels, he's been here for at least twenty years I reckon. I know because he's my Auntie's second cousin."

"He's not here today though, is he?" Dianna asked.

"Nah, he's off sick. Broke his leg last week. He's only just out of the hospital."

"Do you think he'd mind a visit? I'd like to ask him about the other body. Because it was discovered in 2004, the electronic files are patchy at best. I'm waiting for the physical folders to come up from archives, but it might take a while."

"I'm sure he wouldn't mind a bit," Stevie said. "As long as you bring him some biscuits. Bourbons are his favourite."

"Noted."

"Do you think they're connected then?" Neil asked. "The body found all those years ago and this new one?"

"I can't rule it out, much as I'd like to," Dianna said. "It means more work for us, but I want all the files on the previous unidentified body looked at. See if there are any similarities with our case, other than where they were found. If there are we're going to end up working two cases at once. I hope you're all ready for some overtime."

Chapter 9: Mary

Mary was doing Liz a favour. Her friend had called her first thing in the morning to ask if she would go and speak to someone that used to work with Pearson.

"I've got about a million files to go through today and I could use some help," Liz had said over the phone.

"I was hoping to get the housework done when the kids left," Mary had said.

"Liar."

"All right. I was going to have a bath and read the newest Stephen King novel."

"Well, you can do that later. I think you'll like this woman anyway. She used to work at the police station so she might have some inside information on both cases."

"What's her name?"

"Frederica Valentine. Former Tory councillor, now an estate agent in town."

"They won't be open on a Sunday, will they?"

"Nah. I've got her home address. I already arranged to meet her; I think she's dying to give us all the dirt on Pearson. Word is that the local party put him forward for MP instead of her, so she's got an axe to grind."

"Excellent. I'll see the kids off, then I'll pop round."

In reality, it had taken the best part of the morning to get the kids ready for staying with their dad. There were bags to pack and shoes to find and before Mary knew it they were all piled into the car with Matt and waving goodbye out of the windows.

They would be fine, obviously. He was their dad and he was hardly new to looking after them. But Mary might have admitted to feeling a tiny bit anxious about them, while still enjoying the unnatural silence that now filled the house.

A distraction turned out to be very welcome. She skipped the bath and headed straight for Frederica Valentine's place, a modern apartment next to the river.

"I was expecting Liz Okoro," the woman said, looking at Mary with suspicion when she answered the door.

"Liz has another meeting at the moment. I'm Mary Plunkett and I work with her."

"All right then, you had better come in." Mrs Valentine led her into the living room which was double height and in the industrial style with beams in that weird unfinished wood effect that always made Mary think there were spiders lurking in it.

"What a lovely flat," Mary said, thinking – not for the first time – how easy it was to be tidy when you didn't have children.

"Thank you. This building used to be a mill. I just love the sense of space and light. The kitchen is from Magnet, their latest handle-less collection." The estate agent sat down, smoothing her smart linen suit as she did so. She was somewhere between fifty and sixty, but looked like she spent a lot of time doing her hair and make-up in an attempt to appear younger. Mary crossed her ankles to try and hide the scuffs on her shoes.

"You're here to find out about Pearson, is that right?"

"Yes. We are working for a client that has some concerns about a planning project he was involved in recently."

"That monstrosity they are calling a golf course? They are selling it as a leisure enterprise, free memberships for kids, all that nonsense. But of course we all know where the money really is."

"Which is?"

"The hotel, of course. Do you know how much these destination golf hotels make? No one seems to care about the wildlife that gets destroyed in the process. I am the president of the local bat society, you know."

"Fascinating," Mary said. "They did do an environmental assessment, didn't they?"

"So they say. Of course, I shouldn't speak ill of a member of my own party, but it hasn't been unknown for these things to be fudged over the years."

"Do you have any evidence of wrong-doing on Pearson's behalf?"

"Nothing so clear cut. He hasn't kept a marginal seat by being stupid, I'll say that for the old crook. No, everything will have been done legally, on the surface at least."

Mary sighed. "Could you at least give us some pointers in which direction we should be looking?"

Mrs Valentine tapped the heel of her shoe against the tiled floor. "Pearson is careful, but he doesn't always surround himself with people who are equally cautious. Try his associates, at least that's where I would look. That's as much as I can tell you without leaving myself liable."

Mary supposed that was something, although she had been hoping to bring something juicier back to Liz.

"I was told you used to be a police officer," Mary said.

"A long time ago now. And I was a Special, not a full WPC, as they were called then."

"I don't suppose you remember the body found in the farmer's field? The one near the old military road."

"Of course. I helped them search the fields the first time. Would that have been 2002?"

"2004."

Mrs Valentine offered Mary a plate of biscuits and she took two graciously even though there were no cholate ones.

"Ah yes, my last year as a Special. I started the estate agency the next year and became a part time councillor the year after that. How time flies."

"What do you remember from the search?"

"It was piddling down with rain, if you'll excuse my language. We searched a mile radius on the first day, despite the fact there was clearly nothing to find. All the evidence was long gone, washed away by the Scottish weather."

"So you didn't find anything useful?"

"Not a sausage."

"I suppose they will never find out who it was then," Mary said, feeling rather deflated.

"Oh well, the thing is, dear, we did know who the body was in 2004, we just couldn't prove it."

Mary nearly choked on her biscuit. "Sorry, did you say you knew who it was?"

"Oh yes. There was a young man working on one of the building sites. Up from the North of England somewhere, maybe Newcastle way. He gave his name as Paul Dean, but we always thought that it might have been false. Sure enough it turned out that a Paul Crossly had gone missing as a teenager, and it seemed to be the same kid. The kicker was that he walked with a slight limp on his right side and the body they found had a badly healed fracture on the right leg."

"Why didn't the police announce that it was him?"

"As I said, we didn't have enough for a formal identification.

He went missing around the time that the body would have been buried, but we couldn't narrow it down to the exact day. The building site where he worked didn't want to tell us anything. He'd been working cash in hand, and they hadn't been paying any NI or anything for him. We interviewed them a few times but they didn't want to know."

"What was the name of the builders?"

"West Clyde Builders. They've gone bust long since though."

Mary noted it down. "What about his family? Didn't they want to know?"

"Both parents were dead, from what I can remember. Crossly had a sister, but I can't think what her name was. As I said, it's not like we could give the poor girl any closure without proper identification. His face was beaten so badly it was unrecognisable. We tried DNA, but we couldn't get a match."

"Why not?"

"I'm not sure. The body had been in the ground for a while. You'd have to ask an expert. Anyway, the sister didn't want to believe that her brother was dead, we had no proof, so that's where it ended."

"Seems a bit like no one wanted to know."

Valentine shrugged. "Resources are finite. Sometimes, even the police have to move on."

Mary straightened her back. "But not the WWC."

"Is that some sort of sports thing? I play tennis every Wednesday."

"No, it is not. Thank you for your help."

Chapter 10: Bernie

"Well Bernadette, I never would have guessed you were interested in joining the Women's Institute." Mrs Graham, the farmer's wife was giving Bernie some serious Stepford Wives vibes. It was something to do with the fact that she had a frilly apron around her waist. She hadn't seen anyone with one of those since she was a child.

"I had heard that you were looking for some younger members," Bernie said, nibbling on a tiny piece of scone. She hated to think how much butter and oil was sitting in front of her in the form of cakes and biscuits.

"Oh yes, we're always looking for new blood." Mrs Graham grinned with white, gleaming teeth. Too white to be natural. Were they dentures? Surely the farmer's wife was a little young for that. She had to be under fifty. Maybe they were those modern veneer things that everyone seemed to be getting. A few less jam scones and you might have kept your own teeth, Bernie felt like saying to the woman.

Bernie wondered if Mrs Graham was always ready for guests. The farmer's wife had opened the door, lead her into an immaculate kitchen and set out an array of baked goods as if she had expected someone to drop in at any moment. If you turned up unannounced at Bernie Paterson's house you'd be lucky to get an out of date protein bar and a sink full of washing up.

"Why don't you try the lemon drizzle cake? My secret ingredient is poppy seeds. It won first place at the WI fair."

"Oh, I have quite enough here already. I hear you had a bit of a commotion here yesterday. Police cars and all sorts."

Mrs Graham's perfect smile flickered for a moment. "Ah yes. An unfortunate incident."

"The same sort of incident that happened twenty years ago, of course."

Now there were spots of pink on the farmer's wife's cheeks.

"I don't think it's something we should discuss over tea, do you?"

"It can't always be crochet and Victoria sponges, can it?" Bernie said with a chuckle. The silence in the room made it clear the joke had not been well received.

"I hope you're not here to gossip, Bernadette," Mrs Graham said finally.

"Not at all. In fact, I'm here to help you."

"To help me?"

"You might have heard that I have founded a firm of private investigators."

"I had heard that," Mrs Graham said, sniffing as if she had smelt some overbaked bread. "I had rather hoped it was a joke."

"Not at all. Myself and my colleagues work for clients looking to solve unusual problems. Such as finding multiple dead bodies right on your doorstep."

"Hardly on the doorstep. We have three hundred acres around here. The... remains were found nearly two miles away from the house."

"Of course. But it still looks rather unfortunate, doesn't it? One dead body might be considered a misfortune. Two look like carelessness."

"I never thought you'd be quoting Oscar Wilde," Mrs Graham sneered.

"I went to school," Bernie said airily, although she'd always thought the quote was from Shakespeare. Oh well, it sounded good anyway. "I just meant that it won't be long before the press make the connection with the other body."

"Those scavengers. Well, they'll get short shrift up here. Everyone knows that we had nothing to do with any bodies."

"Do they though? I mean, I would hate for it to come up at the next WI meeting."

Mrs Graham put her hands on her hips, reminding Bernie so much of the Happy Families card game that she nearly laughed out loud.

"Bernadette Paterson, I don't think you have any intention of joining our institution."

Bernie shrugged. "Probably not. But I could be an asset to you and your husband, for when the you-know-what hits the fan. Why don't you tell me everything you know about the bodies and I'll see to it that the investigation is concluded as quickly as possible?"

"You can do that?"

"Well, I was at the police station only yesterday, so I think I have some influence there."

"All right." Mrs Graham swept some invisible crumbs off the table. "It was my father that had the farm when the first body was found in 2004. We took over a couple of years later. And now this new body. People seem to think the countryside is the place to dump their rubbish, if it is not old fridges it is dead bodies."

Bernie didn't really see the comparison but she nodded so that the woman would continue.

"The first time we thought it might be someone who had wandered off the road. We're pretty far out of the town, but it wouldn't be impossible for a drunk to come out this far. Maybe trying to hitch a lift or something. But the police told us that wasn't possible."

"Why?"

"Because he was found naked. And it wasn't that the clothes had melted away or anything; he hadn't been in the ground long enough for that. Someone had killed him, then stripped his clothes off."

"To stop him from being identified?"

"I assume so," Mrs Graham said with a sniff, as if the whole thing was a calculated insult to her family. "They never found out who it was. The police put out a sort of digital photofit, you know, the ones that look like badly drawn cartoon characters. It was so generic it could have been anyone. I can't believe our taxes pay those people's wages."

"And there didn't seem to be a connection to the farm?"

"No. As I said, we're just being used as a dumping ground. Just like this new one."

Bernie could sense she wouldn't get much more out of the woman. "So you have no idea who might be behind it all?"

"Gangs, probably. Knife-wielding drug pushers. I saw a documentary on it once. Or… Well, of course, some people think that she had something to do with it."

"She?"

"The witch."

For a moment Bernie was actually speechless. "Sorry, do you mean the witch on the hill? That's just an old story isn't it?"

"Well, Bernadette, when you work the land as long as my family has, you tend to believe in some of the old stories. There is something about that hill. The sheep don't graze there and nothing grows on the Eastern side. There's a ruined croft that used to be the witch's house and I tell you something for nothing, I wouldn't set foot in it myself."

"How far is the croft from where the bodies were found?"

"Maybe half a mile."

"Do you think I could go there? Check it out?"

Mrs Graham shook her head. "I think you'd be mad to go up there. Why mess with things we don't understand?"

Bernie shrugged. "I like understanding things. Why should we be so scared of an old woman who someone didn't like the look of and killed, hundreds of years ago?"

"You think she was just an old woman? She was a witch, and that's the truth. She cursed that hill and everyone who goes there. Why else do you think those men are dead?"

There was no answer to that one.

Chapter 11: Liz

Liz was settling down for the evening with a bunch of the Pearson files loaded up on her laptop and a cup of strong coffee when the doorbell rang.

"Expecting anyone?" She called out to Dave who had just put their son to bed.

"Nope."

Liz sighed and got up from the sofa. She hoped it wasn't Mrs Beetle, the next door neighbour, come to complain about Sean kicking balls against the fence again. The sort of miserable old hag that complained that children were stuck inside in front of screens but didn't want them to play anywhere it might disturb her nap.

When she opened the door she was surprised to see a young woman there instead.

"Hi Alice, how are you?"

"I'm good thanks," Alice fidgeted a little awkwardly with the strap of her bag. "I was wondering if we could have a chat."

"Of course. Come in."

Dave gave them a look and then reached for his tea. "I'll take this upstairs and let you girls chat."

Liz rolled her eyes at the 'girls'. "Thanks."

When Dave had disappeared up the stairs, she turned to Alice. "I wasn't expecting you today. Did Bernie send you?"

"No. I came on my own."

Liz glanced over at her. "Is something wrong?"

"No, not at all." Alice flicked her hair out of her face. "It's just that I've been doing some research on the unidentified body, sort of off my own back."

"Well, that sounds interesting."

"I've written it all up. The thing is, I wanted to bring this to you. Auntie Bernie is great but she's not exactly open-minded."

Liz felt her spine straighten up a bit that this cool young woman thought she was open-minded. She just hoped that she would not prove to be a disappointment.

"I've been looking into the stories about the witch."

Liz tried not to look surprised. "The one that lived near where the bodies were found?"

"Yes. I went to the library today. They had all sorts of old documents that you can't even get online." Alice shook her head in wonder that even the internet had its limits.

"And what did you find?"

"Well, I started off by learning about witchcraft in general. I guess I wanted to know how unusual the witch, or whether the countryside was full of them back in the day. And

62

I found out some crazy stuff. Did you know that there were nearly four thousand men women and children convicted of witchcraft in Scotland?"

Liz was horrified. "Really? No, I had no idea it was that many."

"Mainly in the sixteenth and seventeenth centuries. The witch on the hill – her name was Ruth Macintyre, by the way – was actually one of the last. She was executed in 1703 and they banned killing witches in 1736. And she wasn't burned at the stake. Most witches weren't, not in this country anyway. She was hanged."

"How did it happen?"

"From what I can tell, it started with the woman who lived in the farmhouse. Her name was Esther Finney and she and her husband were the richest people around. So when they said that the old woman who lived in the croft had started killing their animals, people listened. Ruth Macintyre never had a chance at the trial. She was illiterate and could barely speak. She couldn't defend herself, and when more and more of the villagers came up with stories of her witchcraft, they found her guilty immediately."

"This is all really interesting, but I think I know what Bernie's going to say about it."

"That it has nothing to do with the case. And maybe that's true. But there has to be some reason those bodies were left on the hill. And I think maybe the killer or killers knew about the witch and the bodies are telling us something about her."

Liz wasn't convinced. In her experience, people were killed for much more mundane reasons than connections to witchcraft. Money or sex, those tended to be the reasons. Or just a moment of rage.

"Find a connection," Liz said to Alice. "If you can show a link between the body from 2004, or the one they've just dug up, and the stories about the witch, then you should take it to Bernie. As for now…"

Alice nodded. "I know. It's just old stories."

Liz walked her young friend to the door. "Oh, there was something I could do with your help on. Would you mind doing some surveillance on Pearson?"

"The dodgy MP? I'd love to."

"I want to know what he gets up to in his free time. Hopefully lots of affairs and brown envelopes, that sort of thing. But you'll have to be careful. As an MP, he's going to be more security conscious than most."

That earned Liz an eye roll.

"All right," Alice said, "I'll keep an eye on him. And thanks again for the support on the witch thing. It's good to know you'll back me up with Bernie."

Liz nodded and shut the door. She just had to hope that Alice never found a connection between the witch and the bodies on the hill. Liz didn't want to end up caught in the middle between Auntie and Niece.

Chapter 12: Walker

Bob Daniels was a career sergeant. Walker, who was still hoping to make Chief Inspector one day, had always thought of him as a bit of a bore, a man behind the desk who was happy for the younger cops to go out and do the legwork. A police officer already dreaming of his retirement. But it only took five minutes in the man's living room to work out that he had severely underestimated the older man.

"The call came through on a Tuesday morning," Daniels said, his broken leg propped up on an embroidered footstool. "It would have been around ten o'clock because I had finished going through the overnight messages. The caller was the farmer, Tom Bryce. I knew him a little from when we'd had some illegal fly-tipping the year before. He said that he had found some bones on his land. Normally, it wouldn't be a priority you see, but farmers know what animal bones look like, and this wasn't a sheep or a cow. So I put it through as an urgent case."

"Who went up to the farm?" Dianna asked. She had deposited herself in the comfiest chair, a brown leather Eames-style recliner next to the stove.

"Well, that would be Inspector Johnathan Marr, what finished up as Superintendent in the end. I'm afraid he's got dementia though, so he might not be much use to you."

"We'll try him anyway," Dianna nodded to Walker who made a

note in his phone to that effect.

"Maybe you could tell us what you remember about how things went down in 2004," Dianna said. "Especially anything that didn't make it into the file."

The Sergeant gave his cast a scratch. "Well now, it wasn't even that much of a case. We had the body, of course, and there was plenty of forensic evidence. But none of it made any sense. We couldn't even get a definite ID."

"I wonder if we could try again for a DNA match," Dianna said, thinking aloud. "I mean, it's nearly twenty years later, so the lab techs might have more luck."

"Can't hurt to try," Bob Daniels agreed, "although it's a pity the sister wasn't blood-related."

"The sister?"

Daniels raised an eyebrow. "They did tell you about the sister, didn't they?"

Walker could see Dianna sit forward in her chair.

"No, they did not."

Daniels blinked. "The sister of the lad that went missing. Surely someone told you? His name was Paul Dean, but we always thought it might be false. He went missing around the time our unidentified man was killed. Anyway, he matched the description of a young lad called Paul Crossley from down south. The sister was next of kin but they weren't biologically related so we couldn't do a DNA match. We always thought it

67

was him though, even if we couldn't say officially."

"You mean to tell me that we had a likely identification for the first body and no one at the station thought to mention it?" Dianna's tone was icy, but this was somewhat undermined by the fact that she was still reclined on the chair with her ankles crossed.

"I guess there aren't many people left that remember those days. Ancient history. Just like me," Daniels said, smiling to let them know that he was joking.

Dianna's lips parted ready to speak and Walker just knew she was going to say something insulting to the Sergeant so he interrupted them.

"Who else worked the case with Marr? He must have had some Sergeants with him at least."

"Inspector Wardrop was involved I think. Might have been the SIO, but he was a bad one for the drink, so Marr often took over his cases. He retired a couple of years ago. Oh, and there was that teuchter chap, the one that was here last month."

"Detective Inspector Macleod?"

"Aye, that's the one. He was still in plain clothes then, but you could tell he was a canny lad. He was only here for a few months in uniform before he transferred over to the Specialist Crime Division. Course it was plain old CID back then. I remember he was the one that went out to interview the farmer and he was well pleased because the farmer's wife gave him a malt loaf to take back to the station."

Dianna looked over at Walker. "That's the Inspector you were working with on that murder case, wasn't it."

"Yes. Want me to give him a call?"

"Put it on the list," Dianna said. "Thanks for your time, Bob. I'm mindful that this body could have no connection to the earlier one, but you've certainly filled in a few blanks for me."

"I'm hoping to be back in the office next week," the Sergeant replied. "Light duties probably, but it sounds like you might be in need of an old dog around the place."

Dianna finally struggled out of the recliner, not without having to give up a little dignity on the way. "I hope by next week we'll have an ID on our victim and put the whole thing to rest. Maybe it will turn out to be straightforward after all."

The Sergeant gave Walker a Look, with a capital 'L'. The look said that no matter what the higher ranks said, the job was never as simple as it ought to be.

Chapter 13: Mary

Mary managed a video call with the kids before their bedtime. Peter spent most of it trying to show her his tonsils, but it went surprisingly well. Matt seemed to be coping all right and everyone had the same number of fingers and toes they had gone away with. When she clicked off the call Mary sat on the sofa for a few minutes, staring at the wall opposite. It was a strange feeling not to be needed by any of the kids for a day. Four days, to be precise. It left her feeling unsettled, like there was something she should be doing. Washing, probably.

Instead, Mary made a huge mug of hot chocolate and added a generous handful of mini marshmallows. She pulled out her laptop and logged in to fantasy worlds online. She loaded up her favourite character, a bearded wizard called the Great Fandango. Fandango put on his most magical cloak and went out to seek some treasures.

The way this game worked was that you went on quests that had some sort of tangential relationship to a game story of saving the world from the powers of darkness. Walker had explained it all when he had first recommended it to her. Mary wasn't convinced when she started playing – she spent hours wandering aimlessly around in circles – but now she was completely addicted.

Fandango was on his way to an Emerald mine. There were only seven in the whole realm and it had taken her a week of walking and far too many hours watching other people do it on video walkthroughs, but she was there, standing at the gates.

A ping alerted her that another player was approaching. Mary – or rightly, Fandango – spun around to see who it was.

Ugh, some sort of orc-thing was approaching with a crown made of human skulls. Nice. Normally Mary didn't engage in battle, but she really wanted the emerald mine. The quest had been going on for so long that she couldn't remember what she needed the emeralds for, but she was sure that they were important.

The big orc took a step towards her and Mary tapped the keys furiously. The Great Fandango picked up his wizard's staff and started to twirl it like he was in a cheerleading competition. She unleashed her most devastating spell and turned the orc into a very cute pink frog.

Mary rubbed her hands together and walked over to the emerald mine, getting ready to harvest until…

"Damn!"

The orc must have been using some sort of shield spell. He had come up behind her and stuck an axe in her back. Her health line had halved immediately and was still going down. In a few seconds, she would be dead.

From out of nowhere, a tiny elf-maiden arrived with blue hair and improbably perky breasts. A bubble above her head announced her as 'Pixielynn', but Mary knew that already. Pixielynn pulled out a sword that was longer than her body and

71

dragged it through the orc, splitting him down the middle. The body of the orc disappeared and Pixielynn did a little victory dance.

You're late, Mary typed into the chat. *Come over here and heal me!*

Okay the avatar called Pixielynn said, rushing to her side and healing her immediately. Pixielynn gave her a thumbs up and Mary didn't have to try hard to imagine Walker alone in his flat, doing the same thing to the screen.

Just getting some emeralds, Mary said walking back to the mine.

To give the Sorcerer in exchange for a magical tiara, Pixielynn said.

Magic tiara, that was it, Mary remembered now. Although what was the tiara for? Something to do with disguising herself as a princess? She couldn't remember.

Pixielynn took position next to her and they both harvested emeralds until their virtual bags were full. She didn't communicate with Walker – harvesting was a complicated process involving pressing lots of buttons – but she liked the idea that they were working in companionable silence.

Something moved in her peripheral vision and Mary noticed another user standing just to one side of Pixielynn. A tough-looking barbarian woman with plaited hair that reached down to the ground.

Enemy behind you! Mary typed.

There was a pause. The barbarian woman seemed to be looking around, not attacking anyone.

That's Dianna. She's a max-level player. She wanted to tag along!

Mary pushed the laptop away in disgust. The new Inspector, the pretty one, and Walker had taken her into the game with him. Wasn't this *their* thing?

But just as she felt the anger rise in her chest, she realised she was being an idiot. It wasn't a date, was it? Just two friends playing games together. Why shouldn't he bring another friend along with him? She had absolutely no right to be upset.

A hot tear landed on the laptop keyboard. What a fool she was being. Hormones, let's blame them. Definitely better to think of it that way. Just her hormones.

Great she typed, hating herself at the same time. *Tell her about the tiara!*

There was a tinkling noise and the barbarian's hair shimmered into a foot high sparkling diamond.

Already got one.

Of course you bloody well have, Mary thought.

How's the case going? Found any more bones? As Mary typed she knew it would annoy Walker. Well, good.

There was a long pause.

Fine, Pixielynn said. *We're going to the market to buy some new skins, want to come?*

Changing the subject, aren't you, Constable? Mary thought, but at least it gave her a way out.

73

Need to call the kids. See you next week.

Mary shut down the game before the others could reply. Well, if that was what it was like putting herself out there, maybe it was time to get the hell back in again. She pinched the point between her eyebrows and breathed in slowly.

It was hardly the end of the world. In fact, maybe it was a good thing. What was Walker after all apart from a distraction? It was the WWC that really mattered to her now. The only thing outside her kids that made her feel good about herself. That was what she had to cling to.

She pulled the laptop back towards herself and opened the internet. Time to do some more research. She had noted down the name of the sensational journalist that had written about performing an exorcism of the witch on the hill. S Morecombe, was what he had called himself. She started the usual searches.

And didn't get very far. Apart from the website she had already found, there wasn't much out there, at least nothing that was a definite match. As a last ditch attempt, she checked the usual social media sites. She typed in 'Morecombe' and 'Invergryff' and 'Witches' and was surprised to get a result. There was a Stanley Morecombe from Invergryff, could that be the same person? The reason he had appeared when she searched was that he had posted an article on ghost hunts around Scotland. His profile only had a couple of posts she could see without accessing his private account. Along with the ghost hunt one there was a link to an event at a local historical society about architecture in the textile mills. His profile picture was simply a black circle.

There was nothing definitive, but something told her this was the same man that had written the article about the body in 2004. Feeling like she had nothing to lose, she typed out a message, saying that she was interested in the witch on the hill and could he get in touch.

After she had clicked send she realised that it was after eleven pm. The man probably wouldn't be very impressed if she woke him up. Oh well, nothing she could do about it now. She got up from the sofa and stretched out her back.

Ping. She had a message.

Chapter 14: Bernie

It was Sunday night and Finn was out with his pals. Football night. Or was it rugby? Bernie had never been into sport and found it hard to keep up. When they had first got together she used to pretend to be interested in which team was at the top of the league, or who played in red and who in blue, but by now she had given up any attempt to join in.

That was fine. Finn never bothered with her interests either, never made her give up any of the things she liked doing because he was insecure, like she'd seen happen in so many other relationships. They had the perfect marriage. If only he would stop the drinking.

Bernie had taken another bag full of cans to the recycling that morning. She kept telling herself it was a good sign that Finn wasn't hiding them. Not yet anyway.

At least she could get some work done. She checked her emails. One from Liz and three from Mary. Hiring Mary Plunkett was turning out to be the best decision she had ever made, even if she was a bit of a wet blanket. And she was still a slave to sugar. Bernie had given her a keto cookbook, but the woman didn't seem to have taken the hint.

"Anyone home?"

Bernie turned around in surprise as her husband walked in the door.

"I wasn't expecting you until late."

Finn shrugged and grabbed a packet of crisps out of the cupboard. Bernie had tried to encourage him to follow her diet, but so far he hadn't shown much interest. As a builder he had an active job so seemed to think he could eat what he liked.

"Grab us a can out of the fridge will you?"

Bernie tensed her jaw, but did as he asked, watching in silence as he cracked the ring pull. She turned back to the dishes, scrubbing so hard that soap suds were floating in the air.

Finn put his hand on her shoulder. "Look, there's something important I wanted to talk to you about."

Bernie couldn't help her eyes stray to the empty tins on the windowsill. "What's that?"

"It's Ewan."

She breathed out slowly. "What about Ewan?"

"He really, really wants a pet. I know you're not mad about dogs, but what about a cat, or a rabbit even? I just think it would be good for him."

"And who will end up looking after the blooming thing? You? I don't think so. It'll be me. And I've got enough on my plate as it is."

Finn rubbed his hand through his hair so that it stuck up at the front. "I think... Look, Ewan doesn't always find it easy to

77

make friends. You know how kids can be. I just think a wee pal for him at home wouldn't be such a bad thing. It's not like we managed to give him any siblings."

Bernie felt her hands clench into fists. "That wasn't exactly our fault was it? I mean we really tried and…"

"That's not what I meant. I just mean, why don't we give him something for himself? A pet that he can cuddle every so often. That's all."

"I don't want to talk about it."

"Jesus Bernie, it's just a pet. We could get a bloody goldfish if that's what you want. What's got you so riled up anyway?"

She shouldn't say anything, now wasn't the time. But she couldn't help it. "It's the drinking, Finn."

Finn took a step backwards. "I've just had a couple of beers."

"But it's a couple pretty much every night, isn't it? Then a few more over the weekend."

Finn folded his arms. "Look, it's just how I relax, okay?"

Bernie turned away but Finn grabbed her wrist.

"Bernie, I'm not some sort of alkie. I just like a drink in the evening. You are making a big deal out of nothing."

She shook her head. "I don't think I am."

"Listen, I know you like to be in control. But you've got to trust me that I can take of myself on this one."

"I do trust you."

Finn snorted. "Really? You didn't tell me that you were running a detective agency, did you?"

Bernie's eyes widened. "You… you know about the WWC?"

"No one is that excited by a book group. Of course I know about it. It's the talk of the town. Or did you think your labourer husband was too thick to work something like that out?"

"I… no, it's just…"

"I'm going to bed," Finn said and stalked up the stairs. It was a long time before Bernie followed him up.

Chapter 15: Liz Monday

It was just before eight o'clock on Monday morning. Liz had arranged to meet Pearson's former secretary at the beach where they could take a walk together without any nosy parkers looking on. In general, the WWC motto was that if there were any nosy parkers about, it was going to be them. So hopefully she would get the inside scoop on his financial affairs. And maybe if she was lucky she might find a love affair or two, just to spice things up.

The Secretary was called Fiona Lonsdale and she had been 'let go' from Pearson's employment last month after two years working for him. Unlike other members of his staff, she didn't seem to have got a job since, so Liz had figured she might just be bitter enough about the experience to dish the dirt on Pearson. She was right.

"I hope you get the snake, I really do, but he's slippery, that's for sure." Fiona had brought her dog, a little Frenchie type thing, and it snuffled along beside them.

"My clients are hoping that we can prove this latest venture has gone beyond slippery into the criminal."

"Well, I'll be impressed if you can make anything stick. And you would make yourself plenty of friends. None of the locals want that beautiful country park turned into a playground for boring old men and American tourists."

Liz smiled. This was going better than she'd thought. "What I want to know is, why was Pearson so involved in this contract? As an MP, shouldn't he have bigger fish to fry than a local planning development?"

Fiona bent down to scratch the pup between his ears. "I have to be a bit careful about what I say. I mean, if any of this got back to me…"

"It won't."

"Well, you said you were looking at the financial records. You understand that the whole golf course thing was really organised on behalf of a third party."

"That wouldn't be Victory holdings, would it?"

She raised an eyebrow. "You have done your research, haven't you? Do you know who owns the company?"

"No."

"That's because they've kept it very well hidden. It's owned by Immy Blake."

"I've seen that name somewhere."

"That's because she's Pearson's sister-in-law."

"Then we've got him!" Liz said, jumping up in excitement. "He's put through this deal for a family member. That's got to be against the rules."

"If only it were that simple," the other woman said. "I'd have shopped him in myself if that was the case. The problem is there's still no evidence to say that the contract was awarded

81

unlawfully. Yeah, it's cronyism, but that doesn't make it illegal. But I reckon if you can get to the bottom of the environmental stuff, that's where you might just catch him out."

"What environmental stuff?"

"You've seen the environmental impact reports?"

"I've skimmed them."

"Well, they are very conveniently worded. It's amazing that an untouched part of the Scottish countryside can have absolutely no environmental significance, no endangered species, no habitats at risk… It always seemed a bit fishy to me."

"So I'm going to need an environmental expert, is that what you think?"

"It can't hurt. I'm pretty sure there must be something there. But if that is the missing piece of evidence, you can be sure that Pearson is much too smart to let you find it."

Liz narrowed her eyes. "I've spent the best part of a week on this. Do you think I'm just going to let it drop?"

Fiona sighed. "Well, I wish you luck. You might want to try your hand with Immy Blake, Pearson's sister-in-law. She's rich, and not stupid, but she's not as cautious as Pearson. She might just give something away."

"Where does she live?"

"Glasgow. The posh bit."

"Looks like I'm off to Glasgow then."

Chapter 16: Walker

Mondays were always better for police investigations than the weekend. Walker often thought that it was more prudent to get murdered on a weekday when all the laboratories and civilian services were open. The office had a new buzz of energy as reports started to come in from different departments.

"Briefing in two hours!" Dianna had called across the room when everyone had arrived that morning. She had been on the phone ever since, chasing up forensics and giving progress reports to their superiors.

Walker wasn't feeling quite so chipper. It had seemed like a good idea at the time when Dianna had asked to join games night. After all, he and Mary were just two friends hanging out together, and inviting Dianna along proved that it definitely wasn't a date.

What Walker hadn't thought about was how it might look to Mary. It hadn't really occurred to him that maybe she had been hoping for something more than just a games night. After all, it had been her that put the brakes on the whole boyfriend/girlfriend thing. It wasn't until she logged off suddenly that he thought he might have hurt her feelings.

"You've been a prat," Dianna said simply, once he explained his concerns. "Of course she was upset. You basically brought another girl on your date. Prat."

"You're not a girl. You're an Inspector," Walker said, earning himself the sort of cold look that he might have expected from Mary.

"Total prat," Dianna had said and hung up the phone. All in all, it hadn't been a great Sunday night and when he'd added a couple of beers to drown his sorrows, it left him feeling the worse for wear on Monday morning.

Still, the investigation was progressing, even if his private life wasn't. Walker had left a message for Macleod about the earlier body, but according to the Constable he'd spoken to at HQ, the Inspector had gone back up north for a visit and reception was patchy at best. When he had complained about it to Dianna, she had brushed him off.

"To be honest I don't want to waste much more time on the earlier case. We've limited resources, so I'd rather concentrate on what we can find out about this most recent body, for now at least."

Walker could hardly argue with that, but he still felt like there must be something significant about the body from 2004. Perhaps he could ask the WWC to look into…

No, that would be a terrible idea.

Dianna was pacing the office now, still on the phone. She seemed to be giving someone a piece of her mind.

"Well, that's not good enough!" Dianna said, raising her voice. Every person in the room was watching her now. After a few minutes she slammed the phone down on the desk and let out a whistle.

"You're not going to bloody well believe this," she said.

"What?"

"You know our John Doe in the ground? Well, it turns out it's a Jane!"

"The body is female?" Walker leaned back in his chair. "Didn't the pathologist say it was male?"

"Oh he's very apologetic. Decomposition, blah blah, angle of the body, blah blah, but it sounds like a bit of a cock-up to me. Did we tell the press the sex?"

Walker thought back to the official statement. "I don't think so. Just 'human remains'."

"Well, thank god for that. At least we won't look like eejits in public." Dianna tapped away at her computer. "They are going to send the full pathology results as soon as they get them, but he's promised me a brief summary this morning. Obviously feeling bad about the whole sex mix-up."

Just as Walker was going to sneak a look at his exam prep, Dianna rose from her seat and went over to the smartboard.

"All right everyone, gather round. I've just got the initial findings back from pathology. I'm sure you were all lugging in anyway, but our deceased victim has turned out to be female, not male. To be fair to the Doc, there are a few reasons why he made the wrong call at the crime scene."

She made a face that suggested she wasn't convinced. "Firstly, the clothes. The deceased was buried in jeans and a black padded coat. These were pretty much unisex items at first glance. The hair – what's left of it – was cut short. Brunette, and most likely Caucasian, by the way, if the hair is anything to go by. The victim was tall, over five foot ten, so again that suggested a male body. Anyhow, we now know better."

"An initial look at missing persons didn't bring up much, but now that we know she was female, we'll have to start all over again. Neil, I want you to widen the search to missing persons from the rest of the UK as well as Scotland, just in case she's not local."

"Sure," Neil said, already hurrying back to his computer. There was a new energy in the room, now that they had a description to go on.

"Walker, can you check the local media? See if there's anything about a missing woman in the last year or so. Sometimes it's quicker than looking through the official files."

"Right," he said, turning back to his computer. "Did pathology confirm an unlawful death?"

"Not yet," Dianna replied. "They think there might be evidence of trauma to the skull, but they are sending off for more tests to see if they can prove it was deliberate rather than accidental. For the moment, we're leaving it open. Oh, but they did have one more thing to add and I'd rather we kept it out of the media for the moment."

Everyone in the room looked up at the Inspector.

"Our body was missing some bones. Part of the right leg, between the ankle and the knee. It could just be animal interference with the body, but we can't rule out that it happened around the time of death."

"Creepy," Neil whispered as they returned to their computers. Walker couldn't disagree.

Chapter 17: Mary

Stanley Morecombe had already sent Mary seven messages since she'd reached out to him online. At first, he had been suspicious, asking how she had 'found him' and who she worked for. Once she had reassured him that she wasn't some sort of government agent, whatever that might be, he had agreed to tell her everything he knew about the unidentified body.

Unfortunately, Morecombe's particular worldview wouldn't allow him to divulge that sort of sensitive information on the internet. Mary had suggested meeting up, but he hadn't replied yet, so she was waiting to see what happened.

Mary had only just got out of the shower when the doorbell went. For a weird moment she thought it might be Morecombe, but then she realised he didn't know where she lived.

She popped a towel over her wet hair, flung on her best superhero onesie and answered the door.

"Is that the Phantom?" Walker asked, with his usual bewildered face.

Mary crossed her arms. "It is the ghost that walked, yes. Can I ask what you want?"

"I wanted to apologise."

She bit back the insult that had been waiting on her lips. "All right, I'm listening."

"I wasn't really thinking last night. I should have told you I'd said to Dianna to play the game. I feel like... well, like I've been a bit of a prat."

A tiny part of Mary's frozen heart thawed a little. "You were, yes."

"Look, I don't know if we're ever going to be... well, you know what I mean. I know that for the moment it can't happen. But I would hate to think that I had done anything to stop it from happening in the future."

"By being a prat."

"Yes, as you say, a prat."

Mary shrugged. There were lots of things she wanted to say, but she just didn't know quite how to say them.

"It's nothing. Look, I should really get dressed, so..."

Walker didn't seem to take the hint. "The thing is, there was something else I wanted to ask you. A work thing this time."

Now Mary felt more comfortable. "What work thing?"

He shuffled his feet. "Listen, I'm taking a bit of a risk here, but I thought you might be interested in something. In doing something with me. Um. I'm not saying this right."

Mary fought back a laugh. "What are you asking, exactly?"

"Look, I'm about to chat to Paul Crossly's sister. That's the person who might well be the unidentified body from 2004. It's not an interview, more of an informal chat. I was wondering if you wanted to come?"

"Really?" Mary tried and failed not to look too excited.

"We're going to be talking about her dead brother. It's going to be a sad and difficult chat. We don't even have any more answers for her than we did all those years ago. It'll be emotional and I thought a sensitive person in the room might be useful."

"And I was your first choice?"

"Well, Dianna's busy, so…"

Mary decided she would pretend she hadn't heard that one. "I'd love to."

"Great. I've arranged to meet her in the café on West Street."

"The one with the big scones or the one with the homemade tablet?"

Walker laughed. "You really do have a sweet tooth, don't you?"

"Maybe a little."

"It's called Café on the Corner."

"Ooh, big scones. I'm definitely in. Do I get a set of handcuffs?"

"Definitely not. Or a warrant card or anything police related at all. I will be making very clear to the woman that you are simply a member of the public."

"Good to know where I stand."

Walker blinked. "Am I being insulting?"

"No. I'm just winding you up. Let's go, I'm super excited!" Mary grabbed her car keys and went to leave.

"One more thing…"

"Oh, god, you're totally forgiven about the game. Let's just go!"

Walker coughed. "I thought you might want to get changed first."

Mary looked down at her purple onesie with a skull on the front. "Right. I'll be out in five minutes."

Not much more than twenty minutes later they were sitting down in the café, waiting to see if Paul Crossly's sister was going to show up.

"She might not come at all," Walker said, taking a sip of a double espresso.

"Why not? Surely she'd want to know if there's any information on her brother."

"She didn't sound happy over the phone. I kind of got the feeling she didn't want to think about it. Grief affects people in all sorts of weird ways. I see it a lot in the job. Plus, it's not like I've got big news for her. I'm not exactly going to make her day."

"Do you think this new body is connected? Maybe she knows something about it."

But Walker was already shaking his head. "From the preliminary forensics it looks like this body was in the ground for only a year, so they were killed long after Paul Crossly went missing."

Mary was just about to reply when the door to the café opened and a woman stood there, looking around like she had lost something.

"Wendy?" Walker stood up and went to meet her, touching her arm gently and showing her to their table.

"This is my friend Mary," Walker said, "and she is assisting the police with this case."

Mary thought she must have grown three inches taller.

"Hi, Wendy. I'm really sorry about your brother."

"Thanks."

Paul Crossly's sister was not what she had expected. Mary had assumed, because Paul had been a drifter and a drug addict, that his sister would have borne some of the same scars. But she arrived in perfect makeup and a trouser suit. She looked like she was about to pitch something on Dragons Den, not speak about her dead brother.

"I could have done without this today," she said as she pulled out a little pink vape that smelled like marshmallows. "I'm meant to be at a pharmaceutical conference in Basingstoke."

Mary wasn't sure what to say to that. "I'm sorry," she said eventually. "It must be hard having everything brought up again."

"It's not hard it's… very complicated."

"Perhaps we could start with the facts," Walker said, bringing out his phone. "Your brother went missing at the end of March 2004. Is that right?"

"Yes, although it was hard to give a definite date. I hadn't seen him for months before that. He had never had any long-term jobs. So when he skipped out on the job down South, I didn't hear about it until a mutual friend said they thought he had moved up to Scotland again."

"Did you try and meet him?"

"No. By that point, we weren't speaking." Wendy took in a sharp breath, like someone had hit her. "I'm not going to share my childhood with you, but let's just say it wouldn't have made for a heartwarming movie. Both my parents were dead before they were forty, and to be honest, it was no great loss. Drugs, you see. I thought at first that Paul might avoid them, but by fourteen he had started using, and well, that was that."

"You never did drugs?" Mary asked.

"Never. The only way I could survive was to get the hell out of that place as soon as I could. When I was twelve I went to

93

stay with my Aunt in the Lake District. She had tried to get Paul out too, but he was too far gone by then. Anyway, my Aunt was strict as hell but it felt like paradise after what I'd grown up with. I left school, joined a local pharmacy, worked my way up to manager and now I have three shops of my own."

"That's amazing," Mary said, and she meant it.

"Well, that's what happens when you get out. Dead and buried in the woods is what happens when you don't."

They all sipped their drinks for a moment, trying to think of what to say. Walker looked at Mary and gave her a desperate look.

"Why do you think he might be the body in the woods?" Mary asked.

Wendy looked down at the table. "I saw the police report. The photofit was rubbish, but it could have been Paul. And he left the builders' firm around the time they said the man was killed. But that's not the main reason."

"What's that?"

"No one's ever seen him since. Every year that goes past, it's more likely that he's the guy they found. Because Paul would have got in touch with me if he was still alive. Even if it was only to ask for money. So that's how I know."

Mary reached out and squeezed the woman's hand. She gave her a tiny nod.

"Let's go back to when Paul disappeared," Walker said. "He was working for a local building firm called… hang on, I can check the name…"

"It was West Clyde Builders," Mary said.

"That's right. How do you know?" Walker asked.

Mary just shrugged. "I did some research on them. They officially dissolved in 2006, but the same directors started up several companies since then. Companies House states that they are currently operating as Building Pros West Coast. Might be worth getting in touch."

"Are you reopening the case then?" Wendy asked.

"No," Walker said, just as Mary nodded her head.

"Well, is it yes or no?"

"Officially, the case is still open as the body is unidentified. But at the moment there are no plans to allocate resources specifically to the remains found in 2004. If it turns out that they are related to the recent remains that might change."

"What about you," Wendy said, turning her attention to Mary. "You look like you care about my brother's death."

"I do," Mary said. "As Constable Walker said, I'm not part of the police. I work for a private investigative agency in Invergryff. Me and my friends, we're going to do our best to find out what happened to these bodies. We don't like when people get forgotten."

"That's Paul, I guess. Sometimes I wonder if I'm the only one that remembers him. And it's not like I've got particularly happy memories, the poor sod. In fact, I've spent twenty years doing my best to forget about him. But maybe I owe him a grave at least. Somewhere that proves that he existed in the first place."

"We'll get him that," Mary said confidently, while Walker just glared at her.

"He wasn't your biological brother, was he," the Constable said. "That's why they couldn't get a DNA match."

"Nah. His mum was part of the group of… well, they thought of themselves as hippies, but they weren't really. Just druggies. Never knew who his dad was. One day the mum just up and left the baby with my mum, and she raised him. Not well, but as best as she could," Wendy replied.

"Can I keep in touch? If it is Paul, we might get enough to identify him this time. We have better methods than we did back then."

Wendy shrugged and Mary noticed lines on her face that she hadn't spotted earlier.

"Sure. What have I got to lose?"

Chapter 18: Bernie

Bernie picked up a call from Mary just as she was heading into work, but pretty soon she was wishing she hadn't.

"You want me to ask Finn about some builders?"

"Yes. It's all to do with the body they found in 2004. It's looking like it was a guy called Paul Crossly, going by the name of Paul Dean. I spoke to his sister today. Walker invited me along, actually. Not that that's important. What was I saying again?"

"Builders," Bernie prompted.

"Right. Well, when Paul disappeared he was working for a company called West Clyde Builders, but they went out of business in 2006. Sounds like a dead end, but the same directors have started up several companies since then and they are currently operating as Building Pros West Coast. I thought Finn might have heard of them."

"Well, I can ask him, but he's not around today. Working late, you know." Bernie could have told Mary about her row with Finn the previous night, but she hadn't really processed it herself yet.

"That's a shame."

"But I can chase it up. Email me the details."

"Will do. Do you want me to go over everything else I've

done? I've been quite busy."

Bernie checked her watch. She still had twenty minutes before her shift started. "Why don't you come here? I'd rather we met up face to face. I hate talking on these not-so-smart phones."

Mary's laugh cackled down the line. "Sometimes you sound like you're from another generation, Bernie," she said. "All right, I'll drive to the home now."

It took Mary the best part of twenty minutes just to get to the home, but Bernie had already called ahead to the duty manager and she said it would be fine to start a little late.

"I've brought the laptop," Mary said when she got out of the car.

"Great," Bernie replied. "We can sit on the picnic bench over there."

While Mary fired up her laptop – a long process given that the ancient thing seemed to predate the invention of the wheel – she explained to Bernie what she had been up to. Bernie was impressed: between somehow arranging with Walker to attend an interview with Crossly's sister and tracking down Stanley Morecombe, Mary had achieved a lot in a couple of days. It was a just pity that none of it seemed to link together.

"So we have the journalist looking at satanic rituals on the one hand, and the unfortunate, but entirely predictable, death of a drug user on the other. And that's just for 2004."

"That's right. I've barely started on the recent body yet. I have noted down a few relevant names, however, if you want to hear them. There are the dog walker that found the body, the farmer, and the unidentified victim, of course. Apart from that, there's not much to go on."

"I think I might have to contact my friend at the police station," Bernie said. "We need some more information before we can start chasing up leads."

"Do you think this second victim might be drugs related too?" Mary asked.

Bernie considered it. "Could be. It's a dangerous business. But if Paul Crossly was killed because of drugs I can't see how we're going to find out who is responsible. How would we even know who was in charge of the drugs scene twenty years ago?"

The nurse crossed her arms. "I'll have a think. There must be someone we can ask. It's a pity that Superintendent Marr is so far gone. But maybe his wife remembers who the players were back then. Policemen always talk to their wives. Even if they're not meant to. What else do you want me to have a look at?"

"Oh." Mary looked surprised. "I hadn't actually thought you would be working on this one. I've already got Alice helping me out so…"

"I see." Bernie's lips were pressed tightly together.

"I mean, I'm sure I can find something that you could do…" Mary started scrolling back through the spreadsheet.

"Don't worry about it," Bernie said, in a tone of voice that told the other woman the conversation was over.

Chapter 19: Liz

Liz scheduled her visit to Glasgow for the following day. She had made an appointment with Imelda Blake of Victory Holdings on the premise of wanting to set up an organisation of successful women in business. No such organisation existed, of course, but Immy Blake had seemed very excited to be a part of it on the phone.

Now she just had to find something to do today. She was still adjusted to not having a full time job to go to. There was a continual feeling of guilt that she should be running around somewhere in her smart suit and heels rather than sitting on the sofa in jogging bottoms.

Dave came in the door and gave her a kiss.

"Sean go in okay?"

"Yep, no problem."

"What are your plans for today?"

Dave was never in the Opticians on a Monday, preferring to have a day working from home where he could catch up on the paperwork.

"The usual," he said, pouring himself a fresh cup of coffee. "Nothing exciting."

"Fancy a game of golf?"

Dave nearly dropped his coffee. "Damn it, I've got that down my shirt." He grabbed some paper towels and started dabbing at his chest. "Sorry, did you say something about golf?"

"I said, would you like to come for a game of golf."

"With you? Golf? A game of golf with you?"

"Hey, I work out."

"Yeah, yoga class at the gym. But you know that golf takes place outside, don't you? With trees and mud and weather?"

"If you keep this up I won't pay for your lunch."

"Golf and lunch? Are you having an affair?" Dave dropped his arm around her shoulder and kissed her on the forehead. "Seriously though, what's going on?"

"It's for a WWC case. I'm looking into this new development that they're building. I want to see the last one that they did, have a poke around. And it just happens to be a golf club."

"Will I get the playing fee on expenses?" Dave asked.

"Of course."

"Then let's go."

It took a good half hour to drive to the golf course at Beachside Links. The houses got bigger and more expensive the closer they got to the development. Liz, who had been brought up in a tiny two bed council house, was feeling more than a bit of class insecurity.

Dave seemed to have no such compunction, but then both his parents were dentists and he had grown up in a detached house with four bedrooms and a bidet.

In the clubhouse Liz paid an extortionate amount for two day tickets to the course, only a little comforted that she would be getting it back on expenses. By the time they had hired a set of clubs for her – Dave had his own, of course – it had started raining, a slow, steady drizzle.

"Do you still play in the rain?" Liz asked in a low voice.

"Of course. You wouldn't get out much in Scotland if you didn't."

It took them two hours to play nine holes. Liz politely declined Dave's offer to play the full eighteen. It turned out that golf was the perfect combination of very difficult and monumentally tedious. She lost two balls and ruined a perfectly nice pair of boots.

"That was great fun, wasn't it?" Dave said when they trudged back into the clubhouse.

"Oh, awesome. I particularly liked the bit where I slipped on the edge of a bunker and ended up with a face full of wet sand."

Dave chuckled. "Why on earth did you want to come here?"

"I just wanted to get a feel for the place. This was the first development that Pearson was involved with, back twenty years ago. I wanted to get an impression of the man."

"Still think he's dodgy then?"

"Oh definitely. But I don't know how I'm going to prove it. Let's go to the bar."

Liz felt much happier by the time they had established themselves at a cosy table next to the wood-burning stove with a glass of wine in her hand.

"Have you thawed out yet?" Dave asked, pointing at her feet which were pointed towards the stove.

"Just about."

"Do you know, I could get used to this new job of yours," Dave said, giving her a grin.

"Only problem is the pay is half what I got at the old place. Plus, some months we might not have any investigations at all. After the Pearson case, there's nothing coming up apart from a murder investigation, and we're doing that one for free."

"Seems like you need to revise your business model," Dave replied.

"Well, it was only ever meant to be a side hustle. And then I quit my job and here we are."

Dave reached across the table and held her hand. "You know that I don't blame you for that, right? Yes, things are a bit tight right now, but I'd much rather you did something you loved."

"Thanks."

"I mean it. I want our son to grow up thinking he can be anything he wants to be, and you guys with your Women's Co-operative, you're proving that to him. Just keep solving those cases."

"I'll try."

Chapter 20: Walker

Having nipped out for a cup of decent coffee from a nearby café, Walker knew that something had gone wrong the minute he walked back into the office.

"Don't go near the Inspector," Neil hissed, "she's absolutely fizzing about –"

At that moment the door at the other end of the room slammed open and Dianna stormed in, her face red and lips tightly pressed together.

"Walker, my office, right now."

Neil hunkered down behind his laptop and Walker couldn't blame him. When someone was in trouble it was natural to pretend you didn't know them. He only wished he had some idea of what he had done to annoy Dianna.

"Look at this." Dianna threw a copy of the local paper across the desk to him.

"Incompetent police force can't find killer after two tries!" Walker read out the headline. "Well, that's a novel take on the situation."

"They're making it sound like we've got a serial killer here. Some sort of Scottish version of Jack the Ripper. And who is to blame for the bodies? The police force of course."

"Well, that's nothing new is it?" Walker said. He didn't really understand why Dianna was so upset. The press loved to criticise the police. Between that and pictures of celebrities in short skirts, it filled half their pages.

"Turn to page two."

Right at the top of the page was a picture of Dianna. The photographer had caught her coming out of the station. The unfortunate thing was that she had clearly chosen that moment to tuck into a sausage roll.

Walker clamped his lips shut so that he didn't laugh. "That is a rather… indelicate look."

"Indelicate? I look like one of those snakes that can unhinge their jaw to shove more of their dinner in."

The laugh that had been threatening to come out escaped his lips. "Sorry," Walker said, wiping his eyes. "You've just been unlucky, Dianna, that's all."

"Bloody unlucky considering it was the first time I'd had refined carbs in weeks. What a way to fall off the wagon. At least I've provided you with a little amusement. You can just imagine the conversation I've had with Superintendent MacKinnon."

"Surely he saw it was just bad timing."

"Not really. I mean, he's never going to be happy about some article that makes us look like arses and then me looking like a mega arse right on the next page, is he?"

"Oh come on, it's funny."

"Yes, well, I think they surgically remove your sense of humour as soon as you get above Chief Inspector."

"You better remember that when you're running the place."

"I'll be different, of course. What about you, have you been studying for your exam?"

Walker shrugged to deflect the question. "Of course. Now, how are we going to solve both these cases and get back in the Superintendent's good books?"

Dianna threw down the paper. "Search me. That's the worst bit, it's not like we're even making good progress. I refuse to let another body get left unidentified on that bloody hill. This time we're going to solve the thing. And before CID turns up to take it off me."

"Any signs of them coming down from Glasgow?"

"Not yet. But the Superintendent was hinting it wouldn't be long."

Walker drummed his fingers on the table. "Why didn't you ever go down that route? If you don't mind me asking."

Dianna pulled a free strand of hair back into her ponytail. "Because I don't like the twisty stuff. I like cases where you get results straight away. CID or, as we should call it, the Specialist Crime Division, even though no one does, is more work for fewer results. That's the way I see it."

Walker nodded. "I can understand that."

"You should totally go for it though."

"Why?"

"Well, you've always been a bit 'twisty' yourself, haven't you?"

Walker pretended to look offended, but they both knew what she meant. He was a bit twisty, a bit different from most other police officers. And what else should people that are a little bit weird and antisocial do other than become detectives?

Of course, he had to pass the Sergeant's exam first.

Chapter 21: Mary

Stanley Morecombe was more or less what Mary had expected. He was a little older, probably closer to seventy than sixty, and he could do with a haircut, but that wasn't exactly something that she could say didn't also apply to herself.

"Can I make you a tea?" he said, showing her into the house. It had a floral wallpaper in the hall and some very retro kitchen cupboards with Bakelite handles, but the whole place was clean and tidy. Something about the décor made Mary think that this house had belonged to Morecombe's parents and that he had never left home.

Mary accepted the tea and was not totally surprised that there were no biscuits on offer. Apart from the hints of wallpaper and faded pictures on the walls, there was nothing feminine about the house at all. A black leather sofa took up most of the living room and a large desk with a computer took up the other half. A bookshelf overloaded with files sat across the back wall.

"Thank you for meeting with me."

"No, thank you. It's always nice to meet a fan of my work."

Mary hid a smile. That was not exactly how she had described herself. She had told Morecombe that she was a student writing a paper on witchcraft in the present day, and had found his article about the body found on the witch's hill. That had been enough to draw him in.

"I thought we should start with the history of witchcraft from the early modern period and work our way up to the present day." Morecombe had that awkward way with other human beings where he looked down at his feet when they talked, waiting patiently for them to stop so that he could talk again. The definition of antisocial.

Mary had a lot of sympathy with this as a world view. She had been an awkward, geeky child, spending more time with books than human beings. She had eventually found more outgoing friends and developed a liking for other people – some of the time at least – but there was still a big part of her that wanted to spend every day snuggled under her duvet watching vintage Star Trek episodes.

So where Bernie or even Liz might have sneered a little at Morecombe's lifestyle, Mary found herself envying it. Obviously, she was glad that she had learned how to relate to people and fill her house with children and noise, but there was a lovely nostalgia to the silence of the journalist's home. An eighteen-year-old Mary would have been very happy there.

"Perhaps we could skip ahead a little," she suggested. "I'm really interested in how the body that was found twenty years ago relates to the witch on the hill."

"You've heard about the latest find, then?"

Mary nodded. "Yes. How did you hear about it?"

Morecombe tapped the side of his nose, putting his glasses slightly askew. "I have my ways. There may or may not be a police scanner in the basement. Haha."

111

Mary laughed along with him, even though she wasn't sure whether or not he was joking.

"Do you think the most recent body is related to the other one?" Mary asked.

"Undoubtedly. Of course, the fact that it's a woman changes things somewhat."

Mary couldn't hide her surprise. "The latest body is a woman?"

"Ah, you didn't know? Yes, a woman. It does make one wonder what the Satan worshippers are up to this time."

"Um, Satan worshippers?"

"Of course. Who else would be making sacrifices to the witch?"

Mary didn't have an answer for that one. She got up and walked over to the bookcase, mainly to give herself time to think of what to say. There seemed to be a lot of books about the flat earth, and Mary decided that geography was another subject that was probably best avoided, along with the worship of Satan.

"Could you tell me how you became involved in the case, back in 2004?"

"Well, I was working as a freelance journalist then. Physical papers mainly, you understand. It was the early days of web journalism back then. Now I'm all about my video content."

Mary nodded. She had sampled some of Morecombe's videos.

They were seriously strange, veering from the latest conspiracy theories to American politics. Sometimes those things seemed to be one and the same.

"I heard about the first body. The way the police were talking about it was like it was just an accident or something. Of course, I knew better. I made the connection with the witch on the hill before anyone else did. I was the one that told the police about the cottage."

"Who did you speak to?"

"Detective Inspector Marr. Typical copper, not interested in the occult angle in the slightest. But he perked up when I told him about the cottage. He hadn't even known it was there! Well, you can't see it from the road. It's in a little copse of trees. Anyway, that got him all excited and he went barging up there to do a search."

"Do you know what they found?"

"Oh, they didn't share that information with me, even though they wouldn't have found it without my help. But I snuck up there after they'd finished and you can bet I saw the same things."

"Which were?"

"Evidence of satanic worship. Pentagrams painted on the walls, arcane symbols carved into the floor. Perfect evidence of occult machinations."

"Right. And the police never chased it up?"

"Said it was just kids. Hah! They would like to believe that wouldn't they." He started a long rant about authority and public property and Mary found herself zoning out. She asked a couple more questions, but it was clear that Morecombe's theories about the bodies were pure conjecture. Pretty soon, she made her excuses and left.

On the way home Mary stopped off at a drive-through for a hot chocolate and a doughnut, just because she could.

Chapter 22: Bernie

Bernie was the first to arrive at the WWC meeting on Monday night. She let herself into Annie McGillivray's old house with the usual combination of gratitude and sadness. Having their own place to meet without husbands and kids getting underfoot was invaluable, it was just sad that it had come about through the death of their friend.

Still, Annie had never been one to wallow, and Bernie was certainly of the same breed. Mind you, if she was ever going to allow herself a little self-pity, today might just be the day.

Nothing had gone right since she had got up that morning. After she had spoken to Mary, Bernie had phoned Superintendent Marr's wife, hoping to get another interview with him, only to be informed that he was 'much worse' today.

"I think he was overstimulated," Mrs Marr had said, the accusation lurking behind her usual politeness.

"Sorry to hear that. Will you let me know when he is up to visitors?"

"Of course," the woman had replied, but Bernie didn't think she would. Then when she had picked up Ewan from school her son had seemed more quiet than usual. Bernie had asked what was wrong, received a soft 'nothing', so they had driven home in silence. She was a good mum, Bernie knew, in a lot of ways, but working out what was going on inside people's heads had never been her strong point. She would have asked Finn, but they were still not talking. Eventually, she had taken herself to the WWC headquarters an hour early, just to get out of the house.

The thing about being a nurse, Bernie thought as she put the bottles of wine in the fridge, is that you are always needed, all the time. And when she had started the WWC, Liz and Alice had always needed her, always asked her opinion on everything. And then Mary Plunkett had joined, and like a baby lamb, she had needed help every step of the way.

And just look at them now. Even Mary was perfectly capable of solving crimes on her own. And that was a good thing, of course. It just left Bernie feeling a little… deflated. Plus Finn was avoiding her at home, and it wouldn't be too long before Ewan noticed something was up. Bernie's kid might not always be the quickest at making friends, but he was far from stupid.

There was a jangle of keys and Bernie's niece walked into the house. Since the WWC had officially taken ownership, they all had keys. And that was a good thing, obviously. Bernie didn't really miss being the only one with access to the house. Not much anyway.

"You won't believe the day I've had," Bernie's niece called out.

"Is that right?"

Alice walked into the kitchen, then stopped, and did a double take.

"Bernie… are you eating sugar?"

Bernie's mouth turned downwards. "Just a little bit of dark chocolate."

"I mean… I'm not judging. It's just I've never seen you eat chocolate since, well, you know…"

"Since I was fat. Yeah. I just felt like some."

Alice leaned forward. "Auntie, is everything okay? I know you don't like to talk about personal stuff, but we work together and we're family and you got me arrested, so maybe you could actually talk to me, you know?"

Maybe it really was that easy for some people? Bernie put down the brownie and sniffed. "Well, I did have a row with Finn."

"What about?"

"It's not important."

"Auntie, you guys never row. Please, tell me what's wrong."

Bernie sighed. "I don't like how much he drinks."

Alice bit her lip. "Right."

Bernie waited a few moments. "Is that all you're going to say?"

Her niece flinched. "Look, I don't want to get in the middle of this."

"Then why did you ask about it? Besides, surely there's no 'getting in the middle'. If Finn is drinking too much then that's just a fact."

"Well… yes. But then again…"

Bernie could feel her blood pressure rising. "Go on, say what you're trying to say."

"It's just… Okay. The thing is, Auntie, you have very high standards. Like, impossibly high. And sometimes it might be that you see his drinking as a major problem, when maybe you are jumping to conclusions, that's all."

While Alice was talking Bernie could feel herself getting more and more tense in her chair.

"Is that what you think? That I'm making it up?"

"Not at all. It's just that you're so clever, and so strong, and you always know exactly what you're doing every moment of the day. You just never seem to have much patience for anyone that is struggling more than you are."

"Well, I think that you are –"

The front door opened just in time to stop Bernie saying something she would regret to her niece.

"Hello everyone, I hope you've got the gin ready," Liz said, entering the room along with Mary. "I need something to warm me up. Did you know you have to play golf outside, even if it's raining?"

Bernie blinked. "You? Playing golf?"

"I know. I wanted to check out Pearson's first development project. I thought it might give me a sense of what the man's been up to. Turns out the only thing it gave me was chilblains."

Bernie was about to ask another question when the doorbell rang.

"Ah, that'll be the witch," Alice said with a smile.

Chapter 23: Liz

"The what?" Bernie asked.

Alice ignored her aunt and went to open the door.

"This is my friend, Eve," she said when she came back into the room.

Eve looked like someone who would have been called a hippie if she'd been born half a century earlier, Liz thought. She had long ginger hair that was sort of straggly and unbrushed, with a pale oval face and watery eyes. She wore a tie-dyed dress that was covered by a fluffy coat that made her look like an adolescent yeti.

Liz could feel Bernie tense up beside her.

"Eve is a witch," Alice said, earning a little 'ooh' from Mary.

"We prefer the term Wiccan," Eve said, with a smile.

"Liz said it would be okay," Alice said, earning Liz a glare from Bernie. Perhaps she should have warned her friend, but it was too late now.

"Look, there's nothing wrong with bringing in an expert when we're out of our depth," Liz said, giving Bernie a warning look. She definitely didn't want a barny between Aunt and niece.

"All right," Bernie crossed her arms. "But if you try telling us about the healing power of crystals, I'm sending you home."

Eve's smile had hardened somewhat but she managed a nod.

"Eve is a history graduate," Alice said. "She's done lots of work on medieval witches. I got in touch with her about the witch on the hill."

"Ruth Macintyre. I'd never heard of her before," Eve said. "Although that's not altogether surprising. Renfrewshire had a large number of witch killings."

"Is that right?"

"As a county it was almost a local sport. The most famous ones were the Paisley witch trials in 1697. An eleven-year-old child called Christian Shaw accused thirty-five people of witchcraft. Eventually, seven of them were killed. It's a pretty gruesome story."

"But that was earlier than the witch on the hill," Bernie pointed out.

"That's right, although not by much. Your witch was executed in 1703. Mind you, she was pretty unlucky. Thirty years later and the Witchcraft act was repealed so she would have been safe. Well, from legal persecution anyway, not from the mob."

"Did you find out what she did? I mean, to make them think she was a witch?"

"The usual." Eve shrugged. "It was a hard life farming at that time. Any number of diseases could afflict crops and livestock. The farmer had a whole herd of sheep who turned out barren. Of course, now we would do tests to find out why, but back then they just looked for a convenient scapegoat."

121

"The witch."

"She wasn't well liked in the village. Something to do with ownership of the land, it is difficult to understand from the contemporary sources. Anyway, the farmer seemed to have it in for her. He had already taken over some of her fields as 'common land' in the 1690s. Then the accusation in 1703 that she'd cursed his flock. No one stood up for her, and there we have it. An easy way to get rid of an old woman who was an inconvenience to society at the time."

"What about since then?" Mary asked. "People calling the hill haunted, that sort of thing."

Eve sniffed. "Well, I believe that people can leave an essence behind after death, but as for a haunting, some ghost running about the hills trying to scare people, it seems unlikely."

"And the curse?"

"Well now, that is interesting. The reports of the time say that she cursed the town in general, but the farmer in particular. Apparently, the curse has worked as the family has never had a son live into adulthood."

"Wow," Liz said, "is that true?"

"Seems to be. Whether you believe that it is bad luck or the occult, is up to you."

Bernie sniffed, making her thoughts on the matter clear.

"We should speak to the farmer," Liz said. "Ask him about the curse."

"I've never heard anything so ridic–" Bernie said, half-rising from her seat.

"I mean," Liz interrupted, "it'll be a good excuse to ask them about the two bodies. Look, I don't believe in a curse any more than you do. But it'll give us a reason to speak to them. There has got to be some reason that two bodies were buried on the same hill. Whether you like it or not, Berns, the location of the bodies is important."

Bernie's brow creased in anger and Liz wondered what would happen if she lost her temper. Bernie was pretty acidic at the best of times, so it wasn't a sight that Liz was looking forward to. But if she was going to be a proper partner in the WWC, she had to be prepared to challenge Bernie when she thought she was in the wrong. Liz held her breath.

"All right," Bernie said finally, the words escaping from between gritted teeth. "I agree we need to talk to the farmer. But I'll be the one to do it. And none of this witch nonsense. No offence, Eve."

Eve, who did indeed look offended, managed a smile. "None taken. Are those scones vegan by any chance?"

"No they certainly are not," Bernie replied.

Chapter 24: Walker

The police station was a hub of activity when Walker arrived on Tuesday morning. The briefing to the press had just gone out, including the new information that the body had been female. The phones were ringing as the usual suspects came out of the woods to offer up 'information' on the crime. Most of it would be useless, of course, but they had to follow up on every possible lead.

"Another one who thinks it was aliens," a young female Constable called Jane Russell called out. "That's three in the first hour."

"I'd rather little green men than all the people convinced it's because of the witch," Neil said, his eyes on his laptop. "Half the town seems to believe in her."

"Well, if she wanted to show up with a confession I would be happy to arrest her," Walker said, passing out a cup of tea to each of them.

"Thanks," Neil said, gulping down half the cup. "Problem is, we've no better suspects. Although the forensics have come through."

"Have they?"

"Yeah. Full report from pathology. Dianna's going to go over it in half an hour." Neil leaned forward so that his head was only a couple of inches from Walker's.

"Don't suppose you know if she's single, do you?"

Walker couldn't help but look surprised. "Fancy her, do you?"

"Have you seen her?" Neil answered, as if that said enough.

"Probably a bad idea to go out with your immediate superior, though, mate."

Neil shrugged. "Oh aye, a terrible idea. But that's not stopping me thinking about it."

Walker couldn't help but laugh. "She broke up with her partner Ricky a while ago, so as far as I know she's single. Just be careful, all right?"

"Will do," Neil said with a wink. Walker couldn't help but feel that he had no chance. Dianna was far too sensible to get into anything with a colleague. She had the same point of view as Walker did on this one: better to get into bed with a boa constrictor than someone you have to see at work every day of the week.

Walker typed a couple of notes into the computer before he realised he was starving. He went in search of sugar.

Dianna found him by the vending machines as he was collecting a couple of chocolate bars.

"You really should eat something better than that," Dianna said.

"Let me guess. Seaweed smoothies and kale salad?"

"I'm not that bad," she laughed. "But I did make my own

hummus. After the sausage roll picture I'm not touching anything I haven't made myself. It's full of roasted veg. Fancy some."

"I need the carbs," Walker said, ripping off the wrapper and tucking straight in.

"Savage," Dianna said, shaking her head. "How are you feeling about Friday?"

Walker shrugged. "Well, what will be will be."

"You should tell them about… what you told me."

Walker looked around, just to make sure no one could overhear them. "Look, I just need another chance. I know where I messed up last time. I've done a lot more practice for this one."

Dianna frowned at him. Walker could tell she was considering him carefully, like a difficult piece of evidence. He wasn't enjoying it.

"If you tell them you're dyslexic, they'll have to make adjustments. Give you more time, for a start."

Walker just gave her a look.

"Come on, it's nothing to be ashamed of. I bet you'll find there are plenty of other officers that have the same issue."

"But that's the thing, I've not got a formal diagnosis. At school I was always just 'slow'. Now, I know what it is, and that's enough for me. I should be able to do this bloody exam without any extra help. Otherwise, how am I meant to be a decent police officer in the first place?"

Dianna pursed her lips. "Well, I don't agree with you on this one. But if that's the way you want to do it, then I'll help you study."

"Thank you," Walker said. "I better get back to work."

When he got back to the office, there was a note on his desk, scribbled in Neil's handwriting. Detective Inspector Macleod had been in touch, asking Walker to call him back.

Walker got straight on the phone.

"Nice to hear from you," DI Macleod said once he had realised who was calling. "How's life in the deepest darkest central belt?"

"Not so bad," Walker replied. "How's life in the frozen north?"

"Aye, fine. Colder than a penguin's armpit, but I'm surviving. Might not survive another week with the in-laws, mind you. Were you calling about something in particular?"

"Yes. I wanted to know about the unidentified body that was found in 2004. The one on the witch's hill. I heard that you were involved in the case."

"I was. I thought you might be phoning, actually. I hear that another body has turned up."

"A woman this time."

"Now that is interesting. I can't see how she could be connected to our body back in 2004, though. The body wasn't that old was it?"

"No, been in the ground for less than a year. Could you tell me a little about the older case? There's hardly anyone left at the station who remembers it."

"Not many old fogeys like me, eh? Well, I remember going up to that hill and looking for evidence. It was bloody Baltic, even though it was meant to be spring. We combed the whole hillside but we didn't find much."

"No signs of a struggle?"

"No, we always reckoned he'd been killed elsewhere and dumped up on the hill. The locals got their knickers in a twist about a witch's cottage nearby, some kids had painted pentagrams on the walls, that sort of thing. But there were no forensic links to suggest the deceased had ever been in there."

"And the body was never identified?"

"No, although most of the station was convinced it was some lad that had gone missing from a construction site."

"Paul Dean also known as Paul Crossly."

"Aye. Do you know, I always thought it might be something to do with that farmer. Bryce, that was his name. There was something cagey about him, but he didn't seem to have any connection to the body, other than it being found on his land. Well, I suppose he's long dead by now anyway."

"I'll double-check."

"You do that. I hear you've got another crack at your exam this week."

Walker stared up at the ceiling. Was there anyone that didn't know?

"Yes."

"Good luck. I'm sure you'll do grand."

I wish I was as sure, Walker thought, as he put down his phone.

Chapter 25: Mary

It felt like an unimaginable luxury to Mary to be able to go for a child-free cup of tea on a Tuesday morning. While Lauren was still only at nursery part time, she had never really been on her own during the day. So when Liz had mentioned that they should take the opportunity to have a cuppa together on a weekday, she couldn't agree quickly enough.

Mary had suggested the place to meet based purely on the fact that it was completely un-child-friendly. If she was going to go out when the children were away it wasn't going to be anywhere with highchairs and laminated menus.

She had decided on Paulo's, just off the main street in Invergryff. The café looked like it was last decorated sometime in the sixties. In fact, the word café was probably a little too 'foreign' for this place. It was a proper old-fashioned tearoom with lots of glassware on display and sharp edges on the tables. Perfect.

"I think we're the only people here under eighty," Liz whispered when she arrived back with a tray of tea and cakes.

"I know. Isn't it lovely," Mary said, happier than she had felt all week. "Not a high chair in sight. And just look how thin this teacup is. Peter would have it smashed in a second."

Liz gave her a knowing smile. "You're enjoying having some time away from the kids, then?"

"Definitely. I mean, I still spend most of the time worrying about them, but it has been amazing having some time to myself." Mary leaned back in the chair. "Do you know, I never really thanked you?"

"For what?"

"For letting me into the WWC. It's changed my life."

"Really?"

"I had forgotten what it was like to do something outside of the kids. Something that I'm good at. You gave me that back, Liz, so thank you."

Liz drummed her long nails on the table. "I think it saved my life too. I mean, without the WWC I wouldn't have been able to quit my job. I'll probably still have to get another office job or something, but it's given me an option I didn't know I had."

Mary held up her tea cup. "To the Wronged Women's Co-operative."

"To the WWC," Liz smiled back, clinking her cup against Mary's.

"So what did you want to talk about?" Mary asked once they had settled back in their seats.

"Well, there was something." Liz pushed a slice of walnut loaf across the table.

"Okay, now I know I'm in trouble if you're bribing me," Mary said, cutting off a chunk of the cake and popping it into his

131

mouth.

"I want to know what the deal is with you and the handsome Constable."

Mary sat back in surprise. "There is no deal. You know that."

"Come on, it's always been clear that you like him. And that he likes you."

"Or he did until someone else came along," Mary said, admitting the worry that had been hanging around in her brain since the terrible game night. "It's the new Inspector. The very beautiful, very clever woman who doesn't have four children and a debt-ridden ex-husband."

"Ah."

"I know I'm being completely ridiculous. I have no right to be jealous, and even if I did, what sort of person does that make me, glaring at any pretty woman he speaks to. I wasn't ever like that with Matt."

Liz took a sip of her coffee. "Maybe that's why you're feeling so jealous. If you were actually his girlfriend then it wouldn't be an issue. As it is, when you are his… whatever you are right now, it makes you more paranoid."

"Huh." Mary considered what Liz had said. It had the nagging sound of truth to it. "You could be right. What are my options, then?"

"Well, you could avoid him completely, although our work will make that a challenge. You could just see him in a professional manner, cut out all this 'friendship' stuff. Or there's the nuclear option."

"The nuclear option?"

"You take him out on a date."

Mary wrinkled her nose. "I just don't think that's a good idea."

"Oh yeah, why would you want to go out with the available, stunningly handsome police officer that fancies you back."

"You know why."

"I'm not saying marry him. Hell, you don't even have to introduce him to the kids if you're not ready yet. But take him out for a coffee. What's the worst that can happen?"

"Somehow saying 'what's the worst that can happen' always makes me think it's going to be an epic disaster."

Liz laughed. "All right. I'll drop the subject for now. There is something work related that I wanted to ask you about. Your old job before you had kids, wasn't it something to do with the Environment Agency?"

"I worked for SEPA. The Scottish Environment Protection Agency. It was pretty boring, to be honest with you, but at least I didn't have to wash socks all day."

"It sounds perfect. If I send you some environmental impact statements for some of Pearson's developments, could you check them out for me?"

"Of course," Mary replied, pleased to find something she could be considered an expert in.

"Great. I'll email them over right after I finish this scone."

Chapter 26: Bernie

It had taken an effort of will, but Bernie finally made up with Finn enough that she could ask him about local builders firms. She hadn't exactly apologised for having a go at him about the drinking, but then he hadn't apologised for refusing to acknowledge the problem, so she figured they were pretty much even.

She had presented him with a cooked breakfast, a classic way to get on his good side. Bacon, sausage, eggs, black pudding, fried tomatoes and his favourite, a slice of haggis. No beans, because whatever else her husband was he wasn't an animal. While he was tucking in, Bernie asked if he had ever heard of Building Pros West Coast.

"Don't think so. Is it a local one?"

"Yes. They used to be known as West Clyde Builders."

Finn put down his fork. "Those lads? Aye, I've heard of them."

"Tell me everything you know," Bernie said, sitting down next to him.

"Well, the boss is Tam Brown, and he runs it with his son, William. They've got a bit of a reputation."

"A bad one?"

Finn squirmed in his chair. He was one of those people that

hated gossip. Bernie found it very frustrating.

"Aye. There were always a lot of accidents on their sites. I mean, we all push the limits sometimes, but they had a lot of young apprentices being asked to do dangerous stuff on ladders, silly things just so they could save the cost of scaffolding. And people used to say that they would find extra faults on roofs while they were up there, if you can imagine the sort of thing. A lot of my lads wouldn't work with them no matter what they paid."

For Finn, this was a long speech and he didn't look very happy about making it. He stuffed a large piece of black pudding into his mouth as an excuse to stop talking.

"Did you ever know a guy called Paul Dean or Paul Crossly? He'd have been working on the sites in 2004."

"Jesus, that's a long time ago. I'd have been twenty-two, I guess." Finn chewed on a piece of square sausage. "Don't remember him. But that was when I working on that new estate to the East of Glasgow, so if he was in Invergryff I probably wouldn't have bumped into him."

It had been too much to hope that Finn had known their potential victim, but Bernie couldn't help but feel disappointed anyway. "Would you ask around at work if anyone remembers him?"

"Sure."

"And I'd like to chat to this Tam Brown and his son. Do you know where I'd find them?"

Finn shook his head. "No, and I don't want to. Honestly, Bernie, I don't want you messing around with these guys. They're the sort to solve their problems with their fists. You don't want to get on the wrong side of them."

"What exactly do you think I do, now that you know all about the WWC?" Bernie asked, finding it hard not to show her irritation. "The whole point is to get involved with dodgy characters."

Finn's ears were turning red, a sure sign that he was annoyed. "This isn't some silly tart who has been cheating on her husband. These guys are as close as you can get to gangsters around here. I really think you should stay out of their way."

He bent low over his plate, cleaning it with a piece of buttered toast.

Bernie placed her hand on his shoulder. "I'll be careful, I promise."

She waited until Finn had left for work before doing an internet search on Tam Brown. It didn't take her long to find a number for the building firm. She got through to a harassed sounding secretary.

"Tam is on a job at the moment."

"Right. It's just I've got an invoice for him that I've just realised I hadn't fully paid," Bernie said before the woman could put the phone down. "I still owe him about a grand so I wanted to settle up."

"I can take that payment over the phone," the other woman

137

replied.

Crap. "Well… Actually, we had agreed a cash discount so I've got it sitting here in cash. If he's working somewhere nearby I can just pop it over to him. I'm in Invergryff."

"Hang on. Yes, he is in Invergryff today. Over at the new-builds off the roundabouts. The Elm Woods estate."

"I know exactly where that is. Thank you for your help."

She hung up and headed for the car. Bernie knew that Finn wouldn't be pleased about her talking to Tam Brown, but the man could hardly threaten her on a construction site in the middle of the day. It was worth taking a small risk for the WWC, she reckoned. Especially if it led to a murderer.

Chapter 27: Liz

Liz had treated herself to her favourite takeaway coffee on the way over to Glasgow. Seeing as she had already had two lattes with Mary earlier, she felt a happy buzz of caffeine as she rang the bell for Imelda Blake's office. It was in a very posh building in the Merchant City with an upmarket bar on the bottom level and suites of offices up above.

When she made her way to reception, Liz found herself in a waiting room that was all white walls and curved furniture. Gentle classical music emanated from hidden speakers. There were copies of several Interiors magazines and Liz settled in happily to flick through one. A glass of wine and it would have been a lovely way to spend an afternoon.

A Receptionist who couldn't have been more than twenty with giant false eyelashes and a magazine hidden under her computer keyboard picked up the phone. A few muttered words and nods later, then the woman made her way over to Liz's little oasis of calm.

"Mrs Blake is available now if you would like to follow me," the soft-voiced Receptionist said, and Liz did as she was bidden. Mrs Blake's office was large with a long white desk on one side and a conference table on the other. In the middle was a four-seater sofa and coffee table where the woman herself sat, scrolling through something on her tablet.

"Take a seat, please, I'm just replying to a message from the

Deputy Editor of Vogue."

Liz suppressed a grin. It was going to be that sort of interview, she thought. The woman had a tan that came from a bottle and very expensive looking veneers. Liz wasn't against spending money on her own appearance – her collection of weaves had a cost that her husband was certainly never going to be appraised of – but this woman clearly saw it as a competition. Why else mention Vogue before she had even sat down?

"Thank you for seeing me," Liz said, sitting on a chair that was both exquisitely made and completely uncomfortable.

"It's always a pleasure to network with a fellow female entrepreneur." Mrs Blake said with a flash of a smile. She finally put the tablet to one side and folded her arms.

"I wanted to speak to you about participating in this new venture we are creating for women based in Scotland. It's a combination of face to face networking opportunities and an app to encourage social interaction." Liz had been particularly pleased with herself when she had thought to make up an app. Business types always loved an app.

"An app?" Imelda Blake didn't look quite as impressed as Liz had expected her to be. "I have enough of those already. I think the best thing is to get people away from screens, don't you?"

Liz refrained from mentioning that the woman was checking her emails on her tablet for the third time since she had entered the room.

"Of course, the in-person events are just as important," Liz said, trying to get her back on side, but Mrs Blake just sighed.

"I am already a member of several of these bodies. Why is yours any different?"

Liz gave the woman her best winning smile. In her previous job, she had handled multi-million dollar accounts of international companies going through insolvency. This brittle woman with her white teeth didn't frighten her. Mrs Blake, although she would hate to be reminded of the fact, was just a small time player.

"We look at matching people up by industry. Like a dating website, but for professions. For example, I know that Victory Holdings has several interests in the residential and commercial property sectors. We could match you with investors looking to provide funding in those areas."

The mention of funding perked the woman up a bit, and she sat up a little straighter.

"I am always looking to expand the business of course, so if people are willing to invest, I will hear them out."

"You've expanded a lot in the last ten years, haven't you? You started in new builds, is that right?"

Mrs Blake finally put the tablet down. "Yes. Small sites at first, then much larger projects. I'm more of a consultant these days, working to help other people to put through deals. I've cleared six figures already this financial year."

Liz just smiled back at her. At the accountancy firm she had managed the accounts for several billionaires let alone lowly millionaires. She had quickly learned that money was no gauge of what a person was like face to face.

"In your consultancy business, do you work only with businesses, or do you deal with local government? I'm looking to get more people on board from that side of things, you see," Liz explained.

"I have several contacts, of course, many that I have worked with for years."

"I heard that Invergryff council can be particularly... difficult to work with. A client of mine is trying to deal with their planning process at the moment."

"Ah yes, planning departments are always good fun. You just have to know which buttons to press."

"And they are?"

Mrs Blake was not to be fooled that easily. She simply shrugged. "Oh, the usual things. I don't see how this relates to your women's network, though?"

"I should have explained, really," Liz said, keeping her body language open and non-threatening. "I have a client who is currently in a... challenging position with regards to planning in the county. There is a very large, multi-million pound housing development at stake. Very early stages, of course, so I can't say much about it. I suppose I was thinking when you mentioned planning that you might be able to help with the negotiations."

Mrs Blake adjusted one of her earrings, a diamond stud that ended in a teardrop. "I think it was you that mentioned planning, wasn't it?"

"Was it?" Liz said, wondering if all these fake smiles might crack her foundation. "These things are always the same, aren't they? Who you know, not what you know. Like that MP, Pearson, he's a friend of yours, isn't he?"

She had gone too far, Liz knew it the moment the words were out of her mouth.

Immy Blake stood up. "I'm not sure why you're really here, Elizabeth. But it seems to me that you are making some very unpleasant insinuations. My business is entirely professional and I would like to keep it that way. I think it's best if you left."

Liz murmured something about her words being taken the wrong way, but both women knew that the game was up. She had managed to do little more than get Immy Blake's back up. Not a great start to the day.

As she walked out, the Receptionist checked the clock, then turned to Mrs Blake.

"Is it all right if I go for my break now?" She asked in a low voice.

"Wait until lunch," Mrs Blake said, her chin held high. "I don't let people take advantage of me. Not anyone."

The look that she gave Liz was pure poison, just in case she hadn't realised who the remark was really for. Liz was glad to get out onto the pavement. She had a feeling that Immy Blake would be a dangerous woman to cross. At the same time, Liz knew she wouldn't be able to resist trying to cross her.

Chapter 28: Walker

Walker was finding it hard to keep his eyes open by mid-morning. He had resisted visiting the vending machine again, just in case Dianna saw him, and even the frequent cups of tea weren't helping him stay awake. He had been up late studying the Blackstone's Police Manual again. Or not studying. It always took a good hour of procrastination before he could get himself to open the damn things. The online learning resources were even worse, because then he had the whole of the internet to distract him. He had been watching videos of private jet landings for an hour before he went to bed, still no studying done.

Self-sabotage, that was what a previous girlfriend had called it. And maybe it was. After all, no one else seemed to find it so hard to open up a book. But he knew that when he looked at the pages, the words would start to get jumbled up. He would have to read a sentence three times before he could work it out. And it just left him feeling even more stupid than ever. He was a good police officer, he knew that. He liked working out puzzles, using his brain to dig under the surface to find out what was going on. But how could he be so good at one thing, and so thick at something else? It was a different sort of puzzle, and a frustrating one at that.

While he had been feeling sorry for himself, the office had gradually filled up with his colleagues. It was Dianna's voice that pulled him out of his funk.

"All right, I'm not going to stand up here and take you through everything. I want you to shout out what you've learned since we heard about the body's gender."

There was a brief moment where everyone waited for everyone else to talk. Sometimes the police station was like being back at school, Walker thought. And Dianna made quite a good grumpy teacher, glaring at them all to put their hands up.

Finally, Neil stood up. "Missing persons has come back with a few hits. I've graded them from most to least likely. There are two from Scotland and five from England. All Caucasian women between the ages of sixteen and thirty, which fits with what pathology said. I've uploaded them to the case folder."

"Can you tell us who you think is most likely?" Dianna asked.

"My money is on either Kyla Turner or Claire Wright. Wright is from Glasgow, and Turner is from just down the road in Greenock. Both missing for around a year."

"Anything to link them to the site where the body was found?"

"Not so far. Both were drug users, both had histories of living rough. I'm still seeing what I can find out."

"Good work," Dianna said. Walker tried not to notice that Neil was beaming with pleasure.

"What about the phone lines?"

Walker shook his head. "A bust so far. We're following up on a couple of sightings of vehicles, but nothing looks very promising. Unless you're looking for stories about the witch?"

Dianna pursed her lips. "I certainly am not. What else have we got?"

"Stomach contents," Sergeant Suzie O'Connor said, holding up a piece of paper. "Obviously after a year, the lab didn't think they'd get much, but we got lucky. She must have eaten not long before she died. Traces of bread and fish."

"Okay, that's something."

"And there is more. The results show that it was rye bread, not your usual British white stuff. And traces of lemon and poppy seeds."

"Eastern European then maybe?" Dianna said.

O'Connor nodded. "Or eating that sort of food, anyway."

"Good. It's something to go on. Pathology has given me some more details on the probable cause of death. The victim had her skull bashed in, the back of her head. A blow with a blunt object. Could have been a fall, but they found defensive marks on her hands, indicative of a fight, and bruising on her face. Although with the decomposition, they wouldn't state for certain that that was caused pre-mortem."

"It's murder then?" Walker asked.

"Looks like it. Now, normally the Major Incident Team would be down here already, but there has been a big gangland killing over in Glasgow, two dead and lots of weapons found, so half the force is over there. For the moment it's just us."

Walker could see how pleased Dianna was at the prospect of

being SIO for such a major case. He raised his hand. "Just on the unidentified bodies, I spoke to DI Macleod this morning. He worked the earlier case. He thought that the farmer might have been involved. Nothing concrete, but he thought the guy was involved in some dodgy stuff."

Dianna flicked through her notes. "The farmer's dead now though, isn't he?"

"Aye," Walker replied. "It's his daughter that's there now."

"All right then. Can't see him coming back from the dead to kill someone else, even if he was involved in the first killing. Put it on the list of actions, but not urgent, okay?"

Walker nodded. He wanted to follow up Macleod's lead, but Dianna was in charge and she wanted to focus more on the present day. Which he couldn't really argue with.

"What I want you to focus on right now is the discovery of the body. Until we work out who the victim is, there's not much point in spending time on her death. Walker, you go speak to the woman with the dog. And Neil, I want you to go through the forensics again. Check for anything we've missed. There's got to be something."

Five minutes later Walker was in a patrol car heading out towards the area where the body was found. Mrs Cottrell lived in a place called Willow cottage, just a mile from the farm and the witch's hill.

Conjured up by the name, Walker had been expecting a quaint little house, perhaps with roses around the door. Instead,

148

when he climbed out of the car he saw that Willow cottage was a nineteen sixties build on a small estate of similar houses. It had an overgrown front garden and a 'no unsolicited callers' sign hanging above the door.

Walker rang the bell and was greeted by the yapping of a small dog.

"Quiet Lags," a voice shouted from behind the frosted glass. The door was pulled open a crack and a grumpy, wrinkled face peered out at him.

"Mrs Cottrell? It's Police Constable Walker. I wondered if we could talk."

For a moment Walker thought the woman would slam the door in his face. Then her expression transformed into a smile.

"How lovely! I expected you would have come before now. I'm sure the biscuits will still be all right. Come in, please, and leave your boots at the door."

"Don't mind Lags," the woman said, bustling about as she made tea and found some very crumbly biscuits.

The dog in question, a tubby little Westie, was giving Walker's stockinged feet a good sniff. The Constable was just glad he had put clean socks on that morning.

"Unusual name, Lags," Walker said, trying to move his feet under the chair so the dog would stop investigating them.

"Short for Lagavulin, my favourite whiskey."

"Of course." Walker cleared his throat, trying to think how he could regain control of an interview that seemed to already be veering towards the seriously weird. "I wondered if you could go over what happened when you found the remains on Saturday night."

"Certainly. I have it all written down here." She reached into an old-fashioned writing desk and pulled out a notepad.

"That's very organised of you," Walker said.

"Oh yes. One should always be organised, and I'm not just a civilian, you know... I have listened to three seasons of Murder on your Doorstep."

"If you could tell me what you have written down, that would be a good start," the police officer said, trying to keep things on track.

"Yes, of course. Well, here we are. I left the house just after seven and took the path towards the witch's hill. I had nearly reached the top when Lags started barking. At first I thought it might be a fox – we get plenty of them around here, you know. Mrs Hancock in number thirty-two feeds them, if you can believe that! Anyway, Lags was pulling at the lead so hard I let him take me off the path. I suppose I was curious by this point what it might be. Then I'm afraid I smelt it before I saw it. Lags was pulling at something and I tried to grab him as soon as I realised it was... well, it was a hand."

"That must have been very distressing for you."

Mrs Cottrell who had been looking a little queasy sat up

150

straight in her chair. "Not at all. I knew exactly what to do. I picked up Lags and ran to the farmhouse, calling the police on my mobile before I got there. The farmer's wife was all for heading out to the hill, but I told her to wait. I knew we shouldn't touch the crime scene, you see."

Walker had a sinking feeling that he knew what was coming.

"I heard it on one of those podcasts. True crime. Do you listen to any?"

"No," Walker replied, and Mrs Cottrell either ignored or didn't hear the frustration in his voice.

"There's a lovely one about Jack the Ripper at the moment. I listen to it when I'm in the bath. What soothing voices those people have, and ever so clever. I bet they solve more murders than your lot do.

"They have become quite popular," Walker said, with all the diplomacy he could manage. "I did want to ask you about the timings on Saturday. You found the body after seven pm, that's late to be out walking your dog, wasn't it? It must have been dark by then."

"Now that is a very good question, young man. A very suspicious action on my part, being out in the dark on country lanes, wouldn't you say."

Walker pinched the bridge of his nose. "Yes."

"Unfortunately, there is a banal reason why I was doing such a thing. Lags isn't so good at holding his water overnight anymore so I find that we have to make a late visit. I prefer

151

the path near the farm as there's no danger of broken glass. Do you know we were walking by the road once and he got shards of bottle stuck in his little paw?"

"Terrible," Walker said. "So that's why you were walking him so late?"

"Yes. I had my trusty head-torch, of course, but it's nice to be close enough to see the lights of the farmhouse."

"And how did the farmers take the news of your discovery?"

Mrs Cottrell leaned forward so that Walker got just the slightest whiff of the whiskey that the dog was named after.

"If you ask me, you need to start there. There has always been something dodgy about that family, and I don't like that Mrs Graham one bit. She was a right snob, and nobody can possibly care about cake that much, even Mary Berry."

"Did she act suspiciously when you told her about the body?" Walker asked, feeling uncomfortably like he was saying just what Mrs Cottrell expected him to.

"Oh yes. I think she said, 'blast, not another one!'. And that husband of hers never said anything, just sat on the sofa looking at his phone. Ignorant, he is. But she's something else. Sly, just like her father. Mark my words, she's your prime suspect right there."

"Well, that has all been very helpful," Walker said, standing up and heading for the door. He tried not to notice that one of his boots was covered in dog slobber when he pulled it on. "Perhaps you could give me a call if you think of anything else."

Mrs Cottrell clutched his card like it was a precious jewel. "Oh, thank you. I will."

"Good," Walker said, not sure if he meant it or not.

Chapter 29: Mary

After what had felt like an energetic beginning to the case, by Tuesday afternoon Mary had run out of leads to follow on either of the buried bodies. Bernie had taken over the lead concerning the building sites and Alice was still consulting with her friend Eve to see if there was any merit in the witchcraft element. As for the newer body, they had even less to go on. Who was she? Killed a year ago but there had been nothing in the news about a missing woman around that time. Mary had double-checked all the local news websites. So who was she?

In desperation, Mary had even texted Walker. *I hear your body is female! Any connection to Paul Crossly?* But so far, no reply. Despite her chat with Liz, Mary wasn't too keen to poke a pointy stick into that particular bear pit. After all, what if it didn't work out? At least she had the dream of something with Walker, and she wasn't ready to let that go yet.

Matt had texted earlier with a picture of the kids looking very cute in their pyjamas with the title 'pancakes for breakfast' and Mary had had a little weep. Honestly, since becoming a mum the littlest things could set her off. A few years ago she had found herself bawling in the kitchen when she realised Peter was too big for sippy cups. Once Mary had dried her eyes and sent a thumbs up to Matt, she turned on her laptop. Instead of moping about missing the kids it was time to get some work done.

Liz had sent her all the documents relating to the Pearson case.

Mary scanned through them quickly as she hadn't really been following the investigation so far. She found murders and cheatings husbands much more fun than fraud, but as she read further into the case she found that she was becoming hooked.

Pearson seemed like a proper baddy. Politically, he was a member of the party that she would never vote for, a supporter of what he called 'Christian values' which was always something of a red flag and in this case seemed to be supporting the rights of big business all over Scotland. He had supported a certain former President's bid to get three new golf courses approved in Scotland long before he had been involved in Victory Holdings and their own golf course site at Ellenslie Braes.

The client, New Dawn Home Management, was looking to make a case that Pearson had deliberately obstructed their small-scale development of cottages and social housing to ensure that the access to the golf course would be unaffected. And no doubt Pearson wanted the golfers to have uninterrupted views of empty hills rather than the homes of working class people.

Mary paused and drank some of her tea. Of course, it was entirely possible that she was letting her own prejudice shape her thoughts on the case. Just because she didn't agree with the planning decision didn't mean that anyone had done anything illegal.

She clicked down through the rest of the documents and opened up the environmental impact statements. The reports were hundreds of pages long, but that didn't intimidate her.

Before she had become Mary Plunkett and mother to a bunch of crazy children, Mary had been Ms Mary Stewart, part of the technical team at the Scottish Environmental Protection Agency. She had read dozens of these reports a week, and even written a few herself.

An hour later and she had barely scratched the surface. Her notepad was covered in dates and names, but so far it all seemed legit. The flood risk assessments were just as she would have expected for the golf course, and although there weren't many mentions of the hotel complex in the overall development, it was there. If the council had found anything to object about, it would be in these documents.

She moved on to the ecological reports. These were interesting in their brevity. The golf course development was on land that had formerly been agricultural, but left fallow for decades. As such, she would have assumed there would be a high level of biodiversity. But the reports didn't seem to suggest that.

Mary scrolled back through the documents. The name of the company employed to do these reports was Scotia-Enviro Limited, and it wasn't a name she had come across before. She quickly searched for them online.

Her heart dropped a little when a perfectly legitimate website appeared. Mary had been hoping the company itself was bogus, but it didn't appear to be. They even had a report of a recent survey they had done on the Great Crested Newt. A cute little slimy face looked up at her and Mary took a screenshot. She always liked newts with their weird, unfinished faces. A bit like babies, when you thought about it.

Bzzzz. Her phone was buzzing from down behind the sofa cushion. Mary dug down, flinging aside the stuffed toys and empty chocolate wrappers and clicked answer as soon as Walker's name came up on the screen.

"Hi, sorry I took a while to answer. There was a thing about a newt."

"A newt?"

"It's complicated."

Walker laughed. "It always is. Listen, I just wanted to see if you knew anything about the farmers that own the land where the body was found. I wondered if your little group –"

"The WWC," Mary reminded him.

"Yes, that lot. I wondered if they knew anything. Because I just tried to arrange an interview with Nora Graham and she said, and I quote, 'I've already had enough questions from that busybody Bernie Paterson'."

"Ah, well, I think Bernie might have gone up there to ask about the Women's Institute. They do a 'bring and buy' sale every Sunday, you know."

Mary could sense the exasperation in Walker's tone when he replied. "Funnily enough, I didn't know about the 'bring and buy' sale. I wonder if you could remind Mrs Paterson that we would prefer to at least have the chance to be the first ones to question any witnesses."

"You know that we have every right to…"

"Yes, I do. And I know that you understand that this is an active murder investigation. Now, I am more than happy for you to investigate the body found in 2004. In fact, I would be glad of the help. But as for the more recent case, well, it's better if you leave it to us."

"I'll ask them to back off," Mary said, certain that they would do exactly the opposite. Walker might be an attractive, available man, but he was also part of the police force, and that made him the competition, whether he liked it or not. Mary bit her lip. She thought back to what Liz had said and took a deep breath.

"Maybe we could meet up and discuss it? You know, arrange a way for us to work without getting under each others' feet. Um, we could grab a drink together tonight if you want?"

There was a long pause.

"I'm kind of busy this week," Walker said. "Studying, for exams. They're really important and I failed the last time."

That couldn't have sounded more like a brush off, Mary thought, pressing her fist against her forehead. So much for putting myself out there. "Of course," she said, her voice a little too bright. "Well, if there was anything else you wanted…"

There was another pause on the other end of the line, and as usual Mary wondered what Walker was thinking.

"I thought you wanted to know about the female body," he

158

said finally. It was only then that Mary remembered that she had texted him earlier.

"Oh yes! I mean, I don't suppose you can tell me anything."

"I'd rather tell you now than have Bernie Paterson sticking her nose in. The body is definitely female, it was a bit of a cock-up really that they told us it was male in the first place, but there was a lot of decomposition so…"

"Yuck."

"Yuck indeed. Anyway, we don't have an ID yet, but we're working through missing persons. She was probably under thirty. And it's definitely murder. I can't tell you cause of death, but it wasn't an accident."

"Great. Well, not great for the poor woman obviously…"

There was a noise on the other end of the phone, a female voice.

"Look I've got to go. But I'll be in touch, okay?"

"Okay," Mary said, although she couldn't help but feel that he had made it quite clear that he didn't want to be in touch at all. Oh well, at least she knew where she stood. That had probably been the Inspector's voice on the other end. Mary sniffed. They would probably be very happy together. Just like Mary Plunkett was about to be with a large tub of chocolate ice-cream.

Chapter 30: Bernie

It was bitterly cold on the building site and by the time she had got out of the car, Bernie was already wishing she was back at home. Not to mention the mud. It was a typical Invergryff winter – more wet than snowy – and between that and the heavy machinery, the walk up to the building site was like a trip through a swamp.

Luckily, Bernie was married to a tradesman, so she had brought her wellies, but the mud had already spattered up her leggings and was threatening the rather nice woollen coat that she had got in a Black Friday sale.

The site office was a static caravan just at the entrance to the estate which had around thirty houses in various states of development. Bernie had been hopeful of a cup of tea and maybe a heater to huddle at, but when she knocked on the door there was no answer.

She wrapped her coat more tightly around her chest and walked to the nearest house. It looked like it was in the final stages, with scaffolding up and windows in. Bernie wished that she had brought Finn as she had no idea if the work looked any good or not. Were they still cutting corners like the rumours had said when Paul Dean worked there? She had no way of telling.

"Hello!" She called up to a group of men who were standing on the scaffolding. They pointed over to another man in a high-vis jacket who was just coming out of the front door. He was carrying an old-fashioned clipboard so Bernie reckoned he had to be the foreman.

"Can I help you?" he said, showing a set of nicotine-stained teeth.

"I'm looking for the boss. Is Tam Brown about?"

"You'll want young Billy." The foreman shouted out to some of the other lads and eventually one man peeled off from the group and came sauntering over.

'Young' Billy didn't seem all that young to Bernie. He was maybe in his early forties, but he had the sort of pinched, thin skin that made people look older than they really were. One of those young Scottish men whose complexion suggested he had never eaten a vegetable. There was something deeply unlikeable about the man, partly due to the way he swaggered about with his legs stretched wide. He gave Bernie an up and down look that clearly said she was too old and too plain to be interesting to him. Well, she could deal with that sort of man easily enough.

"I want to talk to your father about Paul Dean. Or Paul Crossly, as that was his real name."

"Never heard of him."

"He would have been a bit younger than you," Bernie said, although that was more of a guess. "He worked on one of your sites in 2004."

"I was twelve then," Young Billy said and Bernie tried not to

161

show her surprise. She had thought he was older than that. What a curse poor nutrition was on the skin tone.

"Well, could I speak to your dad? He was in charge back then, wasn't he?"

"Dad's busy. We're running three months late on this site and the windows guys are taking the piss over materials costs. He's got three of them in for a meeting right now."

"I'm happy to wait."

Young Billy sniffed. "I don't see that he'll be able to tell you anything. Lot of lads pass through our sites."

"He'll remember this one," Bernie said, crossing her arms and making it clear that she wasn't going anywhere. "The police interviewed him about Paul, right after they found a body."

The man tilted his head to one side, then nodded slowly. "I'll give him a call. If he's free, maybe he'll come see you."

Young Billy sauntered off, pulling out his phone as he did so. Bernie was left standing in the open air, the wind biting at her cheeks. She kept her legs planted in the same place. She wasn't about to be intimidated into leaving, especially by a loon like Young Billy.

Eventually, one of the lads took pity on her and took her into the site office. At least there was a plastic chair, although the little rotating heater seemed to just emphasise how cold the rest of the room was.

It must have been a full hour before the door opened again.

Bernie immediately closed down the game of Sudoku she had been playing on her phone and held out her hand.

"Tam Brown? I'm Bernie Paterson."

The man hesitated for a second, then shook her hand. Bernie always liked to offer a handshake to men. They never quite knew how to do it with a woman, and that discomfort gave her the edge.

"Sorry you had to wait. I had to put some guys in their place." Brown puffed out his chest. Bernie had to hide a smile. So he was going to be that sort of man, then. All puff and fluster. And what a suit! It would have looked just grand on the set of Only Fools and Horses. The man himself was around sixty, with broad shoulders and the sort of frame that might have been muscular once but was now turning to fat.

"Of course," Bernie said. She tried to give him a simpering smile, but she wasn't sure she quite managed it. Part of her wished Mary Plunkett was here. She would have managed just the combination of vulnerability and flirtation that would have caught the man off guard. Oh well, Bernie had her own style.

"I won't take up much of your time," she said briskly. "I just wanted to ask you about the death of Paul Dean. Now that there has been a second body found up on witch's hill."

The large man blinked. Then he looked at her again, eyes narrowed. "Billy didn't say who you were working for. You're not with the police, are you?"

"No. I work for a private client," Bernie said, not feeling the

163

need to mention that in this case the 'client' was the WWC itself. "We're looking into the circumstances around Paul Crossly's disappearance. Or Paul Dean, as he was called when he worked for you."

Brown snorted. "He didn't 'disappear'. Look, I barely knew the lad, can't even remember his face. In fact, I would have forgotten his name if it wasn't for the police coming and asking questions. There are two types of boys we get here, the ones that work hard, and the ones that dropped out of school and thought going into the trades was easy money. He was one of them. An unskilled labourer, and not even good at that. He'd had two warnings about lateness before he stopped showing up at work. When he didn't turn up one day I assumed he'd found an easier job somewhere else. It was no great loss."

"Is that what you thought when they found the body? No great loss."

"That's out of order," Brown said quietly.

What would I do if he just went for me? Bernie thought, as she watched the man's face turn a darker shade of red. He was around her height, but carrying a fair bit of muscle under a solid layer of fat. Physically stronger, that was for sure. But she wasn't particularly worried. At the care home, it wasn't unusual for dementia sufferers to turn violent. You learned pretty early on how to defend yourself and how to subdue a belligerent opponent. And she could always kick him in the nuts, something she would definitely not do at work.

"Sorry," Bernie said, with no real apology in her tone. "I didn't mean to offend. But you strike me as a straight talker. I wondered if there was anything about Paul that you hadn't mentioned to the police."

"As I said before, I can't even remember what he looked like."

"Well, is there anyone that might remember him better?"

Brown tapped his fingers on the desk. "If I give you a couple of names will you get the hell out of here?"

"Of course!" Bernie gave him a bright smile.

"He used to hang out with a couple of local lads. I can't remember their names, they both left years ago, but they'll be in the files somewhere. I'll get my secretary to call you as soon as possible."

The man walked over to the door and opened it, signalling the interview was over. Bernie was sure he was lying, but then he was the sort of person that probably lied constantly on principle.

"Thank you for your time," Bernie said and moved past him. She had to squeeze past his large frame as she went out the door, and almost laughed at the obvious power play.

"Your husband is Finn Paterson, right?"

Bernie paused, one foot over the threshold. "That's right."

"Nice little business he's got. Just him and three others, isn't it?"

She refused to let her face change. "Yes."

"Then I hope they have a good year. It's tough times for the small business, isn't it?"

Bernie didn't reply. Instead, she stepped outside and pulled the door shut behind her. It took a lot to rattle Bernie Paterson, but she could feel her heart thumping as she walked back to the car. An empty threat, she was sure of it. But she was just as sure that if he chose to, Tam Brown could make life very difficult for her husband. She was beginning to wish she hadn't come to the building site in the first place.

Chapter 31: Liz

In Glasgow, Liz was sitting on a metal bench with a takeaway coffee clutched in her hands. She knew she should probably have headed straight back to Invergryff, but there was something she wanted to check out first.

It was nearly two o'clock before Immy Blake's receptionist managed to slip out of the building to get some lunch. Liz followed the woman, slipping off the bench and stretching out her muscles that had been bunched up for the last hour and a half.

The receptionist was walking quickly along the road, glancing at her phone as she did so. After a few minutes, she ducked into a sandwich shop.

Liz tapped her on the shoulder. "Why don't you grab a table and I'll pay for your lunch," she said, offering the woman her friendliest smile.

"You were in the office earlier, weren't you?"

"Yes. I just want five minutes of your time. And you get a free lunch. I'm guessing you're not paid very much in there."

"Minimum wage," the girl said, tucking her hair behind her ears. "Okay. I'll get a table."

By the time Liz had paid for their lunch, the young woman at the table was drumming her feet against the floor and looking nervously at the windows.

"I'm sorry, I shouldn't have agreed to this. If Mrs Blake finds out…"

"She won't. Honestly, I only want to ask a couple of questions. I won't get you in trouble. What's your name?"

The girl still looked like she wanted to bolt out of the door, but she took a bite of her sandwich.

"Milly. I shouldn't be talking to you. It's probably, like, a confidentiality thing?"

"Maybe," Liz said with a smile, "but then if you're just a temp it doesn't really matter, does it?"

"No, I guess not. I'm going to be out of there on Friday, thank god. I've got a job starting with an Animal place."

"Ooh, is it a cat charity? I love kittens."

"A dog shelter. I'm doing the admin."

"How lovely," Liz said, even though she had always been a bit scared of dogs. It was something to do with the size of their grins.

Milly took a bigger bite of her sandwich and leaned back in her chair. "So are you from a newspaper or something?"

"Nothing like that. I'm actually a private investigator," Liz said, still not over the little thrill that went up her spine every time she said that.

"Wow. That's cool."

"Yes. I'm looking into some of the connections that your boss has. The person I'm interested in is Hugh Pearson. Do you know him?"

"He's that MP isn't he? I saw him on the news last week. He was talking about the bins."

"That's him. Did he ever come and see Mrs Blake?"

Milly nodded. "A few times. I mean, I've only been there six months, and I would guess he's been in maybe three times? She always looks pleased to see him."

"Like, romantically pleased?" Liz said, realising she sounded about a hundred years old.

"No, I don't think so. Mrs Blake's husband is ten years younger than her and he's a footballer. Totally fit. That Pearson guy is an old man."

Liz made a note of this, even though she knew that 'old' to a woman of twenty meant most of the population.

"Do you know what they talked about when he came to the office?"

The receptionist shook her head. "No. He was just listed in the diary as 'Pearson', no subject listed. And when they met the office door was shut and it's pretty soundproof. Except, well, there was one time they seemed to be having an argument and I did hear a bit of that."

169

"Really?"

"But she'd kill me if I told you. I'm not even exaggerating. She's seriously scary when she's annoyed. Like an evil mannequin or something. She can't move her face much because of the botox, but you can tell when she's pissed off."

Liz held up her palms. "Look, I don't want to make you do anything you're uncomfortable with, but if there's something dodgy about Pearson and Blake too, wouldn't you like to see them get what they deserve? I mean, she shouldn't be able to get away with treating people so badly, should she?"

Milly shook her head. "I would like to see her get a taste of her own medicine for once. All right, I did hear a few things during the argument. It was a couple of weeks ago and Pearson had turned up without an appointment. Normally, Mrs Blake never sees anyone without it being arranged in advance, but she told me to let him in. I could tell she was mad though. She didn't pull the door shut, and as soon as he's in there Pearson starts yelling at her."

"What about?"

"I'm not sure. He kept mentioning land, something wrong with the land. I guess that's not surprising given that Mrs Blake is involved in so many developments. And then he said something about someone called Nora, and called her, well, actually he called her a bitch."

"Is that all?"

"Pretty much, Mrs Blake told him to calm down and then I

couldn't hear any more. She was in a rotten mood after he left though. She told me to take the afternoon off and she shut the office. Of course, when I checked my paycheck she had taken the afternoon off from my pay. I won't be sad to see the back of her."

"I don't blame you," Liz said. "Were there any other times…"

"God, that's nearly half past," Milly said, looking at her phone in horror. "She'll kill me for taking this long." With a quick goodbye she was running down the street, hair whipping around her face in the wind.

Liz took the time to finish her coffee in peace. She sent an email with the gist of the interview to Bernie, and made sure that Immy Blake was put at the top of her list for further investigation. Apart from anything else, Liz always hated people who treated their staff badly. Hopefully, she would get enough dirt not just to nail Pearson, but to take down Mrs Blake as well. She just had to find the evidence to pull it off.

Alice text her at that moment and Liz couldn't help feeling that this might be the breakthrough she needed.

Surveillance is a bust. All Pearson does is play golf with other old men. Have sent you their names, but all locals, nothing suspicious.

Liz clicked off the phone in disappointment. Where were the torrid affairs when you needed them? MPs definitely weren't what they used to be.

Chapter 32: Walker

Shamed by Dianna, Walker had brought in some porridge and dried fruit for his breakfast on Wednesday morning. When he arrived for Dianna's briefing he was less than pleased to see that someone had done a run to the local greasy spoon. Neil gave his sad breakfast a thumbs up from behind a large bacon roll.

Walker tucked into his bowl of warm, but bland porridge and tried to pretend that he was enjoying it. It wasn't like the Inspector even noticed his saintly snacking when she came into the room. Dianna had a face like thunder and she slammed her hands down on the desk.

"That's it," she said. "I've just spoken with the Super and we've got until five o'clock on Friday, then he's sending in the Major Incident Team. And we've got no ID on our victim, no leads, no suspects... Come on guys, we need to pull our fingers out. I want to show everyone that we can solve this case just as easily as they can."

Walker joined the murmurs of agreement around him. It would be a feather in his cap if he could be part of the team that presented the MIT with the case nicely worked out and a suspect in custody when they showed up. He knew that Dianna would put a good word in for him at his next promotion board, and a result would help his chances no end.

He opened up his laptop and started scrolling back through the evidence and interviews they had already done. There had to be a clue somewhere, at least a hint of something they could investigate. Walker found himself returning to the crime scene. What was it about the witch's hill? And what was the connection between the two bodies? Even though Dianna didn't like the idea, he was sure there was a link.

"I've got something!" Suzie O'Connor leapt from her seat and rushed over to the smartboard. "I just took a call about a missing person. They saw our appeal. It's a landlord, name of Beatson, they were renting a flat to a young woman and a year ago they just disappeared. Of course, they never thought to report it at the time. But here's the thing though; her employer did report her missing and in the description he said she was tall, with short brown hair."

Dianna's eyes narrowed and she turned to Neil. "Why didn't this woman come up on your search of missing persons?"

Neil swallowed. "I'm not sure."

"No one actually reported her to the police," Suzie said quickly. "She was working for a temp agency, cleaning offices and things. The people in the office reported to the agency she wasn't turning up for work, and they didn't take it any further."

"Why the hell not?"

"They just thought she was kind of flaky. Apparently it happens a lot, the wages are pretty rubbish so people get other jobs, move on and never bother to let them know."

Dianna pursed her lips. "Well, we'll certainly chase that up with

173

the agency. Suzie, will you interview them?"

"Of course."

Dianne walked over to the smartboard. "So what was the woman's name?"

"Mikala Nowak."

"Nowak, that's a Polish name, right?" Neil asked.

"Quite common in Poland, but also across the Slavic countries," Suzie said. "The temp agency said she was Polish but they went quiet when I asked if they'd seen her ID. Paying in cash and not doing any paperwork, I reckon."

"So she could have been from anywhere," Dianna said. "All right, as of now Mikala Nowak is our most likely fit for our victim. Let's find out everything we can about her. Walker, would you go and find the landlord that phoned in? He should at least have some information for us."

"Will do," Walker said, pulling on his coat. He couldn't help sharing a grin with Dianna. This was just what they needed, and about time too.

Chapter 33: Mary

It was her last day of freedom and Mary was determined to make the most of it. Tomorrow the kids would be back and life would return to its usual madness. That was why at nine o'clock in the morning she was still in her pyjamas, drinking a cup of tea and scrolling through old TV shows on streaming. She was just about to play an episode of the Golden Girls when the door rang.

Crap! She looked down at her PJs, to see that it was the very ancient hello kitty ones she had had for a decade that were just about taking leave of their elastic. She pulled on a big fluffy dressing gown to keep her modesty intact and went to the door. She didn't even have time to check her hair, but it was probably just the postman, not –

"Good morning."

Double crap.

"Hello Walker," she said, pulling the dressing gown firmly together at her neck.

"Kids not back yet then," he said with a knowing smile.

"Tomorrow." Mary wasn't sure why he was there, but she certainly wasn't about to let him in. Quite apart from the fact that he had brushed off her enquiry about a date, she hadn't done the dishes and there was half a box of chocolate biscuits on the living room floor.

"I wanted to let you know we've had a development. Of course, it's confidential."

"Right?"

"We think we might have got an ID on our remains. A young woman who went missing around a year ago. Her landlord reported her missing. Well, he did this morning. Apparently, no one bothered when she disappeared last year."

"That's so sad," Mary said, instantly imagining herself in the poor woman's situation. "Imagine no one caring you were missing."

"Well, we're going to find out what happened. I'm just on my way to interview the landlord, and I was wondering if your WWC sources knew anything about him. Local man named Liam Beatson."

"Oh, you better watch out. He's a sneaky character that one."

Walker blinked. "Sorry, are you saying you know Beatson?"

"Aye, he's my mum's next door neighbour. Likes to think he's a bit of a Del Boy character. He owns loads of flats, all kind of rundown. I rented one for a while."

"You did?"

Mary nodded. "Yeah. Just after I left school. I was saving up money to go to Uni, so I needed a cheap place to stay. One storage heater in the whole flat. There was ice on the inside of the windows in December. Pretty terrible, made my student halls seem like a palace."

"Don't suppose you'd like to come with me to speak to him?"

A grin spread across Mary's face. "Of course." Then she held up a finger. "And you don't have to tell me this time: I'll go and change."

Twenty minutes later she was back in the squad car with Walker wearing a more subdued outfit of a black jumper dress and leggings. The police officer had refused to put on the siren or the lights, which Mary felt was a little miserable. It was 'misuse of police equipment'. She wasn't entirely sure that Walker was meant to be taking her on interviews, so Mary didn't protest about it too much. She did take a quick selfie though when he wasn't looking and sent it to Bernie with a jaw dropped emoji.

They had only just left Mary's street when Walker's phone started to buzz.

"I'm going to put it on speaker," the Constable said. "Please don't make a sound."

Mary mimed zipping up her mouth and he clicked on the call.

"Walker? It's Sergeant Suzie O'Connor here. I've just finished up with the temp agency that our missing woman was working for. They're called Office Helpers Limited and I managed to get hold of their HR woman, Phillis Newton. She wasn't keen to tell me much, kept banging on about confidentiality. Anyway, when I mentioned I would get Immigration to come and have a look at her books, she got a bit more chatty."

"I'll bet she did," Walker said.

"Newton said that Mikala Nowak started working for them in the March. Now that would only be six months before she disappeared, and a year and a half before our body was found. The HR woman claimed she couldn't remember the girl, but she's sending over all the files. I asked her what happened when she stopped showing up for work, and Newton said she 'made a note' on the file. And that was it, can you believe it? No one ever followed it up."

"Did she tell you about the company Nowak was working for?"

"A cleaning firm. Macarthur Cleaning. They still seem to be in business, so I'm going to arrange a meeting with them ASAP."

"Great. I'm just heading to visit the landlord just now. I've heard he's a well-known dodgy character in the town."

Mary preened with pride at being the originator of that piece of intel.

"Ask him if he knows where Nowak came from. Neil's been checking but there's nothing coming up so far for when she entered the country. We don't even know if she is Polish, or if that's just what everyone assumed."

"Will do," Walker said and then the Sergeant said goodbye and hung up the call.

"So you still don't know how this woman ended up in Invergryff?" Mary asked.

"Not yet."

"If she's Polish, there's quite a big community in Invergryff. I know a couple of the mums. I could ask around for you?" Mary held her breath, not sure if Walker was going to tell her to butt out.

"That would be a great help, thanks. There's something funny going on here. I mean, it's not unusual for people to disappear, but not a peep out of anyone that knew her when she's been out of touch for over a year? That is strange."

Mary tapped her fingers against the seat. "Could it be that she was into drugs? That would give us a link to Paul Crossly."

Walker frowned. "I don't think we should be jumping to that sort of conclusion. If we get a definite ID, then we can look and see if there is a connection. But we don't know for certain who either of the bodies may be. No point in wasting time until the forensics come back."

They drove in silence for a few minutes. Mary was desperate to provide some insight that would help Walker in the case, but she couldn't think of anything. If the body from the witch's hill was this Mikala Nowak, then no one seemed to know the first thing about her. Mary looked at her phone, but resisted sending a message to the rest of the WWC. She was dying to get their opinion on the newly identified remains, but it didn't seem a good idea to do that while Walker was sitting next to her.

Mary's foot kicked against something on the floor and she picked it up.

"A study guide?" she said, looking at the book. It seemed to be a cheaply printed copy of some exam questions. "What's this, are you sitting exams?"

Walker's hands gripped the steering wheel and she knew she had said something wrong.

"Yes."

The silence in the car lengthened.

"Are they… is it a police thing? Or some sort of evening class."

"A police thing," Walker said, without turning his head to face her. "It's for my Sergeant's exams."

"That's exciting!" Mary said. "You'll make an excellent Sergeant."

"Have to pass the exams first."

"I can't imagine that would be a problem. I mean, you're really good at your job so…" Mary knew that she was poking at an open wound, but she was sure there was something Walker wasn't telling her.

"The thing is… I'm dyslexic." He breathed out a deep breath and pursed his lips.

Mary almost laughed. "Is that all?"

"All? Have you any idea… I mean, I failed my Sergeant's exams the first time, even though I know every single answer, just because I couldn't work out what the questions were asking. And because I only got half the bloody paper finished.

I mean, god dammit, it was just like being back at school, staring at the paper, sweat dripping down my back…"

If they hadn't been in the car she would have hugged him. Instead, she reached out and gave his hand a quick squeeze.

"Walker, it's not that bad you know," she said gently.

"You have no idea."

"That's the thing, I do."

She could see his jaw tense.

"Right."

"No, honestly I do. Peter's dyslexic."

"What?" Walker turned to look straight at her, his eyes wide in surprise.

"Yeah, my eldest son. We found out last year. I mean, I had wondered for a while. But we finally got the diagnosis in July. He's doing fine now."

"Just like that?"

Mary swallowed. "Um, could you look at the road please?"

Walker swore and pulled the steering wheel to the left, just in time to avoid missing a sharp bend in the road.

"Damn. Look, I'm going to pull over."

He eased the car into a layby and pulled on the hand break.

181

Then he looked over at her, his dark eyes intense.

"Are you making this up?"

Mary sighed in frustration. "Why would I make it up?"

"I don't know," Walker said, running a hand through his hair. "It's just... You said it so casually. You're not... you're not embarrassed?"

"God no. Why would I be embarrassed? It's just a thing, like... like the colour of your eyes or whether or not you are allergic to broccoli. I mean, it caused some problems for him, sure, but now that he's got the help he needs... Well, his behaviour is better because he's not so frustrated in school. Sure, it takes him a little longer to do his homework, but we can deal with that." Mary leaned her head to the side and looked at Walker. "Are you embarrassed?"

For a moment, she thought he was going to open up to her. A slight tremor passed his lips, then he shook his head.

"Of course not," Walker said, starting the car once more. "It's just like being allergic to broccoli, right?"

"Right."

"Except no one is allergic to broccoli."

Mary's laugh broke the awkward silence and they sat happily together for the rest of the journey.

Chapter 34: Bernie

Bernie spent an hour updating paperwork for the Wronged Women's Co-operative before she started getting ready for work in the care home after lunch. Admin always put her in a funk. Mainly she tried to get Liz and, since she had joined them a couple of months ago, Mary to do it, but as the boss, there were some things she couldn't delegate. It always made her feel like her brain was leaking out through her ears.

She was just completing the final spreadsheet when Mary texted her a photo of herself in a police car.

Enjoying being in handcuffs? Bernie texted, knowing that it would annoy her friend. For some reason, Mary was pretending that there wasn't a relationship going on between her and Walker. Bernie hated that sort of game-playing. If people fancied each other they should just get on with it, as far as she was concerned.

She turned off her laptop and went to make a cup of tea. Black, no milk or sugar. Her eyes flickered briefly towards the biscuit tin. It was only there for Finn and Ewan, of course, she would never indulge in such a thing.

Her right hand reached out for the tin and opened it. A certain brand of oat-based biscuit was right on the top and she –

Buzz

Bernie grabbed her phone out of her pocket.

"I wasn't doing anything!"

"Are you all right?" Mary asked. She was whispering.

"Yes. Fine," Bernie said, putting the biscuit tin back in the cupboard and shutting the door. "How's it going with the man in uniform?"

"We're about to go and interview someone. I just wanted to let you know that I'm going to be a bit late with the Pearson reports."

Had Bernie known that Mary was working the Pearson case too? She couldn't remember anyone telling her. "Of course. That's fine. Just have them in by the end of the day."

"And I'm waiting to hear back from Morecombe with more details of the witch, but I'll have that for you soon. I'm working on the spreadsheet with the details about the body from 2004. I noticed you hadn't added in the details from your visit to Superintendent Marr."

"Well, I will get around to it. I'm very busy right now and –"

"Yeah, don't worry about it," Mary said, and for some reason that annoyed Bernie even more.

"How are we doing on our recent body?" Bernie asked. "I mean I guess until we know more about who the dead woman was we can't –"

"Oh, I know who she is."

"Sorry what?"

"The body. The police think that they have ID'd the dead woman."

"When did this happen?"

"I don't know. Walker just told me. We're going to speak to her landlord. Hang on, I've got to go. Yeah, yeah, just talking to the school about packed lunches. Sorry, bye."

Bernie stared at the phone, feeling her temper rise. What the hell? Mary knew who the body was and she was too busy to even let her boss know about it. Because whatever else she was, Bernie knew that she was still meant to be the boss of the WWC. Funny how everyone seemed to forget that.

She slammed the kitchen door shut, spilling half her tea down her front in the process.

"Damn!"

Luckily she was wearing a jumper over her uniform so she just pulled it off and stuffed it into the washing machine. But it did nothing for her temper.

Bernie knew she needed to do something to get out of her funk. She glanced over at the sink and saw a bottle of beer, just sitting on the side. It was empty but no one had bothered to put it in the recycling bin.

She snapped.

It barely took any time at all. Just a few cupboards ransacked and there it was. Done.

Finn walked in just as the last of the amber liquid disappeared down the drain with a satisfying glugging sound.

"What the hell is going on?"

Bernie turned around, a flutter of nerves in her stomach. Although why should she be nervous? She was doing the right thing.

"It's an intervention. I saw it on the telly. I'm helping you to do what you aren't able to do yourself."

"Is that my whiskey?"

"And vodka, beer and everything else. Even my gin. I'm going sober in solidarity."

"No you're not, gin is about the only thing that makes you bearable at the moment." Finn picked up an empty glass whiskey bottle. "Jesus Bernie, that was a present from my dad. It cost a hundred quid!"

Finn loomed over the sink, shaking his head like he couldn't believe what he was seeing. Bernie straightened her back. She probably should have thought about how much some of this stuff cost, but it was done now. No point in crying over spilt Laphroaig.

"I'm removing temptation for you."

"You're being a bloody lunatic, that's what you're doing. Bernie, if I was an alkie, I wouldn't be getting drunk on the good stuff. I'd be down the supermarket buying turps. There must be hundreds worth of booze wasted here. I can't believe you!"

"I was just –"

"You were just making up things so that they fit what you believe. I am an alcoholic, so you've got to chuck out all the booze. You never stop to question whether your... what's the word... assumptions, that's it. Whether your assumptions are right in the first place."

Bernie sniffed. She wished that Finn would shout at her and storm off. After all, that was what normally happened in arguments. She certainly wasn't going to change her mind.

"I'm going out," Finn said, and Bernie almost smiled.

"Sure. Listen, I know you think I'm being a bit over the top, but it really is for your own good."

Finn's head dropped low to his chest. "Berns, I used to think you were what was good for me. But now I'm not so sure."

When the door shut behind him, Bernie put her hands to her face. The smell of discarded booze filled the kitchen and for once, she wondered if she might not have been just a tiny bit hasty. At least about the gin.

Chapter 35: Liz

Liz had stalled on the Pearson case. Until Mary got back to her about the environmental reports, she couldn't go much further. Her discussion with Immy Blake's secretary had been interesting, and it had cemented the idea that Blake and Pearson were into something dodgy together, but apart from that it had been annoyingly vague. The argument that Milly had overheard had only mentioned a problem with some land. Liz had downloaded every planning application from Blake for the last ten years, but all it had given her was a headache. How was she meant to tell which one they were referring to?

And then there was the name 'Nora'. Liz had gone through her notes and there was no Nora associated with Pearson, so who was she? A girlfriend, perhaps? Liz had spent half the night scrolling through social media to try and find out, but she had drawn a blank.

It was never this difficult on telly, Liz thought as she scrubbed the dishes. For that matter, the detective never had to do the washing up. Just as she was finishing, a text came through on her phone.

Possible ID on new body. Mikala Nowak. Polish? Disappeared 1 year ago. Out with Walker now. NOT LIKE THAT. M x

This was more like it! Liz practically skipped over to her computer and switched it on.

She keyed in the woman's name into her search engine and her enthusiasm fell slightly. There were hundreds of thousands of results. It was a common name in Poland and other parts of Eastern Europe. Liz's fingers flew over the keys. Even limiting the results to the UK didn't help. On the social media sites there were dozens of women with that name living in Britain.

Liz sighed, then typed in 'Mikala Nowak Invergryff'. Three results. She leaned forward over the screen.

The first result was a link to a local community website. When Liz clicked on it she was taken to a page that showed a group of people at some kind of funfair. The list of names underneath included Mikala Nowak. Liz peered closer, trying to work out which one might be Mikala. There were six women and three men, all of different ethnicities. Two women wore hijab, but even with their headscarves, they were both too old to be Mikala. There was a short black woman who Liz looked at carefully. Being black in a small Scottish town, she normally knew most other people of colour, but this woman was a stranger. So it conceivably could have been Mikala, but Liz seemed to remember that the body was Caucasian. The only other woman was standing on the far right, her head turned away from the camera. She was tall, taller than the men and Liz could make out some short brown hair. Her head was turned so that it was impossible to make out her eye colour, or even much of her facial features.

Well, at least it was something to report back to the others. There were only a few lines of text underneath the photograph. It was a fundraiser for a local refugee group called 'Welcoming Renfrewshire'. The name was vaguely familiar to her, but she couldn't remember why. Liz took a screenshot of the photo and added it to the file.

The second search result was a link to a social media site that Liz didn't use. Taptap, it was popular with kids. Some of Sean's friends were on it, even though you weren't meant to be until you were thirteen. Liz clicked on the link for Mikala Nowak's profile. Apart from the location which was Invergryff, there was nothing else there. No photos, nothing. Liz kissed her teeth. Maybe she needed to be a member to see the profile properly? She suddenly felt ancient. Surely forty was too young to already be out of touch with technology?

She tapped her false nails on the table.

The third link didn't seem to work. It was an out of date link to a website that just came up with an error message. Liz noted down the domain name anyway. It seemed to be in polish, osobzaginionych. She ran it through a translation program, but it didn't get any hits.

Liz messaged Mary: *Found some hits on Mikala Nowak. Should we have a WWC meeting tonight?*

Mary replied immediately with a thumbs up emoji. Probably not a good sign that she's on her phone, Liz thought, when she's meant to be out with the hunky police officer. She needed to give the woman some pointers. The guy was seriously into Mary, but she was in danger of getting in her own way. If she would only –

Liz shut down that train of thought. She was acting like her mother, poking her nose into someone else's personal life. Liz

190

hated it when Grace Okoro tried to run her love life, so it was probably better if she didn't try to do the same for Mary.

Now, why had her brain led her to her mother so quickly? Suddenly it came to her: 'Welcoming Renfrewshire' – hadn't her mother been involved with them at some point?

Liz checked her hair and made sure the room was tidy before she turned on the video call. She took a deep breath and sat up straight. Thus armed, she was ready to face her mother.

"Hello?" A view of her mother's forehead and greying roots appeared on the screen.

"Hi mum, could you tilt the camera up?" Liz asked.

"Oh, like this?"

Liz was treated to a view up her mother's nostrils.

"Maybe zoom out a bit?"

"Zoom this, zoom that," Grace Okoro said. She moved the phone back a little so that Liz could see the whole of her disapproving face. "You're looking tired. Have you been using that new moisturizer I got you?"

"Yes, mum," Liz mumbled. She had the sinking feeling in her stomach she always got from a conversation with her mother.

"So why are you phoning during school hours? I guess you don't want to talk to your poor old mother just to see how she's doing?"

"No. Well, not just that. Actually, it's to do with a case."

Grace leaned forward, like she was about to swallow the screen in one piece. "Ah, now that is interesting. I suppose you want your mother to help you investigate something, hmmn? I always thought I would make a great detective. I'm not above pounding on the odd suspect either."

"I bet you're not," Liz laughed. "Listen, I wanted to ask you about an organisation. The name is 'Welcoming Renfrewshire', wasn't that something you were involved with?

"Not really," Grace said, pulling her hair wrap so that it was less squint. "I did a little volunteering for them a few times. They needed someone who spoke Igbo, so I helped out with that, until they got a proper translator. And I baked a few cakes for a charity bake sale a while ago."

"You baked?"

Grace snorted. "I didn't say they were any good, but people bought them anyway because they were for charity. I put some of those glace cherries on top, that disguised the burnt bits."

"Did you ever meet a woman called Mikala Nowak? She would be young, twenties. Probably at least a year ago."

"Mikala? I don't think so, but as I said, I was only with them a few times. I can put you in touch with Connie MacIver. She runs the charity."

"That would be amazing, thanks. Can you email me her details?"

"Sure. Are you sure you don't want me to use the thumbscrews on anyone? I always fancied myself as a bit of a

192

torturer."

"I think we'll manage without that," Liz replied. "I'll see you for dinner on Sunday."

"Great. Make sure you put more chillies in the stew next time. Your father doesn't like it so bland."

"Of course," Liz said, clicking off the call and managing not to throw her phone across the room in frustration. Just.

Chapter 36: Walker

Dyslexic. It was amazing how easily the word tripped off Mary's tongue. Like it was the littlest thing in the world. It had almost taken Walker's breath away. On the way to Liam Beatson's house he hadn't been able to think about anything else. Mary had chatted to him for a while, then fallen into silence. She probably thought he was being rude, but Walker couldn't think of anything to say. Was it really true that the word that had haunted him ever since he had worked out why he could never do anything at school, was nothing more than a slight bump in the road for today's children? Mary had said there was no shame in it anymore, but he found that very hard to believe. That hunched child sat in front of a worksheet with two scribbled words on it, when everyone else had already long finished? No, it wasn't possible that that ache of shame wouldn't still exist deep in his guts.

Maybe she was partly right though. Diana had been saying for weeks that he should tell the examiners that he was dyslexic, that they would take it into account. But he hadn't, had he? And Walker knew exactly why. He didn't have to be a detective to work out why that shameful little boy still couldn't admit why he couldn't read the questions. Was it self sabotage? Or was it self preservation. After all, he had worked hard his whole life to move away from that shameful little boy. Was it his fault that he didn't want to acknowledge that there was a problem?

"There it is," Mary said, pointing to a large, white-rendered

194

house in the middle of a cul-de-sac of half a dozen similar properties. Walker pulled the car to a stop. He was embarrassed that he had barely even realised they were at their destination. Time to get his head back in the game.

"That's my parents' place next door," Mary pointed to a much more modest-sized property that was built from red brick. "The whole street was livid when Beatson got planning to knock his house down and built that McMansion thing."

It was kind of ugly. Walker quite liked modern houses: much more practical than the drafty Victorian flats he had rented when he was younger. But the scale here was all wrong. The house was too big, too flat-faced and with too many windows. The thing that upset his police officer's heart the most was that the windows had a reflective film so that no one could see inside. It hurt his snooper's heart.

"Let's see if he's home," Walker said, opening the car door.

Just as they were getting out of the car, a woman with wispy blond hair and a beige anorak ran towards them.

"Oh god no," Mary whispered just as the woman swept her into a hug.

"Darling!" The woman said, grinning from ear to ear. "I had no idea you were popping around. And in a squad car no less."

"Um," Mary tried to get a word in, but there was no stopping the woman.

"And this must be the famous Constable I've heard so much

about. I'm Nel, Mary's mother. What a pity her father isn't in. Went to the shop to get well-fired rolls. You know the ones, don't you, Constable? Perfect for extra crispy bacon."

"Mum, Walker didn't come around to hear about bacon rolls," Mary interrupted. "We're not actually here to see you at all."

"Oh." Mary's mother looked like she had been slapped.

"I mean, obviously I would have loved to come and see you," Mary said, backtracking furiously. "It's just we're here to interview one of your neighbours."

Walker felt he couldn't let that pass without some comment. "I'm here on police business, and I asked Mary along."

"It's that Liam Beatson, isn't it?" Nel said, her eyes narrowing. "He's a dodgy character, mark my words. Never takes his bins in, for a start. Saturday morning, quarter past ten, sometimes half past if the weather's been bad, the bin men have been. Of course, our bins are always in by twelve at the latest. Him next door? One time they were out there until Monday! Can you imagine?"

"Perhaps we could have a chat inside," Walker said, looking at Mary in desperation. He just had to hope that Beatson wasn't looking out of the windows.

"Of course. I'll put the kettle on," Nel said, grabbing her daughter by the arm and practically dragging her towards the house. Mary turned her head just enough to mouth 'I'm sorry' before they were all inside.

If Walker had expected the sort of chaotic mess that even the

196

most charitable visitor would see in Mary's house, Nel's place delivered something very different. It was immaculate, down to the pristine white walls and the hoover lines in the carpet. Walker wondered if Mary's children were ever allowed inside the place.

"God, I had no idea she was in. I'm so sorry," Mary said as they sat down on a cream leather sofa.

"It's fine," Walker said while checking his watch. He really needed to get to Beatson's house.

Mary's mother emerged from the kitchen brandishing a freshly baked plate of scones. Walker turned them down reluctantly. How was it that some people were always ready for visitors? If someone turned up at his police accommodation, they'd be lucky to get a wrinkly apple and a furry bit of cheese from the back of the fridge.

"Nel, would you mind telling me what you know about Liam Beatson," Walker said, hoping that they could satisfy Mary's mother's curiosity with a few questions, then head next door.

"Well, let's see now. He moved in around four years ago. That's to say, he bought the house a year before that. Lovely little bungalow it was, roses round the door, that sort of thing. He spent a year building that horrible white box, diggers around all day and night, what a racket it made. Mary's dad went around to complain about the noise on more than one occasion, but he didn't give a monkey's."

"And he's a landlord, is that right?"

"Aye. He was even on the telly once. One of those shows where they buy a place that's falling apart, stick some textured wallpaper over all the cracks and then resell it for a bunch of cash. I've heard all sorts about the flats he rents out. You remember Ollie's sister."

Mary paused mid-scone when she realised her mother was talking to her. "Um, no?"

Nel sighed. "Yes you do. You were in Brownie's together."

Mary's eyes drifted toward the ceiling. "Sorry mother, I can't remember someone I knew when I was six."

"Well now, never mind, I'll remind you. Ollie was the one who used to mow the lawns here over the summer. His mum worked in the hardware shop, the one that closed down and became one of those charity shops that smells of mothballs. Anyway, Ollie's sister got pregnant when she was seventeen. It was quite the scandal."

Walker pretended not to notice Mary rolling her eyes beside him. "Please go on," he said to Nel, hoping she might get to the point sometime this century.

"Because of the baby, she needed a place to stay. I don't think she ever got on that well with her mother, but that's another story. Anyway, she ended up renting a place from Liam Beatson. It was in the town, just near that park with the big fountain. But the whole thing was a disaster. The flat looked nice enough, new kitchen, bathroom all that stuff. But Ollie's mum told me that underneath it all, it was a right state. Apparently the roof on the building had never been maintained

198

and it was leaking like a sieve! Beatson was the factor you see, so he was responsible for the building's maintenance. Well, he'd been collecting their quarterly fees but never using it for any upkeep. The poor girl had to leave in the end, and when she did every single thing she took out of the flat was covered in mould. What do you say about that!" Nel sat back with her arms folded.

"Sounds terrible," Walker said. "Now I think we better speak to the man himself."

On cue, Mary jumped out of her seat and they headed for the door.

"Don't forget to remind him about the bins!" Nel called after them.

Chapter 37: Mary

Mary hadn't been this embarrassed by her mother since she was sixteen and Nel had picked her up from a disco and shouted at her for the length of her skirt. In fact, if she could have just erased the previous half hour, she would have been more than happy. It was so unlucky: normally Nel would be out and about at that time of day, not waiting in the house to ambush her daughter.

Walker didn't say a word about it as they walked up to Liam Beatson's house, but he must have been annoyed. He probably wouldn't invite her to interviews anymore, let alone anything on a more romantic line.

"Ready?" the police officer said, his hand poised over the doorbell.

Mary managed a nod.

Just a second after Walker pressed the button, the door was pulled open by a tall thin man in a suit. "I saw your car pull up, then you went next door. What have that lot been up to, drugs? I bet the back garden is full of cannabis plants. They seem the types." Beatson grinned, showing bright white implants.

"My name is Constable Walker and we were paying a visit to your neighbours on a separate matter." The police officer had spoken quickly as if Mary was going to jump in and defend her parents, and he was probably right to do so.

"You look a bit short to be a police officer," Beatson said, offering Mary another grin.

"Mrs Plunkett is a civilian aid in this case," Walker said smoothly. "I suppose you know why we are here?"

"Well, I did call your lot in the first place. You're here about that poor girl, Nowak."

"Yes. Could we come inside?"

"Suppose so. But you'll have to be quick. I've got a physio session at the gym in half an hour."

Walking into the large central hall behind Beatson let Mary see that despite a large amount of hair gel, he was thinning at the crown. She never understood why men like that didn't just shave off all their hair and have done with it. At least they wouldn't have to spend half their life buying hair products that promised so much and delivered so little, like she did.

"It's a very nice house," Mary said as they walked into a large open-plan kitchen diner with a chaise longue in front of patio doors. She wasn't even flattering him; it was nicely done, even if her parents had spent months moaning at her about the building work.

"My ex was an interior designer," Beatson said. "Just a pity she had the temperament as well as the taste of an artist. Still, I got to keep the house so could have been worse."

He sat down in a low, mid-century style armchair and indicated that they should settle on the sofa. Mary was beginning to realise that they wouldn't be offered tea, a sure sign that

201

Beatson was a murderer, in her book anyway.

"Why don't you tell us why you got in touch with the station in the first place," Walker prompted, his tablet on his knee to take notes. Mary was finding this whole police officer interviewing thing weirdly attractive for some reason, so she angled herself so that she was looking at Beatson instead.

"I saw an article on the web. It said that police were looking for information about women that disappeared a year ago. I suddenly remembered about Mikala Nowak. At the time I thought she'd just run off. She wasn't exactly the most reliable tenant, you know, always late with the rent, that sort of thing. I never imagined she might have… passed away."

"The thing is, Mr Beatson, we don't really know what has happened to Ms Nowak."

"But I thought… I mean, you found a body…"

"The identity won't be confirmed until we have DNA records. Of course, if someone had reported Ms Nowak missing at the time, it might have been easier."

Beatson narrowed his eyes. "Look, none of this is anything to do with me. I had an arrangement with this temp agency that I would let out the flat to some of their workers. I went round to do an inspection, and found a load of mail piled up and rotten food in the fridge. Well, I called the agency and they said she'd done a runner. I was owed three months' rent by this point, so you can bet I was pissed off. I waited another couple of weeks, then I put the flat back on the market. I'm entitled to recoup my losses. Not running a bloody charity, after all."

"Is it usual for a tenant to just disappear like that," Mary asked.

"Oh, aye. When it's not their own home, people are more than happy to treat it like crap. I could tell you some stories about the state they leave the properties in. Filthy, with rubbish piled up the walls. Honestly, it makes you spit."

"You seem to have done all right out of it," Mary said.

"I don't think that's a crime, is it? Not yet anyway," he chuckled. "The key is volume. I've got over sixty properties all over the West of Scotland now. I'm doing coaching on it, I can give you a leaflet if you like."

"Thanks," Mary said, taking the shiny piece of paper and putting it down in the bottom of her bag with the half-open packets of biscuits and spare nappies.

"Can you give me the paperwork related to Ms Nowak's tenancy," Walker asked. "We are particularly interested in any documentation that she was using."

Now Beatson twisted a little in his chair. "The agency dealt with all of that. You'll need to speak to them."

"I will," Walker said, and Mary thought there was an edge of threat in his voice.

"Where is all her stuff now?" Mary asked, breaking the uncomfortable silence. "If she left suddenly, was it all in the flat when you went for the inspection."

"Just clothes and things. These people, they tend to pack light. And well, I'm afraid it all went to the tip."

Walker frowned at this.

"Look, it's perfectly legal," Beatson said, his voice wavering a little. "It's not the first time some scumbag tenant has left town without notice and left all their crap in the property for me to sort out. We keep it in storage for 28 days, then, when no one replies to the warnings we send out, we bin it. My solicitor sent the letters out herself, she'll show you copies if you want."

"Kind of hard for Ms Nowak to reply to the letters if she was dead," Walker said.

Beatson just shrugged. "Guess so."

"What was your relationship like with Ms Nowak?" Walker asked.

Now Beatson looked genuinely annoyed, his scrawny neck turning red. "Relationship? Now you're taking the piss. I met her once, no, two times. The day I gave her the keys and one time a couple of months later when she had a leaking sink. Both times she barely spoke to me, head down, hood pulled low over her face. I thought she was one of those weirdos, you know, that can't make eye contact or talk to real human beings. She spent the whole time looking down at her phone. Bloody rude. But you can't fit me up for anything. I was her landlord, that's it."

Walker stood up to leave. "It is not our intention to fit anyone up, Mr Beatson. We just want to get to the bottom of why a young woman disappeared and no one thought to alert the authorities."

Beatson glanced down at his trainers. "I suppose I thought someone else would do it."

"Isn't that always the way, sir," Walker said, heading for the door. Mary would have liked to say something more. Perhaps give the man a little heads up on social responsibility, but she didn't think that would go down well with Walker.

"I rented a flat from you once," she said, as they were going out of the door.

"Oh yes, nice one was it?" Beatson asked, giving her a wink.

"Not particularly," Mary replied as she shut the door behind them.

Chapter 38: Bernie

Bernie got back from a short shift at the care home and jumped in the shower. While she was getting dressed into her usual jeans and jumper combination, she began to shake off the endless admin that was part of her nursing job, and turn her thoughts toward the Wronged Women's Co-operative business.

She had managed to pop in to see Superintendent Marr right at the end of her shift. This time the elderly man had not been having such a good day.

"I don't think you should see him," Mrs Marr had said, barring the door like Bernie was an invading force. Which, really, she was.

"I'll just be a few minutes. I've brought some leaflets about respite care," Bernie added, brandishing the paperwork in the woman's face. It did the trick, like she knew it was. Spousal carers were always dying for respite care, and there was never enough to go around.

"Oh well, if you'll just be a minute…" Mrs Marr trailed into the living room behind her.

Instead of sitting at the window watching the birds, this time the former police officer was slumped on the sofa, his eyes on the television.

"Morning, Mr Marr. It's me come to see you again. You'll

know why."

"Bossy nurse," Marr grunted.

Mrs Marr looked horrified, but Bernie just laughed.

"That's me all right. Glad you remembered. Now, I wanted to ask you some more questions about the body you found up on the witch's hill."

"Too many sheep."

Bernie looked at his wife in confusion. "Was there, indeed? How about the body, Superintendent. Was there anything you remember, anything unusual that might help us with the case?"

"Too many bloody sheep."

The Superintendent kept glaring at the television. He looked pale and clammy like he was too hot and too cold all at once. Bernie bit her lip in frustration. This didn't seem to be going anywhere.

"At the farm, you spoke to the farmer and –"

"You ask the farmer. About the sheep. Ask why there was too many sheep and not enough people. Ask him."

"I will do," she said soothingly. Bernie stood up to go and tried not to see the edge of despair in the look that Mrs Marr gave her husband, whose eyes had never left the television screen.

It had taken ten minutes of chatter about medications and respite hostels before Bernie had managed to escape the flat.

It had left a bad taste in her mouth, even for someone used to people with these sorts of diseases. There but for the grace of God, and all that.

As she always said, life went on. After her shower, Bernie headed downstairs to make a black coffee and was glad that there was no sign of Finn. Bernie was never one to hide from a fight, but she was secretly glad that her husband wasn't at home. All day she had had a gnawing sensation in her stomach that suggested she might have been a little hasty in pouring away all his booze. The ends justified the means, of course, and she didn't regret trying to help him. But she maybe could have gone about it in a slightly more subtle way.

Still, what was done was done and it was time to move on. At the home today Bernie had treated several warts and a particularly nasty case of athlete's foot. It had cemented in her mind that going forward she really wanted to focus her efforts on the WWC.

Money, that was the problem. If she was to quit her job at the home, there needed to be enough income in the agency for two full time wages, plus the part-time positions of Mary and Alice. Really, they needed to stop taking on jobs like the bodies on the witch's hill where they weren't getting paid at all. But in her heart, Bernie was just as excited about this case as the other women were. The thing is, murder, hidden bodies and – yes, even Bernie could admit it – the whiff of witchcraft was a much more enticing prospect that a cheating husband or a lost dog. But the bills still needed to get paid, so Bernie decided that at the next meeting she would make sure their focus was on the Pearson case, which would be very lucrative, if they ever discovered what the hell the old sleazebag was up to.

Unlike Mary and Liz, Bernie had no particular problem with Pearson's politics, but she was of the opinion that all politicians were generally up to something. Same as estate agents. So she was sure that they would be able to find something dodgy on the man.

Some people might have found it a bit grubby, peering through people's private lives, like she did in the WWC. But those people hadn't spent two decades dressing bedsores and cleaning wounds. No one had a stronger stomach than Bernie.

The front door banged open.

"Bernie, where the hell are you?"

She had never heard that level of rage from Finn's voice. It was like she was frozen to the spot. He was going to end it, she realised with a terrible certainty. She had finally made him so angry that he was going to leave her. And in that moment she saw how awful that would be.

"Bernie!"

"I'm here," she said, in a small voice. She moved towards the door and he barrelled through. He was a huge man and it was like being confronted by an angry bear.

"Oh thank god," he swept her into a hug, that was so surprising she didn't take a breath and ended up struggling to move her chest.

"What…" she gasped.

"Sorry," Finn said, pushing her away from him so she could fill her lungs. "I just… It's been a hell of a day. I just needed to know that you were all right."

"Of course I'm all right," Bernie said, recovering enough of herself to be annoyed that he had frightened her. "Whatever is the matter with you?"

"You went to see Tam Brown, didn't you."

This wasn't what Bernie had expected Finn to mention, so much so that she didn't have time to think of a lie.

"Yes."

"I knew you would. I should have tried harder to stop you. Man, I knew what he was capable of, but I never thought…"

Bernie clicked her tongue. "Why don't you just come out with it and tell me what happened?"

"My van's tyres were slashed. I went to go off for lunch, was going to do the usual burger run, um, I mean salad run. Well. Anyway, when I got to the van the tyres were slashed."

"And you assumed it was Tam Brown? I only went to see him yesterday. Seems pretty unlikely. Couldn't they just have gone flat?"

"Slashed, Berns, not flat. You could see the knife marks. And there was something else."

Finn took out his phone. He brought up a photograph and

210

turned it so that she could see. It was a picture of the front of the van. There was a note pinned under the windscreen wipers. It was a small piece of paper, like one ripped out of a notebook. On it were two words.

She's next.

"Wow. He's not very subtle, is he?" Bernie said. "Mind you, I bet that means that we're on the right track. After all, he's not going to go to the trouble of threatening me if he had nothing to do with Paul Crossly's death."

Bernie's phone buzzed to let her know she had email. She read it while Finn got himself a glass of water.

"Here's a funny thing," Bernie said as her husband came back into the room, his face starting to lose the tomato-red colour it had when he had arrived. "Tam Brown just sent an email with the names of Paul Crossly's friends. Why would he do that if he was warning me off?"

Finn looked at her in shock. "Jesus Bernie, how many people have you pissed off this week?"

"Not sure," she said, "but it means that I'm making progress."

"Will you still call it progress if you're dead?"

Bernie almost went to hug him then, but things were still too weird between them. Instead, she gave his arm a squeeze. "Don't worry about me."

Her husband just shook his head and started phoning around for a mechanic.

Chapter 39: Liz

Liz rubbed at her eyes. She had thought when she quit her high-pressure job in finance that she might get a bit of a rest. It turned out that running a private investigation firm was quite stressful. She didn't remember Poirot having to stay up until two in the morning doing paperwork, but perhaps he had had a secretary to do it all for him. The git.

"Do you want another cup of tea?" Mary asked. She had arrived bouncing with energy after spending the last few hours with Constable Walker. Liz had probed to see if anything interesting had happened between them, but it had apparently been a purely business-like meeting.

"Better not," Liz said, pulling on her coat. "We're booked in to see Pearson in half an hour and it'll take that long to drive over to his office. Thanks again for coming with me."

"No problem. The kids are back soon so I'm taking advantage of the chance to be out of the house. I even blow-dried my hair today," Mary said happily.

They left the house and climbed into Liz's car. "I'd like you to take the lead with Pearson," Liz said, putting the key into the ignition. "The printout I gave you has a list of questions, but I feel like they'll sound better coming from you. You have one of those likeable faces."

Mary stuck out her tongue. "I never realised you were going to employ me to flirt with people for you."

"Then you shouldn't be such an effective flirt. I'm going to play bad cop, so you've got to be good cop. I want to tread carefully with Pearson, he's a politician, so he's going to be used to answering awkward questions."

Mary flicked through the list of questions. "These are pretty thorough."

"I hope so. But if you feel like you're getting somewhere on another track, don't be afraid to just go with it. I mean, I don't think he's going to come out and say what a dodgy character he is, but you never know. Tell me again what you found in the environmental reports."

Mary leaned back in the seat and closed her eyes. "It was weird. There were loads of reports, but although they were long, they didn't have the sort of details I would have expected. Nothing, obviously illegal, but there were a few things that need a bit more investigation. First, there are the newts."

Liz wondered if she had misheard. "Sorry, did you say newts?"

"Yes. Tiny amphibious creatures."

"I mean, I know what newts are…"

"Right. But you might not know about the Great Crested Newt. It's a protected species, you see, and it's very endangered. Every development that is on a green field site has to have a report on the impact on local species, and the newt is a special case."

"Ugh," Liz put her hands to her head. "I'm already lost."

"Well hold on, because it's going to get more complicated. I just used the newts as an example, because they come up quite frequently. But it's all to do with habitats. Special Areas of Conservation are places in Scotland where we have rare animals that need protecting."

"And planning is banned in these areas?" Liz asked hopefully.

"Not at all. It just means that more reports have to be written, and greater care in the development."

"I knew it wouldn't be that easy." The car pulled up outside a row of shops and offices. "We really don't have time to go over all of this now. Look, how about you ask any relevant eco stuff that you think of in the meeting and I'll just try and keep up."

"Right," Mary replied.

Pearson's constituency office was above an estate agency on one of the more run-down streets in Invergryff. The windows were covered in faded election posters and someone had written some not very flattering graffiti about the Tories on the wall next to it.

"He'll see you in a minute," the Secretary had said and Liz and Mary sat down on some hard plastic chairs. It felt very much like a doctor's waiting room, although there were no out of date magazines to browse through while they waited. Liz couldn't help but feel the contrast from Immy Blake's swish place in Glasgow. Was Pearson resentful of his business associate's success? But then this was just the constituency office. His home was probably a lot more stylish.

215

A thin woman with a long raincoat walked out of Pearson's office. "My kids need a new house, you see, we can't stay in this awful flat. Your party promised that –"

"I understand," a voice said from within, "I will look into it with the council. You should hear back very soon."

As she went past the woman muttered something like 'not bloody likely,' and she walked out of the door without a backward glance.

"You can go in now," the secretary pointed them towards the office door, then went back to scrolling on her phone.

Liz was interested to see Pearson in the flesh. He looked older than he had in the clips she had watched of him on the news and on talk shows. He had a smile that almost seemed natural, unless you looked at his eyes, which didn't change.

"Mrs Okoro, how lovely to meet you. And this is…"

"My associate, Mrs Plunkett. Thank you for taking our meeting."

The office itself was an unremarkable room, with a large table that twelve people could have sat around, but instead there was only Pearson, sitting at the far end.

Liz and Mary took seats opposite him. Pearson shifted back in his chair so that his hands were resting on his stomach. All his weight was in front of him, the kind of profile that sometimes appeared on a man of late middle age. Liz wished Bernie was here to give him some advice on cholesterol.

"Would you like tea? Maybe a biscuit?"

"Any chocolate ones?" Mary asked with her best coquettish smile. Liz had to stifle a giggle, so obvious was her friend's flirting.

"Actually yes, it's a rather nice Marks and Spencer's selection. Please, take two"

Perhaps she had got it all wrong, Liz thought as Mary accepted a rather fine chocolate covered digestive. Pearson really didn't seem too bad after all.

"And for you, Mrs Okoro?"

"No thank you," Liz said, even though she would have quite liked one. She figured part of her role as the bad cop was to refuse biscuits.

"Now, I heard that you are writing an article on the revitalisation of Invergryff."

Pretending to be journalists was the WWC's favourite cover story. It was easy enough to mock up a local news website.

"That's right," Liz said. "We've been looking at all the new developments and plans that the council has put in place to update the region. I know that you've been involved in many of them right from your council days."

"I have served this county for a long time," Pearson said, holding out his palms and smiling proudly as if he were some sort of decorated war general.

"And the most recent development is the new golf course over at Ellenslie Braes."

Was Liz imagining it, or did Pearson look a little uncomfortable.

"I am a supporter of that development, yes. I believe it will bring much-needed jobs to the area. But it is only one of a number of strategies we are employing to bring Invergryff bang up to date. If I might talk about the redevelopment of the central shopping piazza…"

"I'd rather come back to the golf course, if you don't mind," Liz said firmly. "Hasn't it been a little controversial? Some concerns about the environmental impact?"

"Well, there were some rather ill-informed people protesting about the site. But we have put together a comprehensive plan to tackle their concerns."

"I know that you are very concerned with nature, aren't you Mr Pearson," Mary said, giving him a broad smile. "You are well known for being seen around the town with your dogs."

Pearson turned to her in delight. "Ah, my prize Weimaraners. There's nothing I love better than taking them for walks in the countryside."

"Of course, I'm sure you are a strong supporter of the environment. And you'll be aware of Natura sites, of course," Mary added.

"Um, yes, I believe so," Pearson said. His face had the look of someone who had been petting a cuddly kitten, only for it to sink its claws into his thumb.

"It's a European designation for unique habitats," Mary said. "On these sites any development is strictly prohibited. There have only been two exceptions since the designation became common use. One was to widen the road to Mallaig, and the other to strengthen a railway embankment on the West Coast Main Line."

"I hope you're not suggesting anything untoward, Mrs Plunkett. I can assure you that I have never had a planning development on a Natura site."

"But you have been close, haven't you?" Mary rustled her papers. "To be specific, twenty feet close. That is how near the site of the new golf course is to the area known as Gleniffer Moss."

"Sorry, are you talking about moss now?"

"That's just its title. What Gleniffer Moss refers to is an area of ancient peat bog, with its own unique habitat and wildlife. One that your golf course comes perilously close to encroaching upon."

Pearson was no longer sitting back in his chair. He loomed over the table, eyes narrowed.

"You are planning on some sort of sensational story that accuses me of being the destroyer of the environment, is that it? I can assure you that we complied with everything the planners required."

"And you weren't even involved, were you, Mr Pearson," Liz

reminded him, "you were just a supporter of the scheme. Despite the fact that it is your sister-in-law's company that is building the golf course."

For a moment, when he clenched his jaw, Liz thought Pearson might crack. But he simply let out a long sigh.

"That is also public knowledge. I have nothing to hide, I assure you. Now I think this meeting is over."

Chapter 40: Walker

After the meeting with Beatson, Walker went back to the office to check in with the rest of the team.

"Dianna is having a meeting at four," Sergeant Suzie O'Connor said as he sat down at his desk. "Think it's going to be a late finish tonight."

Walker didn't mind working late. His head was still spinning about his chat with Mary. It was stupid really. Her attitude towards his dyslexia should have cheered him up: instead of thinking he was stupid, she seemed to view it as completely normal. But the truth was, that was never how Walker had thought of himself. And now he didn't know how to deal with it.

Just before four Dianna walked in and stepped up to the smartboard.

"Gather round. I've got some news."

Walker joined the others around the table, trying not to notice how Neil positioned himself closest to the Inspector.

"Our unidentified body is definitely Mikala Nowak, so good work guys on finding that name. In the last couple of hours, we've also managed to find out some more about her."

She put a selection of photographs up on the screen. There were several of Mikala at what must have been a college, where she was laughing with a group of friends. Walker felt the familiar jolt of sadness that her life had been so abruptly ended.

"For a start, she's not Polish. At least, not by nationality. She's from Belarus. Her parents were Polish emigrants who moved there before she was born, so she spoke both Russian and Polish. She was their only daughter. You can imagine how distressing that particular phone call was. The parents are going to come over to repatriate the body, but that won't be for another couple of days until flights are arranged. In the meantime, we have managed to get a positive ID from her dental records. They match our body from the hill."

"So our job now is to work on a timeline. Mikala's parents told us that she left Belarus and arrived in the UK only around six months before her death."

"Did they say why she came over here?" Walker asked.

"To find work. She was a qualified physiotherapist. Her parents were very upset, and we were talking through a translator, but from what I can gather, she was hoping to get a job as a physio over here. They knew she was working as a cleaner, but they thought it was just temporary."

Dianna took a deep breath. "They last heard from her about a week before she stopped turning up at work. She had been talking about moving on to another position, maybe in London."

"Why didn't they try and find her?"

"Well, here's the interesting thing. They claim that they got a call to say that Mikala had moved to London, but that she wouldn't be able to get in touch for a while."

That made Walker lean forward. "Really? I wonder who made that call."

"They seemed to think it was someone from the agency. We'll check that as a priority"

"And they hadn't tried to find her in the last year?"

"They contacted their government in Belarus a month or so later. They said they would look into it, but this was just before the hostilities in the region flared up. Mikala's father was a soldier, so he was away, and her mother... well, she sounded frightened of anything to do with official processes. I think they were just in denial, hoping that their daughter was safe and well in London somewhere."

"What a way to find out," Walker said.

"I know. How did you get on with the landlord?"

Walker shook his head. "Not much help. It seemed that he had an arrangement with the temp agency to house whoever they brought over. He said that Mikala was late with the rent several times, but we're still checking that to see if it's true. After she disappeared he got rid of all her things, so there's no hope of us examining them. He seemed glad to be rid of her."

"Do you think he's a suspect?" Dianna asked.

"I can't see a motive. But he's definitely dodgy, well known for renting out unsuitable housing. I wouldn't discount him."

"Noted." Dianna brought up a list of items to action. "Okay, here's where we're at. We need to get a firm timeline from when Mikala arrived in Invergryff to when she disappeared. We need to work out the exact day that she was last seen alive."

"I've been trying to get hold of the boss of the temp agency all day," Suzie said. "HR keep passing me from person to person. Their managing director is Theo Fyodorov. He lives in Invergryff, but he has been 'unavailable' since first thing this morning."

Dianna leaned forward over the table. "Now that sounds suspicious to me. What do we know about the company?"

Suzie checked her notes. "They are called Office Helpers Limited. The HR woman, Phillis Newton, sent me over Nowak's files, but there wasn't much there. No passport, which they should have had a copy of. I tried to chase it up, but apparently it was the elusive Mr Fyodorov who handled these things."

"Sounds like we need to talk to him." Dianna checked her watch. "Nearly five. If he knocks off on time, we should get him at home. Suzie, will you take Walker and go and see him this evening? I know it means overtime, but –"

"We'll grab a poke of chips on the way," Suzie said, and Walker perked up considerably. It had been a while since he'd allowed himself a takeaway.

"Did we ever hear from the cleaning firm? The one that the temp agency had sent her to."

"Aye," Neil said, eager to contribute. "Macarthur Cleaning. I'm interviewing them first thing tomorrow."

"Great. Let's wrap up this case before the weekend."

Suzie grabbed her bag and headed over to Walker. "Are you okay to drive? I'm still learning my way around Invergryff."

"Sure," he said. "I'll even take you to the best chippy in town."

Ten minutes later they were happily munching two fish suppers in the squad car. Walker had the windows wound down as the car would smell of fish for the rest of the week otherwise.

"What do you think of this case then," Suzie asked him.

Walker took his time in answering. Suzie was a well-respected Sergeant and he didn't want to come across as a dumb plod.

"I still think we're missing some connection between the two bodies," he said, dipping a chip into a puddle of vinegar. "It can't be a coincidence that they were both buried in the same place."

"Dianna doesn't seem to think it's a priority."

"I know. And I understand why. But I don't think we should ignore it."

Suzie put down her wooden fork. "All right then. Convince me."

225

Walker scrunched up his chip wrapper and squished it into the passenger door pocket. "Okay. We don't get that many murders around here. It's not Glasgow, we don't have the same kind of gangland stuff. So for two bodies to appear in the same spot…"

"It's unusual," Suzie agreed.

"It's bloody weird. That's why I think we need to look at it more closely. Why that spot in particular? And what does it have to do with the witch?"

Suzie groaned. "Don't you start. I've had enough about that blooming witch from the nutters on the hotline."

"I think you'll find the term 'nutter' is frowned upon in present day policing," Walker said in a singsong voice as if he was on a training video.

"Aye, that's true. But if you're telling me some ancient hag is killing people and dragging them underground, you're a nutter."

"But that's the thing," Walker said, voicing something that had been going around in his head for the last couple of days, "our killer could be using the myth of the witch as a cover for disposing of the bodies."

"For their killing spree that happens once every twenty years?"

"I know, it still doesn't make sense. But I would like to spend a bit more time on the older case. I want to know what links these two bodies. There has got to be some reason they were buried in the same place."

226

"Convenience?" Suzie nodded. "Aye, that could be it. Did we look into the farmers?"

"Drew a blank, but it might be worth a second look."

"Okay, I'll back you to the Inspector if you want to interview them again. But we better keep on top of the Nowak timeline too."

Walker pulled the car to a stop. "Here's Theo Fyodorov's place. At least according to his companies house information."

The building was detached, a sixties-style place that had been extended in every direction over the years. There was a new black, four-wheel drive car parked outside with tinted windows.

"No innocent person ever drove a car like that," Suzie said as they walked past. "I don't like this guy already, there's something fishy about the temp agency. I'm just not sure if it has anything to do with Mikala Nowak's murder."

Walker dipped his head in agreement. Suzie rang the doorbell, and they both took a couple of steps back as a loud barking started up inside.

"Crap," Suzie said, "I got bitten just last month in Easterhouse. You can go in first."

"Thanks very much," Walker said. The dog barking quietened down by a small degree as someone started to open the door.

"Yes?"

A tiny woman with east Asian colouring opened the door.

Walker and Suzie identified themselves and then Suzie asked to see Theo Fyodorov.

"He's not in," the woman said. Walker had seen plenty of scared women in his time on the job, but this one was practically vibrating with fear.

"It's okay," Suzie said gently. "We just need five minutes with him."

The woman shook her head so hard it looked like it might fall off. "Sorry, not home."

She closed the door and disappeared back into the house.

"Should we try again?" Walker asked.

"No," Suzie said. "Let's go back to the car. That woman was scared out of her mind. There's something going on here. I think we should talk to Dianna and get a bit more background on Fyodorov."

"Agreed," Walker said and they climbed into the squad car. They drove back to the station in silence, but Walker knew exactly what Suzie was thinking. What the hell had spooked the woman in Fyodorov's house? And was it connected to Mikala Nowak's death?

Chapter 41: Mary

Mary had come to the WWC meeting armed. She had gin, wine, four different types of crisps and even some horrible-looking pea-based snacks for Bernie. Since joining the Wronged Women's Co-operative, these meetings had fast become one of the highlights of her week. A chance to spend time with other adults was always a novelty for a stay-at-home mum, but to her surprise, Mary had found in the WWC not just colleagues, but friends.

Growing up, she had often struggled to make female friends. She had been a bit of a tomboy, more interested in science fiction and computer games than discos and make-up. When she'd hit her teenage years all the boys she had been gaming with started to look at her funny, lowering their gaze and mumbling when she was around. This was irritating. So she'd found herself at a point where she'd lost her male friends, and only had one or two female friends who were just as geeky as her. The years of marriage to Matt had made her even more insular – it wasn't until they broke up that she realised how many of her friends were just the wives of his friends. Not one of them had called since she walked out on her husband.

And so it was that these WWC meetings where they talked about murder and death and misery, were the happiest moments in her week. As she poured the crisps into bowls, Mary wasn't sure if that was a good or a bad thing.

Nuts. They needed some nuts. Those were healthy, right?

She poured a big bag of chocolate Brazils into a bowl.

"Where's the wine?" Liz called from the doorway.

"White's in the fridge, red's on the side."

"Excellent," Liz said, dumping her coat on the chair. "As soon as you left I went back through those environmental reports. Even with your notes, they don't make any sense to me."

Mary laughed. "Weren't you some bigwig financial type? I'm sure you can manage some scientific reports."

"They are just so boring! No, it's worse than that. In finance everything is numbers, you know, black and white. All these reports, they seem to be in the grey area. Everything can be read in a different way by a different person. No wonder Pearson and his cronies are always finding loopholes."

"It's true," Mary said, taking the glass of white that Liz offered her. "If you have enough money you can buy lawyers to argue your way around anything."

"So we still have nothing," Liz sighed. "And I've got a meeting with Iona scheduled tomorrow. I don't think they are going to be impressed with our lack of progress. Hand me those crisps will you, I want to eat some before Bernie starts rolling her eyes at me."

"She gave me a leaflet for Weight Watchers the other day," Mary said with a giggle. "Honestly, from anyone else it would have been an insult, but from Bernie... well..."

"It's just her way," Liz finished for her. "You can hardly blame her, given how much weight she's lost. She a medical bloody marvel."

"Am I?" Bernie said, coming into the room, "Well, that's good to know. I certainly don't feel like one today. Pretty much put my back out lifting Mrs Sullivan at the home today. The hoist wasn't working and the young support worker was about seven stone in wet socks. They need to add an arm wrestle to the job interview. These wee scrawny things have no chance lifting Mrs Sullivan with her penchant for chocolate peppermint creams."

"Ooh, I love a peppermint cream," Mary said, struck by the memory so hard she could taste the tang of the mint on her tongue. "My nan used to keep a bag in the car."

"Why am I not surprised," Bernie said, pouring her usual gin and slim-line tonic. "We might as well get started. Alice is going to be late, she's got an evening class at college."

Mary opened her laptop and got ready to take the minutes. "Are we starting with Pearson or the bodies on the hill?"

"Pearson, I think, seeing as that's the one we're getting paid for. Liz, can you go over your progress for us."

Liz fidgeted in her seat. "It's not going as well as I would have liked. Mary did a great job going through the environmental reports. When we went to see Pearson today he did look rattled by them, but it feels like we're still missing the final piece. The golf course is very close to a protected area, but it doesn't seem to violate it. I'm putting out feelers with the other planners, but so far none of them are biting. And I need to work out who this Nora is that the secretary heard him fighting with Immy Blake about, but there's no one by that name coming up connected to Pearson."

Bernie's face looked like she had sucked on the lemon in her drink. "It's not good enough, really. I mean, I know you've been working hard, but if we don't come up with something soon, we'll have to call it quits. We can't keep taking the client's money if we're not coming up with the dirt, can we?"

Liz's mouth turned down at the corners. "No, I guess not."

Mary looked down at the table. Bernie seemed grumpy tonight, even for her. If she had been the sort of person who would have taken one, Mary would have offered to hug her. Instead, she offered her a healthy snack.

"Would you like a nut?" she said.

"Mary, are those chocolate brazils? They're about sixty calories," Bernie said.

"Ah well, that's not too bad."

"Per nut!"

Mary raised her eyebrows. "Okay, maybe I'll just have a couple more." She made sure that Bernie wasn't looking and grabbed another handful. She needed some brain food.

"I've got a couple of potential clients next week. Both extra-marital affairs, but if we lose Pearson then we'll need to take them for the cash. Let's put that on next week's agenda."

232

Mary dutifully wrote it down.

"Now let's talk about our buried bodies."

"The bodies on witch's hill," Mary said solemnly.

"That sounds like a famous five novel," Bernie snapped. "Anyway, let's go over what we've learned. Mary, can you start with the identification of the more recent body."

"Sure. It looks pretty likely now that Mikala Nowak is the woman that was killed and buried around a year ago. We've been trying to find out as much as we can about her, but she didn't have much of an online presence. Liz found a couple of things, didn't you?"

Liz nodded. "She was involved with a charity called Welcoming Renfrewshire. My mum volunteered with them a couple of times. She's given me the name of the woman who runs it, Connie MacIver. I'm going to go and see her first thing tomorrow."

"Good," Bernie said.

"Me and Walker went to see Mikala's landlord today," Mary said, determined not to blush when she mentioned the police officer's name. "He's a right creep. Liam Beatson. I rented a flat from him years ago. Very much the slum end of the market. He didn't care one jot that Mikala was dead, he was just happy to get his flat back on the market."

"Do you think he was involved?"

Mary shook her head. "I can't see a motive, unless we've

233

missed something. But if he did have a good reason to kill her, I bet he'd know the right people to dispose of the body. He's shady as anything."

"All right," Bernie said, "let's leave him in the suspect column. It's not like we've got many others. How are we meant to find out who Mikala was in contact with a year ago? It's bloody tricky."

The front door opened and Alice came through into the room.

"Hi everyone," she said, "sorry I'm late, we were doing some low light photography, so we can only do the assignments in the evenings. Did I miss anything?"

Bernie rubbed her face. She looked more tired than normal. "Not really. We're close to giving up on Pearson, and Mikala Nowak's a closed book.

"Well, I've been speaking to a guy called Stanley Morecombe," Mary said. "He's the one that wrote the article about the bodies on witch's hill. He's kind of an oddball, but he's got some interesting ideas about the witch's cottage and –"

Bernie held up her hand. "We've already wasted enough time on this witch nonsense. I'd rather concentrate on something that isn't complete rubbish."

"That's a bit rude, Auntie," Alice said, echoing what Mary was thinking but too scared to say.

"Look, this might all be a wee hobby for the rest of you," Bernie said, straightening up in her chair, "but it's my business. We can't be getting a reputation as a bunch of silly women running around after fairies."

There was an awkward pause.

"I don't think any of us view the WWC as a hobby, Bernie," Liz said. She had kept her tone light but her face was stern and still like a statue.

"Maybe not, Liz, but that's what it'll become if we don't get a handle on these cases."

Liz looked like she was going to say something else, but then she stopped and smiled. "It's been a long couple of days. Why don't we call it quits and get some sleep."

Bernie opened her mouth to argue, but Liz gave her a glare and the other woman quietened down.

Mary watched all of this with horror. She grabbed her coat and left with only the briefest of goodbyes. As she walked to her car, she found herself reaching for a tissue. Please don't take it away from me, she prayed to whatever God or spirit might be listening. Please don't let the WWC fall apart. I just couldn't bear it.

As she pulled away from the house she saw Bernie and Liz arguing in the doorway. It wasn't until Mary was halfway home that she realised she'd left the packet of chocolate Brazil nuts, and then she really did feel like crying.

Chapter 42: Bernie

"You shouldn't have sent the others home," Bernie complained to Liz after Alice and Mary had left. "We still have a lot of work to be getting on with."

"Not while you're in this foul mood we don't," Liz said.

Bernie rubbed her eyes. She wasn't in the mood for a big fight with Liz. She was tired and fed up and just wanted to go home to bed. Without her husband who was still sleeping in the spare room. Just great.

"I'm just not sure how committed everyone is to the WWC right now," Bernie said, keeping the subject away from her private life. "Oh sure, Mary is working her socks off now, but when her kids come back she'll disappear again. And Alice couldn't even make the meeting. And let's face it, you're just using the WWC until you get another real job, right?"

Liz looked shocked. "Is that what you think? Yes, I might have to get another job in finance, but that's because someone needs to pay the bloody mortgage. It's not that I'm lacking commitment or anything."

The gin bottle was empty when Bernie went to fill her glass, so she put it down with a clink. "Maybe you're not, but what about the others? They never check in with me, I never know what anyone is up to. It seems like no one cares that I'm the boss anymore."

"Berns, you are talking utter balls."

For a moment she was about to call her friend out, but after a second, Bernie shrugged. From anyone else that would have been an insult, but she knew that Liz was probably just being truthful. From the minute they had started working together, neither Bernie nor Liz had ever held anything back. It was part of the reason the WWC had done so well.

So why was she trying to ruin it now?

Bernie slumped back into her chair. "Sorry, Liz. I'm having a bloody awful week. And the cases have stalled, and it feels like we're going nowhere on them."

Liz still stood with her arms folded, despite the apology. "That's no excuse to treat everyone like crap, Bernie."

"Yeah, you're right. I'll apologise tomorrow, okay? But it's not all my fault. You guys have been working the cases without keeping me in the loop. And Finn went off on one just because I poured his whiskey down the drain."

"I'm sorry, you did what?" Liz's eyebrows nearly jumped off her forehead.

"He's been drinking too much recently, and I know that if it's in the house, then he'll just drink it, so I decided to get rid of it."

"You don't think that was a little extreme?"

Bernie didn't understand why Liz couldn't get it. "It was the only thing to do. He wouldn't listen to me."

Liz let out a long sigh. "Bernie, you know that I think that you're completely amazing, don't you?"

Bernie raised an eyebrow. "All right, give me the sucker punch."

"It's just… Sometimes you're maybe a little too perfect. You can be a little intimidating, in that you are always right and always know everything. I mean, Finn is a nice bloke, he works hard, and maybe he does drink a bit too much. Maybe that's a problem, I don't know. But the thing is, you see the world as being problems and solutions, and if you see one you always want to supply the other. Maybe in this case you need to let him find his own solution."

Bernie didn't say anything.

"Sorry. Maybe I shouldn't have said anything," Liz added. She looked worried that she might have put her foot in it.

"No, I'm glad you did. I'm just going to think about it for a little while, if that's all right with you."

"Sure." There was another awkward silence.

"Shall we talk about murder?" Liz said finally.

"Yes, let's do that. That is one thing that I do not 'know everything about'." Bernie said, with an edge to her voice.

Liz let out another sigh.

Chapter 43: Liz

On Thursday morning Liz woke up with a terrible hangover. The sort of fuzzy mouth, thumping head hangover that makes you wish you had never been born.

"Cup of coffee?" Dave asked.

Liz poked her head out of the duvet. "God, yes. And some painkillers, please. What time did I get home last night?"

"After two I think, I was asleep."

Liz groaned. "On a school night too. What the hell was I thinking?"

"It's okay, I'll take Sean into school today."

"Would you?" Liz sat up to see that Dave was already dressed in his suit, his tie slightly squint. She felt an almost overwhelming love for him. "Thank you."

"It's no problem, I was getting up for work anyway. Did you crack the case?"

"What?" Liz's brain felt like it was stuck at half-speed.

"Isn't that what they say on the telly? I thought maybe you were late because you were all celebrating."

"Uh, no. Quite the opposite. Bernie was in a terrible mood and had a right go at everyone. I stayed late to calm her down.

239

Honestly, sometimes I wonder why we are friends. I think she's feeling insecure because Mary has turned out to be such a star for the agency. So now Bernie doesn't know what to do with herself, and she's taking that out on everyone else. Poor bloody Finn and all."

"I wouldn't imagine she'd be an easy person to be married to," Dave said diplomatically.

"Damn right. But then she's got lots of other good qualities, I'm just struggling to think of them right now. Did you say there was tea?"

Dave gave her a mock salute. "On the way."

It took another two cups of coffee before Liz felt able to get into the shower and get ready for the day. She hadn't done her hair – that was a time-consuming process reserved for Sundays – so she put on a colourful wrap and plenty of makeup to try and disguise her dull, hungover skin. She chose a red dress and a long tweed coat and checked herself out in the mirror. She was probably horribly over-dressed. When her mother went on her volunteering positions she always wore a simple tunic of geometric-printed fabric, no makeup, and the sort of earrings that could poke an eye out from across the room.

Liz was not her mother and she had spent too long as an accountant to become a flamboyant dresser overnight, but she did enjoy not having to wear the obligatory trouser suit anymore. Perhaps the funky prints would come later.

At the last moment, she grabbed her briefcase. She might have left financial services behind, but she wasn't ready to leave the house without a laptop. And if she found some information on Mikala Nowak, she wanted to be able to update the files straight away.

She drove into the town centre with the windows of the car open, letting the crisp breeze blow away the last vestiges of her hangover. By the time she had paid for parking and arrived at the small doorway that marked the entrance to the offices for Welcoming Renfrewshire, she was feeling almost entirely like herself again.

The charity was squeezed in between a vape shop and a place that claimed to sell ice-cream desserts but that Liz had never seen with the shutters up. It was in an area of town that might be described as 'up and coming' if you were being kind. Bernie would have called it a dump.

Liz rang the bell and waited as a large woman in her late fifties or early sixties with hair cropped short around her face answered the door.

"Lovely to see you," the woman said with a strong accent, possibly Yorkshire, although Liz always got the Northern English ones confused. "You must be Grace's daughter."

"That's right," Liz said, slipping into the building and closing the door behind them. The premises seemed to be half office, half meeting place with a collection of desks at one end and a large table and chairs at the other. In the middle of the space were a couple of sagging sofas and a coffee table and it was here that Connie MacIver led them.

By the time she had settled down with a cup of slightly cloudy instant coffee and a chocolate biscuit, Liz knew this was going to be an easy interview. Connie was one of those women that never stopped talking.

"You picked a good day to come and see us, it's normally manic in here. We're a staff of six now, even though I'm the only full-timer. When I started it was literally just me running about trying to help people, totally unpaid. We've got a bit of lottery funding now, but that barely pays the electric bills. So that's why it's quiet in here today. We've a big fundraising event next week, so it'll be back to full power then."

"Yes," Liz said, interjecting while Connie took a breath. "I was wanting to hear your thoughts on Mikala Nowak."

"Ah, the poor girl. It's not easy you know, coming to a new country. Well, your parents went through all that of course. And so did Mikala. We bonded over that, you know. I felt like an immigrant myself when I first moved up here, even though I only came from Leeds. Married a Glaswegian, you see."

"Mmn," Liz said, not really seeing that the two experiences were the same. "Could you tell me about when you first met Mikala?"

"She was very quiet. Clever, with a decent level of English which isn't always the case. She was a qualified physiotherapist in Belarus, but her parents didn't keep well, so she came over here to earn more money. Of course, it wasn't quite the life she had imagined. Poor things, it never is. Mikala came along with another girl, Kristi Villi, who has been living here for a few years now. Kristi's from Georgia, so they both had Russian as a second language. It's nice really, when people hit

242

it off. And then Mikala left, which was very sad for Kristi. She stopped coming along as well not long after that."

"You say that Mikala left," Liz said, "Do you know where she went?"

The older woman sighed. "Many of our clients here are transitional. They work the sort of jobs that no one does for very long. Their housing situation is often unstable, and they get very little support from official channels. It's never a big surprise when someone moves on. If I remember rightly, Kristi said that Mikala had taken up a job in London."

"I'm sorry to tell you this, Mrs MacIver, and it's not official yet," Liz said, hoping that she wasn't about to get herself in trouble with the police, "but I'm afraid it looks like Mikala died almost a year ago."

Connie pressed her right hand to her mouth. "Oh heavens, are you sure?"

"Pretty sure. You know the body that was found up on the hill?"

"That was Mikala? That's just... but what happened to her?"

"As I said, the police haven't officially released this to the public, but it looks like she was murdered."

Connie fumbled in her pockets and brought out a tissue which she pressed to her eyes. Liz sat for several minutes, letting her gather herself.

"I know it's a shock, but if there's anything you can tell us, anything at all that might help us catch whoever did this to Mikala…" Liz ran out of words. Connie's eyes had dropped down to the table, where her cup of tea had gone cold.

"I just… you try so hard sometimes to make lives better for these young women and… Well, some of them never stand a bloody chance. The men that take them over here, sell them on the dream of a better life, they're the ones that should be locked away for the rest of their lives. But they never get caught, do they? And now it ends up like this."

Connie looked Liz directly in the eyes.

"I can't give you any definitive evidence, you understand, but I would stake my life on it that the people that brought Mikala here are responsible for her death. People trafficking, that's what it is, although they disguise it as 'work placements' or 'apprentice schemes'. It's nothing more than exploitation of the most vulnerable people they can find."

"You wouldn't be able to give me any names, would you?"

"Off the record? Damn right I will. The agency that she was working for, Office Helpers Limited, or something equally unremarkable. Thing is, there are only so many cleaners this town needs. And they're all young women, often with no English at all. And if they get word that any of them have been visiting places like this, or other outreach centres, they close ranks."

"You think it's a front for what… human trafficking?"

Connie was already nodding. "Yes, and what it leads to.

Prostitution, modern slavery, all that sort of thing, hidden behind a respectable agency. There's a whole underworld going on that most people wouldn't even dream exists. And because it's happening to people who can't advocate for themselves, no one cares."

"You care," Liz said, giving the woman's hand a squeeze. "And now my team do too. Can you send me an email with everything you can think of on Office Helpers and their workers? And I'll make sure we find out what happened to Mikala."

Connie nodded. "I will. But you look out for yourself too. Mikala wanted something more for herself. She was always talking about how she could have done better than her crummy flat and her cleaning job. If someone killed her it was because she was a woman that stepped out of line. Just like you are. Don't let the same thing happen to you."

Chapter 44: Walker

It was twenty-four hours before his exam, and Walker was starting to feel the effects of nerves when he arrived in the office on Thursday morning. He had spent half of Wednesday night watching videos online about dyslexia, after his talk with Mary. It turned out there was a whole internet community of people that had developed tips and 'hacks' for living with reading problems. Walker couldn't decide how he felt about it. Part of him was pleased that other kids wouldn't have to deal with the same stigma that he did, but mostly he just felt disappointed that he hadn't found this stuff earlier.

He had even managed to get a little studying in. Mary had sent him a link to a text to speech reader with the message: *This might be easier than reading the material. Feel free to ignore if you don't want to use it.* And then she had sent a Christmas tree emoji.

Walker had stared at it for a few seconds. Was this some sort of good luck message? Then his phone had buzzed again.

Sorry, that was meant to be a thumbs up!

Still smiling, he had downloaded the screen reader and set it to read out loud his ebook copy of Blackstone's Police Manual. He still found his attention drifting, but by forcing himself to take notes at the same time, he could feel the information seeping into his brain in a way that it never did when he tried to read from a page.

Just a pity it was all too late. The exam was tomorrow and he had only got through a quarter of the material. He stared at the picture of Mikala Nowak that had been pinned to the wall of the office. It was one of the ones sent through by her parents. She had just finished college and her parents looked so proud in their neatly ironed, but well-worn clothes. Walker could only look at their beaming smiles for a few seconds before he had to look away. Maybe he would fail the test tomorrow, but at least he knew he was a good officer. He would find whoever killed that woman and it would mean more than some stripes on his arm.

"Briefing in five," Dianna said as she swept in carrying some sort of horrible looking green smoothie in a plastic cup.

"Wheatgrass," she said as she passed Walker. "I walked past the press pack five times this morning just in case. Not one of them took a bloody photo."

"They're waiting for another sausage roll," Walker replied, happy in the knowledge that he had cooked himself eggs and sausages before seven that morning to try and wake up. He hadn't got to bed until after three.

"Right everyone, gather round," Dianna said once the rest of the team had arrived. "I'm going to start with some good news. The lab has taken another look at our unidentified remains. We've got a match this time. They found some dental records for Paul Crossly from when he was fifteen. There are a few more fillings in the body in the ground, but there is a definite match. Something to do with some upper bridge-work. Sounded painful, but the point is that Paul Crossly was our man in the ground in 2004."

"Yes!" The shout went up around the team. Now they could really get their teeth into that case.

"Pull out everything we have on the earlier investigation into Crossly. If we get ahead on this one it's something I can take to the Superintendent."

Walker felt his energy seeping back. He had always felt that the earlier body was important, and now they would get the chance to find out why.

"Having said that," Dianna went on, holding a finger in the air, "we still can't let our focus slip from Mikala Nowak. She's still our first priority, but if we can wrap up the Paul Crossly case, too that can only be a good thing. Now, Suzie, I want you to take the lead on the Crossly case. Go back over what we know. Let's start with the basics. Known associates for Paul Dean, aka Paul Crossly."

Suzie tapped at her laptop. "No family apart from the sister, parents are both dead. We do know that he was working for West Clyde Builders at the time."

"That's Tam Brown's business," Neil said. "He's a local 'character'. There have always been hints of trouble at his sites, lots of falls, no health and safety, that sort of thing. People say that he doesn't pay his workers properly, but we've never been able to get anyone to bring charges against him. His son is a nasty little thug too. Known for thinking with his fists. A few aggravated assault charges, but nothing that made it to court."

"Right. Neil, you look into this Tam Brown and his son, and

any other people from the building sites that might be suspects. Paul Crossly was into drugs, is that right?"

Walker nodded. "According to his sister."

"Okay, let's find out who was in the drugs scene at the time. We might need to speak to a few of the older officers again. I'll get back in touch with Sergeant Bob Daniels and I'll see if Superintendent Marr is able to have visitors. They should be able to give us the info on who the major players were back then. If his death is drugs related, then it shouldn't be a problem to find some suspects."

"I'd like to talk to the farmers," Walker said, "I know the old farmer died, but I still think there might be something the family members know that they haven't told us."

"All right. But make it a quick interview. I need as many people as possible still on finding known associates of Mikala Nowak. She's still our number –"

"One priority, got it," Walker said, giving Dianna a smile. "Me and Suzie went to try and get hold of Fyodorov last night, but no luck."

"He's the one that's head of the temp agency, right?"

"Right," Suzie said. "And there's something off about him. The woman that answered his door looked absolutely terrified when she saw it was the police."

"Then we should try and talk to her. Suzie, will you camp out at the house after we finish up here? Try and get her to talk. She might be more willing if it's just a female officer.

Suzie nodded. "We're still working on finding out Mikala's movements in the days before she disappeared. We know that she spent her mornings cleaning, but her afternoons are a blank. No one from the other flats remembers seeing her about the place. By all accounts, she was a ghost. Oh, we did find out that she was involved with a refugee organisation called 'Welcoming Renfrewshire'," Suzie added. "I gave them a phone this morning, and they are going to send us a list of associates of Mikala. It's kind of funny though."

"What's funny?"

"The woman said I was 'late to the party' and that someone called Liz Okoro had already 'beaten me to it'. Any idea what that means?"

Walker couldn't help but let out a groan. "I have a fair idea," he said. "Liz is part of a private investigation agency. The WWC, it stands for Wronged Women's Co-operative. They are a local group and I know that they are interested in the bodies on the hill."

Dianna's cheeks reddened. "What? Some amateurs are getting involved in our cases? And you knew about it?"

"I had some idea," Walker said, not meeting her eye.

"Oh, are these the women that got the suspect to confess in the Sam Jones case?" Neil said, in an unwelcome moment of clarity.

"Yes. They aren't as bad as you think, Dianna. In fact, they often share information with us. Um, with me."

250

The Inspector's face was now resembling a fine ripe tomato. "I will discuss this with you later, Walker."

"Sure."

Suzie cleared her throat. "I'm going to send some constables around the flats where Mikala lived today, just in case we missed someone who remembers her. And Neil managed to get hold of the manager of Macarthur Cleaning."

Neil stood up, "It was a bit of a bust, ma'am. The guy who ran it, Mr Towers, he didn't even remember Mikala. None of the people working for him now were there when she was. But I did a bit of digging on Mr Towers and it turns out he spends a lot of time with his good friend Mr Fyodorov. They go golfing together every Friday afternoon, according to the secretary."

A grin made its way across Dianna's face. "That's nice work. So here's a theory for you. Fyodorov's company gets cheap labour in from Eastern Europe, maybe legal, maybe not. They funnel the immigrants through their temp agency into Towers's cleaning company. Paying the whole lot of them next to nothing, no doubt."

"Sounds about right, sir."

The Inspector tapped her pen against her teeth. "But there must be more to it than that. I don't believe that Mikala was killed for being a cleaner. Let's keep digging."

Meeting over, the officers started to move back across the office to their desks.

"Walker, come and see me in my office," Dianna said, and she turned around not checking to see if he was following.

Without meeting the gaze of his fellow officers, who knew fine well he was a mile deep in crap, Walker walked into the Inspector's room and closed the door behind him.

"Explain. Now."

Walker did. He started with how the Wronged Women's Co-operative had been instrumental in solving the case of Sam Jones's murder. He mentioned that the women involved were discrete and reliable. He may have overegged the pudding a little, but he knew he was on thin ice. In the end he was quite pleased with his description of the WWC's many talents, but the frown was still fixed on Dianna's face.

"Hang on," the Inspector said once Walker had finished talking. "Did you say one of the women was called Mary? This wouldn't be the same Mary that you were playing games with the other night."

Crap. Walker felt a bead of sweat trickle down his back. "Actually, yes."

Dianna dropped her head to her hands and groaned. "You know, you really are trying to sabotage your career, aren't you? First your exams, now this. You are in a relationship with a woman who is using confidential information from you for her own private investigation practice. Jesus, if internal affairs heard about this they would sack you on the spot. I should suspend you right now!"

Walker tried to think of something to say. He had always

known it was a risk being involved with the WWC, but they had proved crucial in finding out things that the police themselves weren't able to discover. But there didn't seem to be any way to explain this to Dianna.

"Look, we're friends, so this makes things tricky. But I'm not going to go down with you. If any of this comes out, I didn't know anything about it, okay?"

"Of course."

Dianna pinched the skin between her eyebrows. "So here's what I'm going to do. I'm not going to suspend you, because you have your exam tomorrow. Unlike you, I don't want to completely screw up your career. But I want you off the case and out of my sight until this is over. First thing on Monday we'll have a meeting about what the hell I'm going to do with you."

Walker opened his mouth to argue, but no sound came out.

"I'll tell the others you've gone home sick. They won't believe it, but they know your exam is tomorrow so they'll just think you're swotting up. Which is what I want you to do. Go home to your studies and don't show your face until Monday."

Numb, Walker stood up and made his way into the corridor. He was barely out of the office before Dianna slammed the door shut behind him.

Chapter 45: Mary

Mary was beginning to wonder if it was all falling apart. Her kids were due back that afternoon, and by nine in the morning she had heard nothing from the other members of the WWC. She had just made herself a big bowl of soul-comforting porridge when her phone rang.

"Hi," Liz said.

"Good to hear from you," Mary said, her voice full of forced cheerfulness. "What's up?"

"I feel like death, that's what's up. Look, I'm sorry about what Bernie said last night. She's being more of a nightmare than usual at the moment."

"I don't think it's you that should be apologising," Mary said, more sharply than she had intended.

"That's true, but if you wait for an apology from Bernie Paterson you might as well wait for all the potholes in Invergryff to be filled. It's not going to happen."

"Right."

"Anyway, that's not what I wanted to talk to you about. I've just been sent the details of a friend of Mikala Nowak's from the refugee charity. I've got to take Sean to the dentist, so I can't go and see her this morning. Could you go?"

Of course she could go! If it meant that she still had a job with the WWC, Mary couldn't agree quickly enough. "Yes. I'm meeting Stanley Morecombe after lunch, then the kids are home at four, but I could definitely squeeze her in this morning."

"Great," Liz said. "I'll send you over the details. Make sure you ask about this temp agency they were all working for. There's some dodgy stuff going on there. Connie at the charity thinks it might be human trafficking."

"Wow. Okay, I will."

Mary hung up the phone and got straight onto an internet search on human trafficking in Scotland. It wasn't as rare as she might have thought, and of course it was hugely under-reported. Mary hadn't realised it was something that went on in her hometown. In London maybe, or possibly Glasgow, but not in a town like Invergryff. Turns out she had been incredibly naïve. From nail parlours to carwashes, it seemed like there was a whole underbelly of these places through which people were moved without any input from the authorities.

An hour later and not feeling much more prepared, Mary had driven to a small hotel in a village ten miles out of Invergryff. When she went up to reception and asked for Kristi she was shown into a small staffroom that smelled of microwaved food.

After a few minutes, a thin woman who could have been anywhere from fifteen to thirty came in. She had a pinched face and a black cardigan that she wrapped tightly around her chest.

"Can we go somewhere I can smoke?" Kristi said after Mary had introduced herself.

"Sure."

They walked around the hotel. It was a crumbling Victorian building that seemed to be on its last legs. A sign outside proclaimed 'teas and lunches', but there didn't seem to be many people taking the place up on the offer.

"She's dead then," Kristi said, her tone more of a statement than a question.

"Yes, I'm afraid so."

"Damn it." Kristi spoke softly. Her English was good, with a strong accent that Mary might have thought was Russian if she didn't know that the woman came from Georgia.

"Was Mikala a good friend of yours?" Mary asked after they had been walking in silence for a few minutes.

"Yes. The only friend I had in Invergryff. After she… left, I knew I had to leave too. It took me six months, but I got the job here. I don't like to talk about that time."

Mary had the sense they were skirting around something very terrible for the woman who was drawing on her cigarette like it was oxygen.

"I know it's really difficult for you, but I need to find out everything I can about Mikala. You see, my friends and I are trying to find out who killed her. If we don't they will get away with it."

Kristi blew out a cloud of smoke. "And she will just be another dead immigrant. No one will care."

"We care. I know it might not feel like that but… A few months ago I came here with my kids. To Invergryff, I mean. And I had a little money and I got a house but I was still lost. I didn't have any friends and I had left my husband…" Mary trailed off, searching for the right words. "Then I found some women that liked the same things I did. That wanted to help other people. And they gave me a job and now I feel like I have my life back, you see? And those are the people that are going to find out who killed your friend."

The younger woman nodded. "Your friends will help my friend. I see. I will tell you what I can. But you must understand that the men that brought us here do not like me talking about these things. If it ever got back to them that I was talking to you…"

"It won't."

"All right. Well, for me it started three years ago. That's when I was brought to Invergryff. I had been in London before, and in Albania before that. It was not a good time, do you understand? I had left Georgia because my mother had a new boyfriend that I didn't like, and he certainly didn't like me. By the time I got to Albania I had hardly any money left, but I met some men that told me there were better things in Scotland. I should have known that things do not get better, they are just the same problems in a different place."

"Is that what happened to Mikala too?"

"She did not come from Albania. She was from Belarus, but I think she was picked up in London. She was smart, did you know that? She was qualified as a... not a nurse, someone who helps people with exercise, I think."

"A physiotherapist."

"Yes, that's it." Kristi let out a grim chuckle. "They made a mistake with Mikala, I think. Normally they go for girls that are not so smart. Like me. But Mikala had brains. And that meant that she was trouble for them."

Kristi took another deep drag of the cigarette. "She asked questions. No one was meant to do that, you see? And even though they gave her the easy work, the cleaning and things, not the... other stuff, she still asked about what the other girls were doing, about what the men were doing too."

"There were men trafficked as well?"

She nodded. "We didn't see much of them, they did work like building, labouring, that sort of thing. But Mikala wanted to know what was happening to them too. She went to English classes, not that she needed them, she was so good. But she got me to go along too."

"Your English is great," Mary said.

"Thank you, I am still learning. For a while, it was okay. Mikala kept asking the bosses for more money, and sometimes they would tell her to shut up, but I don't think they really thought she would do anything. They thought we were all harmless."

258

"But something went wrong?"

"Something was always going wrong. They kept moving people around, girls you were friends with would disappear overnight, come back weeks later looking sick, or on drugs. One time there was a young lad, maybe sixteen? They sent him to work with us for a few days because he was too skinny to be a labourer. Mikala saw that he was black and blue all over, like they had been beating him. She went up to the boss and shouted at him and he didn't say a word, but I was scared. She should not have done that."

"Who was this boss?"

"We were told to call him 'sir', but mainly we just called him the Russian. I think his name was Fyodorov. That's what the other men called him. The Russian didn't beat Mikala, but he gave her worse jobs, twelve hour shifts cleaning toilets, that sort of thing. And then one day they brought a big group of us out into the hills."

Mary found the hairs on the back of her neck were standing up. "What happened?"

"We were in a truck that stank of animal crap. It was dark and they took us all to this ruined house. Then they said that they had a warning for us. They said that if the police found us we would be sent home in… in shame? Is that the word? In disgrace, that was it. Our parents would learn what we… some of the things we had been doing here to earn money. And we would be in big trouble with the police. They said they would send us to prison because we had come here illegally. And we saw the news, the detention centres and everything. We knew

259

it was true."

Mary looked at the ground. She wanted to say that it wasn't true, that the police wouldn't lock these women away in detention centres, but the truth was she didn't really know if they would or not.

"On that day they took us up to the place in the middle of nowhere. It was… creepy. Really creepy. And they kept talking about witches and things. Some of the girls were scared out of their minds. But Mikala grabbed my arm. She told me that they were lying and trying to scare us. She made me feel better."

Kristi had to stop for a second to wipe her eyes.

"Sorry. Anyway, Mikala was right. They took us to this creepy place, and they told us what happened to bad girls, girls that did not have a flat, like they gave us, jobs, like they gave us. All we had was what they had given us, do you see? Then they started telling us that they would look after us. Like, we wouldn't have to worry about being captured by the police, or being sent home, just as long as we did what they said. The whole time I'm getting more and more scared, but for Mikala it was different."

"In what way?" Liz asked.

"She was getting angry. The rest of the girls, they were shaking with fear, and I could see that the men thought Mikala was the same. But I could see her face. It was white, like a skull and her lips were pressed together so that there was no blood in them. She was even scaring me a little! After that they made us work in the fields for a week, sixteen hours a day, barely any food. I just kept my head down and so did she. But when we were taken back to the town, back to the tiny flats they kept us in, it was like something had changed in Mikala. She was fierce, like a bear. And I was scared then because I thought she was going to do something bad."

Kristi sniffed. "And then a week later she disappeared."

Mary shifted position in her seat. "And you didn't... I'm sorry to ask you, but you didn't think that something bad had happened to her?"

Kristi looked down at the floor. "I didn't want to. They said that she sent a message to the agency to say she had to leave for London. She got a physiotherapy job there. And I really, really wanted to believe it was true. But she had a secret mobile, you know? We weren't meant to have one, but she had got one from somewhere. One day I asked a friend of mine to send her a message, but she never replied. And then I knew she was gone."

Mary waited while Kristi sobbed into a crumpled tissue. She thought of her safe little life with her kids and her middle-class divorce and she wanted to weep too, for this woman that never even had the chance of that. But mainly Mary felt what Mikala had felt. She felt angry.

Chapter 46: Bernie

When Bernie heard her doorbell ring at lunchtime on Thursday, she would never have guessed who would be standing at her front door.

"Can I have a quick word?" Constable Walker asked.

"Mary isn't here," Bernie said, blocking the doorway. She wasn't someone who hated the police, but she still didn't particularly like the idea of them turning up at her house unannounced.

"I know. It's you I would like to speak to, as the head of the Wronged Women's Co-operative."

Mollified, Bernie pulled the door open and showed the Constable into the living room.

"Would you like a tea? Do police officers drink tea? On the telly they always drink beer. Or whiskey. And that's all gone down the sink." For once, Bernie was feeling a little flustered. The feeling was not one she welcomed.

"Actually, I could have a beer if I wanted, although it's a little early. I've been suspended."

Bernie turned to him, jaw hanging open. "What? Suspended! What did you do? Let me guess, slept with someone you shouldn't have. A murderer probably. One with blond hair and big boobs and a tight red dress slit to the thigh."

262

"Christ, no!" Walker looked horrified. "I would never do that. And by the way, that sounds more like Jessica Rabbit than a human being. No, I didn't do anything like that. I was suspended because of you."

"Me? But we haven't slept together. You are very much not my type."

Walker frowned at her in a way that reminded her of her husband. "No one slept with anyone, Bernadette. I was suspended because my Inspector is worried that I am behaving in an unprofessional fashion with the WWC."

"Oh." Bernie looked at the man. He seemed a bit lost, with big sad eyes like a puppy. Maybe she could recruit him for their agency once he got fired?

"I was wondering if you could talk to her. The Inspector is clever, I reckon once she sees you she will understand that the Wronged Women's Co-operative is totally harmless."

Bernie's lips pinched together. "We are, are we?"

"Of course!" Walker grinned, not realising that he had made a bad move. "Once she sees that you are a bunch of mums, she'll realise that you are no threat to the police."

There was a long pause where all Bernie could hear were her back teeth grinding together.

"Maybe that came out a bit wrong," Walker said, with the slow realisation of a building avalanche. "I just meant that you wouldn't pose any problems for the police force."

"Damn right we will," Bernie said, "when we solve both murders, your police force is going to look more foolish than when your Inspector went on her little sausage roll binge. Saturated fat and carbs, what the hell was she thinking?"

"I shouldn't have come here," Walker said.

"Yeah, you shouldn't. Seems to me like you've been making plenty of mistakes recently. Messing up your career, taking our Mary for granted, and now you insult us."

"I didn't mean to do that."

"Well, I hope you enjoy your suspension. Drink protein powder and watch sports on TV or whatever it is you people do."

Getting the not-so-subtle hint, Walker got up and headed for the door.

"I'm sorry to have upset you, Mrs Paterson."

"I'm not upset. I'm angry. Now off you go," Bernie said, shooing him out of the door like an errant pigeon.

"And, um, what did you mean about taking Mary for granted?"

Bernie just gave him a final glare and closed the front door. At that moment her phone pinged with an email from Mary. It turned out that the dead woman, Mikala Nowak had been a victim of human trafficking. For many people, the idea that these things were going on in a normal town in Scotland would be a surprise, but Bernie had been a nurse for long enough to know that the worst parts of humanity were in evidence everywhere. Thankfully, the same could be said for the best.

She peeked out of the living room window. Walker's car drove off down the street. Bernie phoned Liz.

"You'll never guess what that police constable just said to me," Bernie said and then launched into the story of how Walker had said the WWC was harmless. Liz was just as annoyed.

"I can't believe that guy. Mary is better off without him."

"Damn right. Now, I want to show him just how 'harmless' we really are. I want to solve these cases before the stupid cops get their funny hats on. We need to drop everything else and get it done."

"Maybe you should have been a bit nicer to everyone else last night, then," Liz said. "You were a bit of a bitch, Bernie."

"I tell it like it is," Bernie said. She wished Liz would get over her huff. They needed to focus on what was important.

"You tell it like you think it is, Berns, just like you did with Finn and his drinking. Maybe you're right. But maybe you're not."

Bernie pressed the phone to her forehead. She didn't have time for this. "Okay, I'll apologise to Mary and Alice. But please, let's get going on this case."

There was a long pause on the other end of the phone, then she heard Liz sigh.

"I suppose that will have to do. Look, there's a list of things

265

we need to do for both cases. I've got to see Pearson today, so you could take over my tasks. I was going to interview the temp agency that employed Mikala. You could go around to her block of flats and see if anyone remembered her. Oh, and I was thinking about having a chat with the farmer and his wife. The site of the burials still seems to be the only thing linking the two bodies, so it might be that they know something."

"I'll take that one. I don't like that Mrs Graham. She's hiding something. No one bakes that well without some sort of deep dark secret."

"Okay. And about the other things I said –"

"Speak soon," Bernie said quickly and ended the call.

Five minutes later she was driving up the road to the farm. It was amazing how it only took a few miles for the town to disappear behind the hills. All of a sudden you felt like you were in the middle of nowhere.

A crow yelled at her when she got out of the car and Bernie gave it one of her Looks. She had never been particularly fond of nature: she was always fighting the urge to disinfect it.

"You again," Mrs Graham said when she knocked on the door. Bernie felt this was rather unfriendly and not really befitting of a representative of the Women's Institute.

"That's right," Bernie said and she shifted her position a little so that her foot was in the doorway. "I wondered if we could have another chat."

266

"Want to borrow my walnut loaf recipe? Or maybe a knitting pattern," the farmer's wife said with her arms folded.

"Never got the hang of knitting," Bernie replied, "too much sitting around. No, I wanted to talk murder and buried bodies."

"And you won't just go away if I shut the door in your face?"

"Not a chance."

"Then you better come in. But I'm not making you a cuppa."

Bernie followed her in, and was struck once more at how organised the place was. Every item in the kitchen was labelled and placed on a shelf, facing the right way, like a picture from a magazine. It was unnerving.

"What a lovely big kitchen. It's just you and your husband here, isn't it?" Bernie asked, noting that she could count eight different sizes of copper pans.

"That live here, yes. We have Jackson who works on the farm and he's here for all his meals. And there's always a couple of labourers about. It's busier than you think."

"I'm sure," Bernie said. "Your husband is called Andy, isn't he?"

"Andrew," Mrs Graham said. "He's out with the cows."

"I don't think I've ever seen him."

"Well, farmers work hard. Dawn until dusk."

Bernie tried to seem sympathetic, even though it wasn't usually her strong point. "It must be hard for you, being on your own all day."

The other woman shrugged. "I was a farmer's daughter before I was a farmer's wife. I knew the score."

"And this was the house that you grew up in, wasn't it?"

"Yes. It was a bit messier then. I've tidied the place up a bit."

There was a strange sound coming from somewhere. Bernie looked around but couldn't see anything and Mrs Graham didn't acknowledge it.

"I came to ask you some more questions about the two bodies found on your land."

"I cannot possibly think what more I can tell you."

"I suppose the police have already told you that they identified the most recent body."

"Yes. A young woman, apparently. Very sad."

Bernie was about to ask another question, when she heard something again. There was definitely a series of mewling noises coming from under the sofa.

"What's that?"

"Kittens," the farmer's wife said. "The cats around here are half-feral. We thought we'd found them all and got them neutered, but we discovered these little ones last week. Of course, in the old days they would have drowned them."

268

"Would they indeed," Bernie said, her expression unreadable. "And what will you do with these ones?"

"Oh, they learn to fend for themselves soon enough. Keep the rats out of the barn, that sort of thing. You can't be sentimental about these things when you live on a farm."

Bernie nodded. "I have never been sentimental about anything myself."

"A good motto. Never let the past rule the present, that's what my dad used to say."

"And did he follow that?" Bernie asked. "As a philosophy? Because it seems to me like there might be a few things in your family's past that you might want to make sure are forgotten."

"What on earth are you getting at, Bernie?"

What was she getting at? Bernie wasn't too sure. "I mean, if there was anything that your dad was into, anything dodgy, you could tell me about it. After all, he's long gone isn't he? Nothing can hurt him now."

A tiny head appeared from the top of the box and Mrs Graham tutted before shoving it back in.

"They only want the warmth, you know, cats," the woman said. "No loyalty. Not like dogs."

For some reason the tiny meows were distracting Bernie. It reminded her of when Ewan was a baby. That feeling like the cries were ripping you open from the inside out. Hormones, that was probably the problem. They were responsible for

269

many irrational thoughts.

"So there's nothing you saw when you were younger that worried you? Nothing your dad might have done?"

"He certainly wasn't a secret murderer. He was a farmer, of the old breed. He lived his life just as his father had done and his father back to the dawn of time."

"The rumours about him being not entirely on the level then, they were all just made up?"

"Probably. People around here are always jealous of success. And that's what my family were, they were a success. And my father made sure of that."

Bernie leaned forward. "I think you're too scared to tell me what went on here. I think there's a reason that those bodies were buried on your land. And if it's not me that finds it out, it'll be the police. Have you seen them? All brought up in Glasgow or worse, Edinburgh, no idea what life is like out here. Do you think they'll understand what your life was like?"

Mrs Graham's gaze dropped to the floor and Bernie had to stop herself from screaming 'gotcha!'

"There were some things... long before I took charge of the farm. Nothing illegal, but maybe some things that dad did would be... frowned upon now."

"Like what?"

"I honestly don't know the details. But there used to be meetings up near the witch's cottage. There are two big laybys, long enough to park trucks in. Big trucks. They would show up in the night and that was kind of... unusual. I was never allowed to go near them."

"But a clever woman like you wouldn't do what she was told, would she?" Bernie prodded.

Mrs Graham pushed her hands into her face. "There was all sorts of stuff. A few times it was trucks with diesel. Sometimes it was animals, sheep and cows. I think... well, I think it was a way of selling them off without going through the auctions. Saving the tax."

"You didn't see anything other than animals in the vans?"

"Like I said, diesel maybe, and wood. Stuff that fell off the back of a lorry."

"What about people?"

Mrs Graham's doughy face creased into a frown. "I guess there must have been someone that drove the van, but..."

"I mean in the van. Did you ever see people in the van?"

The farmer's wife's face paled. "I have no idea what you're talking about. There might have been some things my dad did to avoid paying the frankly unreasonable taxes that the government demanded from him, but that was all. Now I think you should go."

"But..." Bernie didn't want to leave. She knew she was getting somewhere with the woman. At that moment the door to the farmhouse opened and a huge man in padded clothes and welly boots came into the house.

"Hello, Mr Graham," Bernie said cheerily while his wife jumped up and walked over to him. The farmer had aged better than his wife, with deeply tanned skin and the sort of broad chest that people who spent half their life in the gym never managed to achieve.

"Bernadette was just leaving," Mrs Graham hissed, pointing to the door.

"Is this woman bothering you, Nora?" the hulk in the doorway asked.

"Not at all."

"I'll get out of your hair," Bernie said, not wanting to push her luck. The farmer looked like he would happily throw her to the pigs. She made her way outside and as the door shut behind her Bernie tried to pretend she hadn't heard a final pathetic meow.

Chapter 47: Liz

Liz spent lunch eating a sandwich with one hand and typing up notes with the other. Between what Mary had sent her about her meeting with Kristi, plus Bernie's comments about the farm at the witch's hill, she felt like they were finally getting somewhere on the buried bodies case. And finally she could say the same about Pearson.

The breakthrough had come courtesy of a last minute re-read through of all the notes on the development at Ellenslie Braes. She had been back and forth over the notes and hadn't spotted anything, until she had taken a final look at the maps. Now, Liz hadn't paid too much attention to the maps on her earlier investigations, because she had always found them a little confusing. Luckily she had a much more spatially aware son.

"Sean, you do geography in school, right? Any good with maps."

Her son had looked up from his homework, glad of a distraction. "It's all online maps in geography. But I do them in Scouts. Let's have a look."

It had taken them half an hour before they spotted it. Liz noticed the discrepancy first, then checked with Sean.

"Yeah," he said, peering over the piece of paper, "the scale is wrong here. Like, it suddenly goes from counting the contours in tens, then in thousands. It shouldn't do that on one map," he added, then ran off to check out what was happening on a

273

football match that his dad had on the telly next door.

That little chink of light was all she needed. She traced the map back to the survey company that had performed not only the geological surveys of the area, but the environmental impact ones too. The ones that Mary had found so lacking in detail. The ones produced by Scotia-Enviro Limited.

Liz did a search on Companies House and when she found out the details of who owned it, she punched the air. Now she just had to get her evidence in order and go to see the MP.

Half an hour later she had just parked her car when her phone buzzed with the Darth Vader theme from *Star Wars*.

"Bernie, I can't talk. I'm just about to go and see Pearson. I've only got a second."

"I just need one. You were looking for someone named Nora, right? Well, the farmer's wife up where the bodies were discovered is Nora Graham. Born Nora Bryce."

Liz nearly tripped over the kerb. "What? Are you sure? I guess you are. But it could be a coincidence, right?"

"I don't think so," Bernie said. "I've just got home and turned on the laptop. When I searched for their names together it turned out that Nora's father, Tom Bryce, was a big supporter of your man Pearson's. Put money into his campaign, all that stuff."

"Jesus. I don't have time to look into this right now. I'm right outside Pearson's office."

"Don't worry. I've called Alice and she's going to do a deep search on the net while you're in the meeting. Just keep your phone on you."

Liz had to take a couple of calming breaths before she went into the building. She had thought that she knew what she was going to say to Pearson, but what Bernie told her put everything up in the air. Was there a connection between Pearson and the bodies on the hill? She had known he was a sleazebag, but could he also be a murderer?

Somehow she couldn't see it. He seemed like the sort content to let others do his dirty work. And they still didn't know what Nora had to do with anything, even if it was Nora Graham from the farm. Best thing to do was stick to her script. Unless Bernie texted her with anything juicy along the way.

Pearson's smile was a little more fixed for this meeting.

"Mrs Okoro. How nice to see you again," he said. Liz noted there was no offer of tea this time around.

"Thank you for seeing me again. There were just a few more things I wanted to speak to you about."

"I had hoped I had answered your questions the first time."

"Just a few more," Liz said, feeling like she was a raincoat away from being Columbo. "I wanted to ask about some of your associates."

"I don't really see how that's relevant."

"Well, I'm afraid I do. You see, I've already found out about

275

your connections to Imelda Blake. It seemed pertinent to me to consider who else you might be working with."

"You do realise that making connections with local businesspeople is critical to the job of an MP? You seem to be determined to see nepotism and favours, where there is only a sensible working practice."

"Sure," Liz said, not believing a word of it. "And I'm sure you have the details of everyone that you have any financial association with, just for transparency."

Pearson stretched his legs out in front of him. "Of course, it's necessary for my parliamentary position."

"And what if there was a question mark over a developer that you had personal connections to?"

"I can assure you that Immy Blake is perfectly kosher."

"She might be. But can the same be said of the people she employs?"

"We… that is, the developers have always employed reputable local tradesmen."

Liz allowed herself a small smile. "Do you have a list of them?"

"I'll get my secretary to check for you."

"Actually, if you wouldn't mind checking for me now, that would save some time."

Frowning, Pearson spun his chair around and typed into his laptop. "This is all public knowledge, of course, but here is the list of contractors."

"Interesting," Liz said, leaning over and noting down a pertinent name. "This is all very helpful, Mr Pearson. Oh, hang on, someone's trying to call me, let me just message them to say I'm busy." Liz took her phone out of her pocket and messaged Bernie instead of the non-existent caller:

Guy who slashed Finn's tyres, was it Tam Brown of Building Pros West Coast?

There was a pause of a few seconds while Pearson coughed impatiently.

That's him. Why?

Liz didn't answer and instead slipped the phone back into her bag. "I see that one of the contractors is Building Pros West Coast. Run by Tam Brown. Are you aware of that?"

"If they are on the list, then I suppose it must be so."

"The thing is, Mr Pearson, it's looking very likely that the building firm run by Mr Tam Brown is involved in some illegal activities. There have been death threats, and we think it very likely that they were involved in a man's disappearance in 2004."

Pearson looked genuinely horrified. "That is terrible. I had nothing to do with that firm."

"Are you saying they aren't the people that you have lined up to build the golf course? The one that came up on the screen a second ago?"

"Yes, but…" Pearson took a moment to recollect himself. "I'm not sure. That is the business of Victory Holdings, who are running the development. And even if this builder is… engaging in unsavoury practices, that is hardly the developer's fault."

"The thing is, the police have identified the body from 2004. What was a disappearance is now a murder case."

"You can't possibly think…"

"Oh, I'm sure you had nothing to do with all that. But if we were to find that Mr Brown was one of your long-time golfing buddies, that might not look too good."

Now Pearson had started to sweat. "You've been spying on me?"

"Oh yes. I have the photographs to prove you spend a good deal of time together, mainly trying to get out of the rough, from the looks of it. But it's not just Tam Brown that I'm interested in. I wondered if we could return to the environmental reports for the Ellenslie Braes development?"

Now Pearson couldn't help but let out a groan. "My dear woman, we have already been over this. Several times in fact."

"Yes, of course. But you see, my good friend Mary Plunkett used to produce these sorts of environmental reports. And we found that yours were somewhat thin on detail. Not inaccurate, but not up to the standard she would expect."

"Does that really matter?"

"Not by itself. But I had a closer look at the information pack, and there was something funny about the maps. They look like standard OS maps, don't they? At least, that's what the planners must have thought when they were submitted. I mean, who is going to check the maps, right?"

Pearson's chin had dropped to his chest. "Let me guess, you checked the maps?"

"I checked the maps."

"And what did you discover?"

"That the maps were false. The boundaries of the area of special interest, the Natura area, had been moved so that it appeared that your development fell just outside the protected region. When in fact they overlap. And then I checked out the company that produced the maps for you. The same that produced the underwhelming reports. Scotia-Enviro Limited. And guess who the director of the company is."

Pearson pressed his palm to his forehead. "It's Pete Brown."

"That's correct. Tam Brown's brother and another one of your golfing partners, isn't he? My surveillance tells me that you play together once a week. Quite a cosy little relationship, really."

The MP had a look of a man whose world was crashing down around him. "Well, I'm sure you're very pleased with yourself. Have you any idea how many jobs that development would have given this region? And now you're going to shut it all down to protect some crappy bog land that no one even cares about? Look, Pete Brown fudged the reports for us, I'll admit that. But I didn't know the details: I just asked Imelda to sort it out. And I certainly didn't know that Tam had any connections with a murder! You've got to believe that I wouldn't be foolish enough to associate with him if he did."

Liz sniffed. "So you're not a criminal, just your bog standard sleazy politician."

"No hang on a second," Pearson said, his jowls turning a deeper shade of red. "You can't come around insulting me like that."

"Yes I can. Because I'm assuming that you don't want any of this on the record."

Pearson seemed about to argue with her, then he sighed and crumpled into his chair. "I knew it was too good to last. I mean, to get ahead in life you have to take risks. I've always believed that. But this was just one risk too far. The stupid maps. I should never have let Nora persuade me to do it."

"That would be Nora Graham, right?"

"Is there anything you don't know? The farmer was the one that sold us most of the land. At first we thought we would be able to build the golf course without impacting on the protected zones. But when we looked at drainage, and how we were going to reroute the road, there was no other way around it. Unless we could alter the boundaries of the zones, just a little."

"Around five square miles, by my reckoning," Liz said.

"In a countryside full of nothing more than bogs and trees. Hardly a great loss. And now I suppose you'll go to the press and I will be the big bad nature killer. They'll probably throw avocados at me."

"It'll be worse than that when they find out about Tam Brown. The police are looking into him right now and it seems like he's got a reputation for breaking the rules across the board. This could be a national scandal."

"What do I do?" Pearson asked, his face pale so that he looked like he might through up.

Liz felt it was time to get him on her side. "Look, our clients just want this development stopped. They don't care about your career."

"So?"

"So maybe we can make a deal. Kill the golf course. You make the development go away, but you get to keep your job."

Pearson's eyes narrowed. "And let me guess, there's something in it for you."

Liz grinned. "Now that's why you've stayed in Government for so long, Mr Pearson. You are very good at reading people."

"What do you want?"

"I want Tam Brown."

Chapter 48: Walker

What a boon it had been, Walker thought, to get suspended from his job the day before his exam. All this extra study time was simply wonderful.

Of course, that's what he should have been thinking. Instead, he was engaged in an activity that his mother would have described as moping. He was alternately slumped on the sofa or pacing the flat, mainly thinking about how hard done by he was and feeling sorry for himself. None of which was helping with either his study prep, or the apology he was going to have to give to Dianna to get himself reinstated at work.

When his phone rang he jumped on it inhumanely fast, hoping that it might be the Inspector.

"I heard you got suspended," Mary said.

Walker burrowed back down onto the sofa. "Yep. It's unofficial so far. But Dianna is pretty peed off about the whole WWC thing."

"And I just had Bernie on the phone. Sounds like you got her back up too."

The memory of telling Bernadette Paterson that she was 'harmless' flashed across his mind. "Ah, I might have spoken a little out of turn there."

"She said that you called us a 'totally harmless bunch of

mums'.""

"I'm sure that wasn't the exact wording…"

"Well, I thought you might like to know what exactly the harmless bunch has discovered in the last few days. Let's start with Mikala Nowak, shall we? I'm just back from interviewing her best friend. Her name is Kristi Villi and she works at the hotel in Johnstone. They met through the charity 'Welcoming Renfrewshire'. You'll need to talk to Kristi, but be careful. She'll be terrified of the police and she's been through a hell of a lot."

Walker, who by this time was taking notes, felt that he should butt in. "We have specially trained officers who can deal with this."

"Good. Because you're going to need them. Mikala and her friends were the victims of human trafficking. I've been doing some research on it. It seems like there's a group of locals organising it, but they keep themselves out of direct involvement. One of the names Kristi mentioned was Fyodorov, a Russian."

Walker felt his neck tingle with excitement. "She mentioned Fyodorov? We went to see him. He was listed as the boss of the temp agency that Mikala worked for. We couldn't get to see him though. He's been avoiding us."

"Well, you need to track him down because Kristi was seriously scared of this guy."

"Did she see him hurt Mikala?"

"I don't think so. But she implied that he might be involved."

"We're going to need more evidence than that."

"Well," Mary said, her voice taking on a stony tone. "You can do that bit yourself. We've done enough of your investigation for you already. And you can tell that Inspector of yours that I'm telling you this because we're not in competition with the police. We just want justice for two murder victims who no one else seems to give a crap about because they didn't lead the kind of lives that got them on the front page of the newspaper. Do you know where they printed the article about Mikala's identification in today's *Gazette*?"

As usual, Mary's quick change of subject had wrong-footed him. He hadn't even remembered that they were running a piece about Mikala Nowak's identification today. "Um, no…"

"Page six. Under the opening of a new garden centre. That's how much the press cares about people like Mikala. And that's why you need the WWC, 'harmless' or not."

Walker pressed his fingertips into his eye sockets. "Mary, you know I didn't mean…"

"Goodbye."

He flopped back onto the sofa. This was probably worse than when he had brought Dianna along on their date. Which hadn't been a date, and totally wasn't his fault anyway. I mean, the woman was a nightmare. Still married to her ex, so many children that she never had any free time, and a frankly ridiculous attitude about the detective agency. And yet…

Who else would wear a onesie with the Phantom on it? There was something about Mary Plunkett that he couldn't resist. Which meant he was going to have to apologise to her about the 'harmless' thing. Oh well, she would just have to get in line.

He clicked the number for the station on his phone.

"I'm very busy and you should be studying," the Inspector said the moment he was transferred through to her office.

"I know. But I just got a phone call from the WWC."

"Are you kidding me?"

"Please just hear me out. They've been speaking to a friend of Mikala Nowak's. She's confirmed the connection to Fyodorov and suggested that he was involved in people trafficking and modern slavery. I think we need to follow it up ASAP."

Dianna was silent for a few seconds. "Send it to me in an email. I'll get Suzie on it straight away. Did this friend of Mikala's see what happened to her?"

"No. Just suspicions."

"All right."

"And, um, the WWC wanted to tell you that they were giving us information as they want to help the force, not hinder it."

"Oh, I never questioned their motives for a moment. It was yours I was worried about."

"You don't want me to come back in, then," Walker said, more in hope than expectation.

"At the moment I never want to see your skinny arse in here again. You just focus on your exam tomorrow and we'll have another chat on Monday."

If Walker thought the Inspector might have mellowed towards him, the way she hung up without as much as a bye showed that she was really annoyed. He stared at the dark phone screen for a few seconds. He wasn't used to getting into the level of trouble he couldn't talk his way out of. What if the Inspector did report him to their bosses? He could find himself in front of the Professional Standards Department, and that would be his career over. And who would be to blame? Not Dianna. She was just covering her own back. He was the one that had put her in this position.

The thing was, he knew that he would do it again given half the chance. The WWC were capable of finding out things that the police could never uncover. That was what he had meant when he had used the unfortunate word 'harmless'. People underestimated them: a group of mums could get information out of people much more easily than a burly man in uniform could. Now that the police was a national force, with few officers knowing the area they worked in, the local knowledge that the WWC had was pivotal to their investigations.

He knew he had been skirting around the rules when it came to working with Mary and the rest of them, but it was getting results. He just had to get Dianna to see it.

Chapter 49: Mary

Mary had been putting off a phone call for nearly an hour. She had hoovered the stairs, put away a mountain of kids' clothes and even cleaned the oven. Eventually she could delay it no longer.

"Hi Bernie, how are you?"

"Fine," the woman on the other end said.

"I just wanted to let you know that I talked to Walker," Mary explained.

"That patronising git. What did he say?"

Oh dear. Well, there was nothing for it but to confess. "Actually, it was me doing most of the talking. I told him what we found out about Mikala Nowak."

"Did I hear that right? You gave away all the information we had? Just like that?"

Mary had rehearsed this in her head, but now it came to the moment, she was struggling to find the words. "It was the right thing to do. The police need to know what's going on. What happened to Mikala is still going on. If we can help out women like her, we need to do it. Without waiting."

"You should have asked me first."

"It was the right thing to do," Mary repeated stubbornly.

There was a long pause on the other end of the line. Mary hunkered down in her seat, as if Bernie was glaring at her from across town.

"I suppose that's right," the other woman said eventually. "We can't leave someone else to end up like Mikala did. I just think it should have been a WWC decision."

Mary breathed out slowly. "Sorry, Bernie."

"What are you apologising for? It's okay to have a different opinion than me. I'm not going to tell you off for that. You're a grownup after all."

"Thanks!" Mary said, pleased.

"It's a fact, not a compliment. Now I think we should have an emergency WWC meeting. What time are the kids back?"

"Any time now," Mary said, looking out the window for the hundredth time to see if Matt's car was there.

"Can you ask Matt to watch them while you sneak out to a meeting?"

"Of course not. Bernie, I'm not going to leave the kids tonight. I haven't seen them in nearly a week!"

"Then we'll come to you. Around seven o'clock all right?"

Mary didn't have time to think of a reason to say no. "I guess so."

"See you then," Bernie said and ended the call.

288

She stood in the kitchen for a moment, trying to resist the urge to chuck the phone out of the window. Then the doorbell went.

"Mum!"

A delicious few minutes of hugs and kisses followed, with one child showing her a new scratch on his knee, another chattering excitedly about how many toilet stops they had had to make on the way South. Mary drank it all in with pure joy.

"I missed you guys," she said wrapping her arms around all of them, despite their protests. Ten seconds later they had all run off to watch telly or investigate their rooms to check that nothing had been moved since they left.

"Sorry we're a bit late," Matt said, trailing in behind the kids.

Did she allow herself a little moment of smug satisfaction that Matt looked completely exhausted? Mary would not have been human if she hadn't felt that way. But she did manage to squeeze her ex-husband's arm and whisper, "Well done for surviving."

"Oh, it wasn't so bad," he said, heading back out to the car. "I've got three bags of washing for you."

Even that couldn't dampen Mary's mood. She knew that by tomorrow morning the kids would be annoying her once more, but for the moment she had her little angels back and she couldn't have been happier.

"Do you want a cup of tea," Mary offered.

"No thanks. I'll just say goodbye to the kids and head back up the road. I've actually… Well, I've got a date tonight."

Mary stared at him, speechless. She almost felt like laughing, although it wasn't funny. She wasn't sure what it was.

"Are you okay? You look like you're going to faint."

"I'm fine," Mary said, trying to pull herself together. "It's just… I suppose I didn't really think you were dating."

"Neither did I. Only I met a woman from work and she asked me out and I thought, well, why not? After all, we're not together anymore."

"Right. So why not?" Mary agreed. They looked at each other for a moment, each person looking as confused as the other. Finally Mary cracked a smile.

"There's no guidebook on how we do this, is there?" she said.

Matt returned her smile. "I guess not. I'm sorry if I sprung that on you. It's just… I didn't want to go behind your back or anything. Jeez, I thought this would be easier."

"Me too. You know, I think one day we might even manage to be friends."

Her former husband blinked. "I would like that. Maybe you could give me some tips for tonight. I mean, I was thinking about wearing a shirt but –"

Mary interrupted him, shaking her head. "Not yet, Matt. A little too soon."

"Of course. Well, I'll call the kids in a couple of days."

He said his goodbyes to the little ones and Mary watched him drive away. The weird feeling in the pit of her stomach was something she wouldn't be able to explain to another human being, or even herself. But it felt like something had changed, and hopefully for the better.

It was pizza for dinner, the kids' favourite treat, even though Mary insisted they have some broccoli on the side. Peter managed to finish his plate and nobody threw anything at each other or ended up sulking under the table. It was a homecoming miracle.

An hour later they were all tucked up in bed, if not asleep, then at least pretending to be. Mary felt that weird joy of motherhood that almost made her weep. Then she picked up the pile of discarded clothes and headed down to the washing machine.

Her phone buzzed. Stanley Morecombe was calling.

"You said you would come and see me today."

Mary pressed her palm to her forehead. "Sorry Mr Morecombe, it's been a crazy day. You were going to tell me about the exorcism on the witch's hill."

"I was. But I wanted to explain my methodology first. You see, people say the word 'exorcism' like there's a simple ritual to follow. It is much more complicated than that."

Mary tried not to sigh loud enough for the man to hear. With Bernie and the others due any minute, she didn't have time for this.

Morecombe carried on. "I believe in the classics. You can't go far wrong with Leland or Frazer, although their approach was scholarly rather than, ahem, practical. Of course, Crowley wrote the definitive work on the matter."

"Who is Crowley?" Mary asked.

"Aleister Crowley? The most evil man in Britain? How can you be an occultist and not know about the most famous witch ever to have lived in Scotland?"

Uh-oh. Mary tried to backtrack. "Oh, I just forgot for a moment."

"Who are you?" Morecombe's voice went up an octave. "What are you really doing here talking to me? Are you an agent of the state?"

"Of course not," Mary said, alarmed at the sudden change in his temperament. "I'm just someone who is interested in the witch…"

"Liar!" Mary could almost feel his anger heating up her phone. She waited a few seconds to see if he would hang up, but she could still hear him panting down the line.

"Stanley," she said softly, as if she was talking to Lauren after a screaming tantrum, "I'm sorry I upset you. You were right to question who I am. I should have been honest with you from the start. I'm actually working for a private detective agency. Nothing to do with the government. We're just trying to find out who killed those people they found in the ground."

"You're police?" he grunted.

"No, not at all. In fact, we're trying to beat the police at their own game. They don't care about who died up on the hill. They certainly don't care about the witch. But we do." Mary stopped, wondering if she was laying it on a little thick.

"Never trust the police. They're just agents of the state. I was out protesting when Stephen Lawrence died. We knew the truth then." Morecombe paused for a few seconds, then said. "Sorry I lost my temper. My mum always told me not to."

"That's all right, Stanley," Mary said. "I really would like to know about the exorcism though. Anything that you know about the witch's hill could help us find out why those people were buried there."

"It was Father Gannon who did the ceremony. He used to be head of a church in Ayrshire before he retired. He charges quite a reasonable amount for exorcisms."

Mary resisted the urge to ask about the priest-for-hire. She had already put the phone on speaker so she could clean the kitchen counters while they talked. The WWC would be turning up in twenty minutes.

"We did the ceremony at midnight. I did have to correct the father on some of his pronunciation of the incantations, but he did admirably well. Of course, the fact that another body turned up there years later means that the spirit was too strong even for us. We could feel her malignancy even then, and the farmer told us that he could often sense her when he was bringing in the cows."

293

"This was the old farmer, right, the one who died? I bet he was angry that you were up there."

"Actually, he was happy to see us. He knew all about the witch. Said she had cursed his family for generations. No, he wanted us there."

"Oh." Somehow that didn't fit with Mary's idea of what the old farmer was like, but maybe she was wrong about that.

"He didn't believe in the priest, though. He said that no exorcism would stop the witch and that people should keep away from the hill. It would always be a cursed place. And he was right."

"Okay," Mary said, feeling that she hadn't learned much of anything. "Well, if that's all you can tell me…" she trailed off.

"You were never really interested in the occult, then," Morecombe said, his voice so forlorn that Mary could have hugged him.

"Not really, I'm afraid. You've been really helpful though. And I'll tell you what, once we've turned this all over to the police, you could write it up on your blog."

"Like an exclusive?" Morecombe perked up a little.

"Exactly."

By the time Mary managed to get off the phone with Morecombe, Bernie's car was pulling up outside.

Chapter 50: Bernie

"Are you sure this is slim-line tonic?" Bernie asked as Mary set a drink down on the table.

"Yes Bernie."

Bernie gave it a suspicious sniff. She didn't trust the woman to have slim-line anything. Still, she felt in need of a drink. It had been a long day.

"Right. We better get on with things. First of all, we have to give Liz a pat on the back. The Pearson case is officially concluded."

Mary let out a whoop of pleasure while Bernie and Alice applauded. Liz gave a fake bow.

"Thanks guys. I phoned Iona today. Looks like New Dawn Home Management will get their social housing after all."

"Shame we couldn't get Pearson sacked," Mary said, popping a biscuit into her mouth.

"That's not our job," Bernie reminded her. "But I get the feeling that there will be plenty of other people looking at his track record from now on. The rest of his business partners aren't going to be happy with him either."

"And I did get him to talk to me about Tam Brown," Liz said.

Bernie perked up at the name. "The tyre slasher? What did he tell you?"

"Well, he was pretty shocked that we were looking at Tam Brown being involved in Paul Crossly's death. He said he never knew he could be violent."

"Sounds like arse covering to me."

Liz inclined her head in agreement. "Yeah. Especially as he then went on to tell me some of the things that he did know Brown was up to. Turns out that Immy Blake has been working with him for the best part of two decades, mainly because he works on the cheap to get massive profits. He seems to have an endless supply of cheap labour that isn't too worried about health and safety. There have been a few accidents over the years, and Pearson has helped to keep it all quiet."

"How kind of him."

"Yeah. I might have sent a little anonymous tip about that to a large national newspaper this afternoon. Anyway, I asked Pearson where Tam Brown got all those cheap labourers from and he said he didn't know."

Bernie was already nodding. "But we can guess. What was the name of the Russian guy again, the one running the dodgy temp agency?"

"Fyodorov," Mary reminded her. "Walker was trying to track him down just before he got suspended."

"Suspended?" Liz looked shocked. "What happened?"

"Apparently he was hanging out with us too much," Bernie said. "You wouldn't think that would matter seeing as we're so 'harmless'."

"I don't think he meant it that way," Mary said, defending her lover-boy as usual. Bernie just ignored her.

"It's all coming together. Paul Crossly was working on Tam Brown's sites. Maybe he had some sort of accident at work and they didn't want it getting in the paper so they buried him up on the hill. Then, when Mikala starts making trouble for the same people they do away with her too."

"It makes sense," Liz said slowly, "but we still don't know exactly who killed either of them. And we've no concrete evidence to give to the police. It's all just a theory."

"That's why I think we should go up to the witch's cottage, tonight," Bernie told her.

"Are you mad?" Liz said. "It's already dark."

To her left, Mary made a tiny noise like a cat when you step on its tail.

"What was that?" Bernie asked sharply.

"It's just... I can't exactly go out and leave the kids, can I? They just got home." Mary said, her lips pouting.

"I'll phone one of the nieces. They'll come and babysit."

"Oh, I really don't think..."

"Mary Plunkett will you stop being such a wet blanket. Your

children are asleep. They won't even know you're gone. I'll get one of my nieces to come and keep an eye on them. Now go get your stuff together so we can get going."

For a moment, there was total silence. Then Mary rose from the table, pink spots in her cheeks.

"I am not a wet blanket. If I was, I would let you tell me what to do. Now, I am a paid member of this team, and I will happily work all hours of the day. But my kids have been away for the best part of a week and I want to be here for them. I want to settle them if they cry and tuck them in if they roll out of bed. So no, I won't be coming with you. And if you want me to choose between the WWC and my kids, then I'm afraid there is no choice at all." By the end of this speech, Mary's voice had developed a distinct wobble.

Bernie looked to Liz for support, but her friend was staring at her with her lips firmly pressed together.

"Oh all right," Bernie said finally, breaking the silence. "There's no need to be so dramatic. Liz, Alice and I will go up to the witch's cottage. You can stay home if you want."

Mary sat back down, mumbling 'don't need your permission' as she did so. Bernie chose to pretend she didn't hear a thing.

"Are we really going up to the cottage?" Alice asked. She had to be excited as she had put her phone down for a second.

"Yes. I want to see where the bodies were buried."

"And Stanley Morecombe said that the old farmer was encouraging them to do exorcisms and warning them about

298

the witch," Mary added. "Which all sounded a bit weird to me."

"The current farmer's wife said she believed in the witch too. But nothing else about her suggested she was into that sort of rubbish."

"I thought we agreed you wouldn't call it rubbish, Auntie," Alice reminded her.

"All right, there was nothing to suggest that Mrs Graham was into occultism. Either way, I want to get a good look up there. There's something weird about that farm and I want to know what it is."

Mary traced a pattern with her fingers on the wooden table. "You know, when I was talking to Kristi she said that the traffickers took them out to a creepy place in the middle of nowhere to scare them. Do you think that could have been the same cottage?"

Bernie stared at her. "I mean, it could be, right? In which case, the Grahams are in this up to their eyeballs."

"Then we better be careful when we're up there," Liz said. "I mean, if two people are already dead, then they might not like us sniffing around."

"Message me when you get home safe," Mary said.

"Yes, mum," Bernie rolled her eyes. Honestly, sometimes she thought she was the only one in the WWC that had any cojones.

Chapter 51: Liz

An hour after Bernie had suggested it, Liz found herself high up on a hill with freezing rain and wind whipping at her woollen coat. It was darker than she had expected, a thick layer of cloud cover obscuring the moon and the stars. As they walked up the hill from the layby, Liz kept her mind off the cold by imagining all the ways she was going to get back at Bernie for this.

"No phone reception here," Alice moaned as she put the device into her pocket. Liz kept her phone on as the torch function was the only way she could navigate the uneven ground in front of them.

"I think it's magical," the fourth member of the team said.

"Thank you, Eve," Liz said to the young woman, but without really meaning it. The only reason she hadn't acted as angrily as Bernie had when they had collected the self-styled witch was that Liz didn't want to look uncool in front of Alice. "And thank you for coming. It's good to have an expert with us."

"An expert!" Bernie said with a laugh, and Liz gave her a dig with her elbow.

"Be nice," she told her friend.

"What? I was being serious," Bernie said. "Look, we're nearly at the cottage."

There was a brief gap in the clouds and the moon poked out. How do you know if a moon is waning, Liz thought as they walked up the hill. It was almost full, looking down on them like a bulging melon about to go bad. Did that mean it was waning? Or was it waxing? And wasn't there something about gibbons? Liz was so far out of her comfort zone she was starting to feel a little light-headed.

It had been Bernie's idea to visit the cottage, and Liz wasn't entirely sure why they were here. Even though there were still traces of police tape fluttering about in the wind, it had been over a year since Mikala had been buried here, and considerably longer since Paul Crossly had met his end.

At least they were nearly at the cottage. Although, even that was a disappointment. Somehow the word cottage had conjured up somewhere that might be a cosy refuge from the hill, a place they might get a little shelter. It certainly suggested that there would be a roof. Instead, when the members of the WWC and their witchy companion arrived, they found that the so-called cottage was nothing more than three ruined walls and a jumble of old stones.

"There is a negative aura about this place," Eve said as soon as they walked into the cottage.

"Is there?" Bernie said sweetly. Liz didn't like this new, diplomatic side her friend was showing. She knew at some point the nurse would drop the act.

"These stones have seen many tragedies," Eve continued, giving Bernie a look.

Something caught Liz's eye on the wall. "This is recent, isn't it?"

The others crowded around. It was some sort of mystical symbol, painted in blood red.

Bernie touched it. "Yeah, I don't think they had spray paint back in the eighteenth century."

"This is all wrong," Eve said, tracing the shape with her fingers. "I mean, it looks like they're trying to do the eye of Anubis here, but they've got the shape on the bottom all wrong. And look on the floor."

Alice shone a torch downwards so they could all see.

"I thought as much," Eve said. "The symbols in this pentagram mix Chinese I Ching with Western astrological signs. They don't make any sense."

"So what does that mean?" Bernie asked.

"It means that no self-respecting Wiccan had anything to do with this. Kids, probably, or someone that watched too many fantasy shows on TV. These symbols are completely meaningless."

Liz rubbed her freezing hands together. "Are you saying they are fake? Like maybe somebody wanted to make it look like witchcraft?"

"Or they just didn't know what they were doing. Trying to play at being Satanists or something."

Bernie held her phone in front of her face so that everyone could see her. "Okay, so we have someone faking witchy stuff. Why would anyone do that?"

"The witch herself was real enough," Eve said, "I've checked the records myself. She really did live up here."

Alice, who had been peered out of the one remaining window in the cottage, let out a cry. "I think I know. You can see right down to the farmhouse from here. It's a perfect view down the valley."

The rest of them came over to join her.

"Then it must be the same for the Grahams. I just hope they haven't spotted us up here."

As one they turned off the lights, which left them in near-total darkness.

"Well, this isn't creepy at all," Alice whispered. "The thing is, maybe the old farmer wanted to keep people away from here. What could be better than telling everyone it was cursed?"

Liz frowned. "That could be it. But what about the Grahams? Could they be in on it too? And what's the connection with our dead bodies?"

"I don't know, but we're getting close. I can feel it!" Bernie said.

"Can we go now," Eve said. "My toes have gone numb."

"Not until we work out what happened here," the nurse said,

stomping around in the dark.

"Fake or not, there's definitely a negative energy here," the Wiccan said, making for the door to the cottage.

"I'll give you some negative energy," Bernie said, taking a step towards Eve.

"All right, let's all just calm down a wee bit," Liz said, grabbing Bernie by the shoulders. "I think that Eve is right. It's dark and freezing cold. We're not going to find out anything else tonight. Let's go home."

"Okay," Bernie said. "But we're going to have a little chat with the farmer and his wife tomorrow. I want to hear what they think about all this. And what new excuses they are going to come up with this time."

Chapter 52: Walker

By the time Walker came out of the examination, he could barely remember what day it was, let alone the time. It was only when he checked his phone that he saw it wasn't even lunchtime on Friday yet. He had been in the tiny airless room staring at a computer screen for three hours, but it felt like forever.

He was exhausted, and just wanted to curl into a ball and sleep but when he stepped out onto the pavement he had a vision of an angel.

There was Mary, sitting on the wall opposite him, holding two takeaway drink cups.

"I got the weirdest message," Mary said, handing over one of the cups to Walker. It was full of hot, sweet, milky tea, like you might give an invalid. "It just told me when and where you were sitting the exam, and that I might want to meet you outside. Do you know who sent it?"

Walker smiled. "I think it was Dianna. She's really annoyed with me right now, but she still wanted to look out for me, I guess. She probably thought I needed someone to commiserate with, and you're kind of here as her surrogate."

"And is it commiserations?" Mary asked gently.

"Honestly, I'm not sure. It went better than I could have imagined. When I went in, they asked if anyone needed any accommodations, and I put up my hand." Walker chuckled. "I still can't believe I did it. If you knew how much of school I spent hiding at the back, hoping that no one would notice I couldn't do any of the work... Anyway, they took me out into the corridor and asked me what I needed. I said I didn't have an official diagnosis, but I was dyslexic. And just like that, the guy running the place found me a private room with a computer so that I could have the program read the questions out loud."

"That's great!"

"I know. They couldn't give me extra time without a letter from a specialist, but just having the questions read out to me made it so much easier. But as for whether or not I passed..." Walker's shoulders dropped. "Who knows? I still don't type fast, but I managed to get an answer down for everything. I should find out in a few weeks."

Mary pulled him into a hug. "I'm so proud of you."

He leaned back, not wanting to let her go, but still feeling awkward about touching her. "Thanks. Now tell me what's been happening with our cold cases."

"Our cases? Does that mean that you don't think the WWC is harmless anymore?"

Walker groaned. "I'm never going to live that down, am I?"

"Nope," Mary replied, but she said it with a smile. "If it makes you feel any better, you're not the only one in the bad books with Bernie. They all went out to the cottage last night but I

306

told her I had to stay home with the kids. I still can't believe I managed to stand up to her."

The Police Constable almost spat out his tea. "Hang on, they went up to the cottage? The one near where the bodies were buried?"

"Aye. Don't get your knickers in a twist though, they didn't go up to the burial site. They just had a look around."

"Let me guess. They found a man standing there holding an axe crying 'I did it!'"

"Sadly not. But it's looking more and more likely that the farmers are involved."

"What makes you think that?"

"Well, our witch thought that the Satanic symbols at the cottage were fake, made by someone who had no idea what they should look like."

"Sorry, did you say a witch?"

"Don't worry, she's a friendly one. She makes her own granola."

Walker rubbed at his eyes. "You were saying about the paintings on the cottage walls…"

"Oh yes. Well, they were made to look like Satanic stuff was going on, but by someone who didn't know what they were doing. And the old farmer told Stanley Morecombe – that's the guy that wrote those articles about the witch – that the cottage was cursed. It seems to me that maybe they had some reason to keep people away from the cottage."

This was something he could work with. "Why would they do that?"

"I think they might be connected to this human trafficking thing. Kristi said that the Russian guy that ran the whole horrible enterprise took them up to somewhere in the middle of nowhere to scare them. What if that was the cottage?"

"Seems a lot of effort just to scare some people."

"They did some work up there as well, I think, for the farmers and –"

Just then Mary's phone started to play the theme tune from *Murder She Wrote*.

"Hang on, it's a text from an unknown number. Oh crap!"

She held her phone up to Walker so that he could read it.

In Fyodorov's car. He has my phone but I have spare. He is taking me somewhere, he says he has job but I am scared. K.

"What do we do?" Mary said, her eyes wide like a cartoon pixie.

"We call Dianna. Get in the car."

Chapter 53: Mary

This time Mary felt no excitement at speeding through town in the passenger seat of Walker's car. She couldn't help thinking about all the terrible things that might be happening to Kristi right at that moment. And how it was all her fault. The Russian must have heard that Kristi had talked to her somehow, otherwise why would he suddenly be interested in the woman again? Mary chewed her thumbnail. What if she ended up like Mikala?

While he drove, Walker talked to the Inspector on his police radio.

"We have no idea where he is taking her. I need you to trace the mobile number. There is a real risk of harm."

"We're on it," Dianna replied. "I've put out an alert on Fyodorov. Suzie is heading over to his house now and I've got Neil going to the temp company. Any other ideas?"

"We could try the farm," Walker said. "Like I told you earlier, that's where the WWC reckon she was taken there before to work."

"Is that woman with you now? Can she hear me?"

Walker looked at Mary guiltily. "Yes, she's in the car. It was her phone that Kristi texted so…"

"All right. Now, Mrs Plunkett, I know all about your agency,

309

but I'm going to take the lead on this, do you understand?"

"Of course. I just want to find Kristi before anything happens to her."

"Then we have the same objective. Walker, you are temporarily unsuspended, but prepare yourself for one hell of a bollocking when this is all over."

"Noted," Walker replied and his ears turned red at the tips. "Do you think we should call Kristi?"

"No, if her phone rings it might alert whoever she's with that she's in contact with us. Hopefully we'll get the trace through soon then we can find her location. Now, bring me up to speed on this trafficking business."

Between herself and Walker they explained to Dianna everything they had learned about the people Mikala had been working for. In her turn, Dianna told them that she had been in touch with the Human Trafficking Unit since they had heard Mikala's story from Connie MacIver.

"Turns out that Fyodorov was already known to them. He used to live in Edinburgh in the nineties, and had links to international smuggling gangs at that time. When he moved over here he seemed to be keeping a lower profile, so they stopped watching him. But it looks like he started up again over in Invergryff. Maybe he thought a smaller town would keep him outside of police notice."

"It worked for long enough," Mary said. "If we're right about these connections, then he's been doing this for nearly two decades."

"I wouldn't assume anything," Dianna replied, a hint of disapproval in her voice. "We're going to get these people for Mikala, but we still don't have a link to Paul Crossly."

Mary was about to argue, but then she snapped her mouth shut. Now wasn't the time: they needed to focus on Kristi.

"Another interesting thing I learned from the Human Trafficking guys was the names of some of Fyodorov's known associates," Dianna continued. "These include Liam Beatson and Tam Brown. They've been involved in various schemes together over the years, but nothing we could get to prosecution."

"We'll get them this time," Walker said, with more confidence than Mary felt. These were career criminals, not just ordinary people who had made a mistake and committed a crime. For the first time since she had joined the WWC, Mary felt out of her depth.

The radio went silent for a few minutes. Walker was driving them out of town towards the farm, but there were roadworks all over the place and it seemed to Mary to be taking forever.

They were stuck at a red light when the radio beeped once more.

"We've found her from triangulating her phone. You were right. She's at the farmhouse."

Walker glanced at the sat nav. "We're only five minutes away."

"Don't even think about it. I'm heading there myself right now. We'll be there in twenty. When you get there, park out of sight and do not approach the suspects, understand?"

"Understand."

The radio crackled off again and Mary and Walker drove in silence for a few minutes.

"You're not really going to wait outside are you?" She asked finally, not able to keep quiet. "I mean, if they've got Kristi captured somewhere in the farmhouse, we can't just let them hurt her."

Walker pulled the car onto a verge and cut the engine. "We're going to do exactly what we're told. Look, I'll admit that you guys are very good at what you do. You find out things that the police would never be able to uncover. You're nice to people, and because they like you they tell you all their secrets. But this is my job now. These are really bad guys we're dealing with. You could get hurt or you could do something that jeopardises the investigation. We need to make sure these people go away for a very long time."

"I know. I'm just not willing to let Kristi get killed so that that can happen."

The police officer didn't look happy, but he opened the car door. "Let's just see how close we can get without being seen. From the look of the map, we're on the other side of the farm from the witch's cottage, so they might not be expecting us to come this way."

They were lucky that this side of the hill had some tree cover. Mary felt like she was in a James Bond movie, crouching low and following after Walker who was jogging over the uneven ground much faster than she was. Every few minutes she stopped to check her phone, but there were no more messages from Kristi.

After ten minutes scuttling through the trees, they came around a hill and were looking down at the farmhouse.

"Stay out of sight," Walker said, reaching for his radio.

"Dianna? We're in view of the farmhouse. There are four cars outside and a large van. I'm going to text you the number plates. One of them is an SUV, white, with –"

"Crap! That's Liz's car!"

"Hang on a second," Walker muted the radio. "Are you sure?"

"Yes. It's still got the dent in the front where... there was a little incident one time. Anyway, it doesn't matter. The point is, Liz is there, and probably Bernie too."

"Well isn't that just great," Walker replied. He got back on the radio to his boss to tell her that as well as multiple suspects, it looked like there were at least two civilians there.

Meanwhile, Mary was frantically texting her friends. She sent a group message to Bernie, Liz and Alice.

Are you at farmhouse? Is Kristi there?

No reply. Then Mary realised that her reception was showing

313

one measly bar.

"Damnit, there's barely any reception here. Kristi could be trying to contact us right now, but we wouldn't know."

Walker sighed. "Well, that's crap. Dianna says she's only five minutes away. What the hell are you doing?"

Mary was waving her phone in the air. "Trying to get reception."

"Did I not explain the whole 'try not to let them see us' thing?"

"Sorry. Hang on, I'm getting a message."

Just me, Alice and Liz. Having tea with farmer's wife. Trying to get her to talk about father. Fruit loaf clarted in butter. Why would Kristi be here? B.

"Bernie says it's only them in the farmhouse. No sign of Kristi."

Walker stared down at the building as if he was trying to use x-ray vision. "There's a barn just next door. It might make more sense for them to take her in there. Especially if they didn't want the wife to see."

"No windows in the barn," Mary said, hopping from one foot to the other. "I reckon we could run right down there without anyone seeing us."

"Okay. But we're not going in. We'll skirt around the back of the farmhouse so that we can get a view of the barn entrance.

That's as close as we're going to get."

Mary didn't answer because she had already started running down the hill. Or, more accurately, slipping down the hill as the Scottish weather had turned the path into a mudslide.

"Wait for me!" Walker yelled from somewhere behind her.

"I can't," Mary said desperately. It wasn't long before her feet slid out from under her and she was bouncing down the slope on her bottom. She could feel the mud splattering up the back of her coat, but she was mainly trying to keep going in the right direction. From the cursing behind her she could tell that Walker wasn't faring much better.

Eventually, the slope evened out so that she could get back on her feet and scurry around behind some scrubby bushes, out of sight of the barn and farmhouse. After a few moments, Walker joined her.

"I really hope that was just mud I stepped in," Walker grumbled, peering past her to look at the barn. "Let's go over to that hedge. We should get a better view from there."

Walker spoke a few words into his radio in a low tone, then beckoned Mary over to another bush.

"The door to the barn is ajar and the lights are on. I've checked the number plate of the van and it belongs to Fyodorov's cleaning business. I think that's where Kristi is."

"Then we need to get in there," Mary hissed back.

"What, you and your Swiss army knife keyring? They could

have weapons in there, and we're already outnumbered. Not to mention that you are not, in fact, a police officer."

Mary sniffed. She was quite proud of that keyring. It had a bottle opener as well as a screwdriver and a set of scissors. She was just about to say something nasty back to Walker when a group of people walked out of the barn.

There were three men and a woman. Mary had to press her hand over her mouth when she recognised Kristi. She was being held up by one of the men, a guy in a suit and heavy black boots. The other two men walked close behind them, one had a beard and had to be pushing seven feet tall. The bearded man was slightly younger than the others, closer to Mary's age while the other two might have been in their fifties. The third man was skinny and wiry with a very expensive-looking suit. Kristi stumbled as they walked and the man holding her arm pushed her roughly.

"Steady now," Walker said, his hand on her shoulder as if he knew she was going to charge at the men. "Dianna should be here any minute. Now, I want you to stay here. I'm going to go down and have a word with them. Whatever happens, don't you move from this spot."

"Are you crazy? Didn't you say they could have weapons?"

"Yes. But if I'm not mistaken that girl's already taken a hell of a beating. We're running out of time. Promise me you'll not move an inch."

"Okay," Mary said, feeling sick to her stomach. "But –"

316

Before she could say anything else, Walker was off. He walked towards the barn slowly, with his arms by his sides. Like any man out for a pleasant stroll.

The group from the barn stopped when they saw the police officer approaching them. For a moment, the skinny man moved one hand towards his pocket and Mary bit her lip so hard it drew blood. Then he dropped his arm with a shrug.

"My name is Police Constable Owen Walker," Mary heard him say, voice clear and strong. "Can I ask you all to put your hands where I can see them. I would like to have a word with Kristi Villi. Could she come over here, please?"

For a moment, no one moved. Then Kristi took a step forward. The men didn't stop her, and she managed to walk all the way over to stand next to Walker, hands clasped in front of her chest.

"All right. Now, I think we should all go into the farmhouse. My colleagues will be here shortly and we would like to talk to all of you."

The skinny man cleared his throat. "It seems to me," he said in a voice that only had the smallest hint of a Russian accent. "That with only one of you, and three of us, there's not much you could do to stop us from driving away."

"Not at all," Walker said, not moving a muscle. "But my colleagues will just pull you in for questioning at the station instead."

"Or maybe you have an accident," the big man said. "It's very

317

muddy today. You might just slip over. Farms are dangerous places, after all."

"We don't need that kind of talk, Mr Graham," Walker said calmly. Mary recognised the name and was surprised to learn that the man mountain was the farmer himself.

"Oh don't we? Let me tell you something –" Graham took a step towards Walker and Mary couldn't help but gasp. The police officer still didn't move away, but he gently pulled Kristi behind him so that she was shielded by his body.

Mary was frozen to the spot, but she knew she had to do something. She reached into her handbag for her keyring. Maybe the corkscrew attachment could…

At that moment three police cars screeched into the farmyard. Mary saw Walker's shoulders relax with relief.

The Inspector jumped out of the first car and jogged over to Walker.

"Everything okay, officer?" She asked, looking around at the men from the barn.

"Yes. I was just about to commence questioning. Perhaps we could get everyone into the farmhouse and out of the rain? And I think we should have a paramedic look at Kristi."

"I'm all right," the woman said softly.

Feeling like she would be allowed to move now, Mary emerged from the hedge. "It's okay, Kristi, these guys will look after you."

The other woman smiled in recognition, and Mary gave her a gentle hug. Kristi's lip was swollen and she had the beginning of a black eye.

Dianna walked over to them and gave Mary a nod. "Nice to meet you, Mrs Plunkett."

"It's Mary."

"Dianna. Let's get Kristi inside and get her examined." She turned to the quivering woman. "Do you think you're up to talking about what happened?"

Kristi glanced at the men who were being marched into the farmhouse by police officers in uniform.

"Yes. I would like to tell you all about it. If you will make sure that they stop doing these terrible things."

Dianna placed a hand on her shoulder. "After today, the whole lot of them are going to be going away for a long, long time. With your help."

Kristi smiled. "Then I will have a chat with you. And a cigarette please."

Chapter 54: Bernie

If Bernie had thought that the day might contain some pleasures, she had never imagined one as great as watching Kristi smoke a cigarette at the immaculate farmhouse table. Tiny flecks of ash were settling on the doilies that were scattered around the surfaces. Mrs Graham, banished to the kitchen to make tea, was going to have a fit.

"Now, I just want a quick word before the paramedic arrives," the young female Inspector said. Dianna, that was her name, and Bernie rather liked her. When the woman asked for something to be done, it was done straightaway, something Bernie very much approved of.

"What happened this morning, Kristi?"

"They came to the hotel. I had just started my shift, but Debbie from reception put out a call that I was to come back downstairs. If I had known I would have run away, but when I saw them there, what could I do? They still have my passport, all my papers… Anyway, I knew I was in trouble, but maybe I thought now was my time, just like Mikala. I got in their truck and they took me here. When I saw the barn I panicked, tried to run, and that is when the big man hit me."

"The farmer?"

"Yes. Then they took me into the barn. They wanted to know what I had told the police. Of course, I told them I had not spoken to the police. I did not say that I had spoken to the nice Mary woman," at this point she paused to give Mary a smile. "I did not want to get her in trouble too. But I think they knew anyway. They told me they were taking me to London tonight. For a new job. Well, I know the sort of jobs they have women like me do in London, but what could I say? I said I would go. Then they took me out of the barn and the very handsome policeman was waiting for me."

Dianna smiled. "Well done, Kristi. Now, the paramedic has just pulled up outside. I want you to go with Constable Rihanna Beattie here and she'll take you out to his car. Then I want you to stay with Rihanna until we're done with the men. Okay?"

"Okay," Kristi said, following the female constable outside.

"Suzie, will you get Walker to bring the men in here?"

Suzie, a Sergeant with black hair that looked like she straightened it, went out of the kitchen into the sitting room where the others were being kept.

A second later, the Russian named Fyodorov, Mr Graham the farmer and Tam Brown walked into the room, followed by Constable Walker.

"Kristi is going to testify about the human trafficking," Dianna said, her voice hard. "We'll get the others to talk too. I've just heard back from one of my Constables. They were in your house, Mr Fyodorov, with a warrant. Your maid was happy to let us in when we told her what we were looking for. Passports, dozens of them, hidden away in a drawer. Men and women. Now, it won't take us long to link those men to your building sites, Mr Brown. I expect the list of charges will be quite extensive."

If looks could kill then Dianna would be dead three times over.

"We'll wait and see what our lawyers have to say about that," Fyodorov replied.

"Indeed. And there is the other matter. The discovery of not one, but two bodies on your land, Mr Graham."

"Nothing to do with me," the big man grunted.

"Is that right?" Walker said, stepping out of the doorway. "I guess you could keep quiet like the others. I'm sure you'll be able to afford the most expensive lawyers, just like they will. And I bet they won't drop you in it as soon as they can."

You could almost see the thoughts collecting in Graham's mind.

"That lad that died, that was when the old farmer was alive. Nothing to do with me."

"Why don't you tell us what happened?"

Graham was sweating now. "Can I talk to you alone, for a minute?"

"Don't be an idiot," Tam Brown hissed at him.

Dianna smiled at them. "Why don't I take Mr Brown and Mr Fyodorov outside and give them a tour of our police van."

When the others had left, the farmer turned back to Walker.

"Like I said, I was just a labourer on the farm at the time. Mucking out, all the crap jobs. So I just had to do what I was told, right?"

"How did that body end up in your field, Mr Graham?"

"Tam Brown was meant to be fixing the roof on the barn, but between the old man and Tam, they were doing it on the cheap. They sent a bunch of lads over, including that Paul Dean. He was working on the barn roof with a couple of his friends. Well, we told them not to do the work off ladders, but of course they were young lads and they wanted to finish up early."

"First I heard was the other lad yelling. When Paul fell off the roof he landed on a pile of old farm parts. It made a hell of a mess. I'm not surprised you think he was killed, but it was an accident. It was the old man, my wife's father, he was the one that suggested we bury him. Put him in the field near the witch's cottage. I went along with it, but it wasn't my idea."

"And Mikala Nowak?"

"Don't know nothing about her. Fyodorov said he had to hide something up there in the field and I didn't ask what it was."

"How convenient," Walker said. "Let's get you to the van."

Bernie watched them go, then turned to the other members of her team

"I can see why you like him," she said to Mary, "that was a pretty sexy thing to watch."

323

Mary turned pink, but she didn't deny it.

"Now, where's the farmer's wife? I want a word with her."

On cue, Mrs Graham emerged from the utility room and sat down at the table.

"They've taken him away! What am I going to do?"

She flopped into a chair and started sobbing quietly.

"I didn't know about any of it," she wailed.

It had been a long day, and Bernie had had enough. "Well now, Nora, that's not going to wash is it?"

Mrs Graham peeked out from her hands. "What do you mean?"

"It's pretty clear that this has been going on in your family for generations."

"Not the… the stuff with the girls. My father, it was such a hard time for farmers, you wouldn't understand. We had been through BSE, foot and mouth… By the end of the nineties we were in danger of losing the farm."

"So he found some ways to supplement his income?" Liz asked.

"It was just low level smuggling. Cigarettes brought in from Europe, that sort of thing. They needed a place to switch the stuff between trucks, or sometimes to store contraband. So they used the cottage. It was perfect because if anyone complained about people being up there at night, they could

324

say it was weirdos obsessed with the witch. But my father just let them use the land, he didn't know what they were up to."

"Is that right," Bernie said. She almost admired the woman for the bare-faced lies, but it was time for the fibs to stop. "It's funny, you know, I was talking to Superintendent Marr the other day. His memory isn't quite what it was. It's bloody awful, in fact. But he said something to me that struck a chord. He kept saying: too many sheep. And of course, at first I thought he was barmy, not that we use that word in patient care anymore. But then I realised he was trying to tell me that something was very wrong up at the farm. I've had a look into your books, and for a farm this size, you barely have any staff wages. How do you manage that?"

"Um, well, I'm not sure. You would have to ask my husband."

"Come on now, let's not pretend that you're an idiot. I know that you do all the bookkeeping for the farm, so it's your responsibility."

Mrs Graham squirmed in her chair. "Well, perhaps we don't always put everyone through the books. Many of our workers prefer cash in hand payment."

Bernie leaned forward over the table. "But what I would like to know is: whose hands was this cash going into?"

The farmer's wife pressed her lips together, like she was afraid to say anything more. At that moment Dianna walked back into the kitchen.

"How's it going ladies?"

"Just fine," Bernie said, smiling at her. Yes, she really did like this Inspector. And she had never called the WWC harmless, which propelled her to the top of Bernie's list of favourite police officers.

"I was having a little chat with Mrs Graham. And I was thinking about poor Mikala's last meal. Could you remind us what it was, Inspector?"

The Inspector clicked on her tablet and brought up the pathologist's report. "We know she ate rye bread and fish. A taste of home, I suppose. But then there were other things in there too."

"Ah, that's right. And then I remembered your wonderful lemon cake. The one that won the baking category at the WI fair. With its special ingredient."

"Poppy seeds," Mrs Graham said, "but I don't know what…"

"Lemon zest and poppy seeds were found in Mikala's stomach," Dianna said, spelling it out for her. "She ate your cake just before she died. Now unless you want us to arrest you on suspicion of murder, perhaps you should tell us what happened to the woman."

The sobs started again, but in between them, Mrs Graham began to talk. "I just felt sorry for them. That's the truth. The ones that my husband brought them up to do some work on the farm. The year before it had all been men, and they coped well enough. Nearly a dozen of them, barely any spoke English. But that year they brought women too and… And those girls were so skinny, and so frightened… So I gave them some cake. They needed something to eat. I would smuggle it out to them wrapped in kitchen paper. But I swear, when they left here they were alive and well."

"And you never saw anything happen to Mikala? Come on, Nora. Your husband is going to prison for a long time. You don't want to join him, do you?"

"I think... that Tam Brown, he came up one day with his son."

"Billy?"

"Yes, that was his name. Anyway, they were checking on the girls and that Mikala, the one who... she was arguing with them. Telling them that they were being worked too hard. She even talked about going to the police! I don't know what she was thinking. The rest all knew to keep their heads down. Anyway, Tam says to Billy to take her out in the van and get her to 'calm down'. But then... it was dark when the van came back and Billy, he was in different clothes. And they asked my husband if they could bury something for them and I... I never asked what it was."

"But you knew?"

"No. Not for certain."

Dianna pulled her up by the arm. "All right, I think you should come with me. I'll have my Sergeant pick up Billy Brown. Ladies, thank you for your help."

Bernie watched her leave the room and shut the door behind her. She turned to Mary, Liz and Alice.

327

"Well now, wasn't that exciting? Who's for a gin?"

Epilogue: Bernie

It was late when Bernie got home from the farm and Ewan was stomping around the house, getting his bag ready for school. How all his school items seemed to disappear from one day to the next, Bernie wasn't sure. She never saw him take them out of his bag, and yet water bottle, homework, library book... all would disappear by the next day. It had to be some sort of children-specific magic.

"Where's your dad?" she called out.

"Shops," Ewan said. "Can I play computer games?"

"Sure, just till he gets home."

Bernie went out to the car to get the box she had left there. Her back was killing her. Mrs Graham's dining room chairs were the high backed wooden types that forced your spine straight in an unnatural way. She needed to do some serious stretching to get rid of the kinks.

Still, it was nothing compared to what poor Kristi had been through. When Bernie thought about those men with their schemes to keep people like her crushed beneath their feet, it made her want to spit.

Mind you, Bernie wasn't worried about Kristi in particular. That girl had survivor written all over her. And now that Fyodorov would soon be locked away for a very long time, she could sleep soundly for once. Bernie was already thinking she might be well-suited to work at the care home. They needed tough women like her, and she could live in the staff accommodation for reduced rates. Yes, that would sort that problem out quite nicely.

"Hello?" Finn called as he walked in the door.

Excellent, Bernie thought. Time to fix another problem.

When Finn saw Bernie standing in the kitchen, arms crossed and waiting for him to come home, he put down his workbag with a sigh.

"Are we about to have another row?" Finn said, his shoulders sagging. "Because honestly, Berns, I'm not sure I'm ready for one."

"No. Not today anyway."

"Really?"

"Do you know, in a lot of ways it's been a really crappy week," Bernie said, walking over to her husband and grabbing a tea towel. "Some of the lives that people have are so miserable… But it makes you realise that we don't have things too bad at home. Do we?"

Finn turned to face her. "I don't think so."

She craned her neck upwards and kissed his stubbly cheek. "Well then. I'm not going to say I won't keep trying to make things better. Because that's just not in my nature. But I'm going to try and stop viewing you as one of my projects. How does that sound?"

His lips quirked up at one corner. "That sounds pretty great."

"Right. I've got something to show you. Will you clear the table for me?"

"Sure."

It only took a few minutes for her to come back in and then Bernie put the small beer box down on the table.

"The thing is Finn, I'm still worried about the drinking. But maybe I have to let you sort it out yourself, not try and do it for you."

"Hang on, you want me to drink less, so you bought me a case of beer?" Finn laughed. "I mean, I'm liking the new Bernie but it feels like maybe you're taking it a little too far."

"Oh, this isn't beer," Bernie said, pointing to the box. "I just needed a box for something. Do you want to give Ewan a call? He's upstairs."

Finn gave her another quizzical look as he went to get his son. Bernie was starting to quite like being mysterious. It wasn't her usual manner, but maybe she should do it more often.

Ewan bounded down the stairs and ran into the room. His hair was getting too long and his skinny legs were poking out of the bottom of his trousers. Why did kids keep growing? It wasn't fair that every day they moved further away from the babies that you had brought into the world, breaking their mothers' hearts.

Well, that's the way it goes, Bernie thought, shaking off the moment of sentiment that was so unusual for her. Time for a new phase.

"Dad said there was a surprise."

"There is. But it's a surprise that comes with a few conditions. Mainly that you will be feeding it, and we will all be helping with the litter tray, because I do enough clean ups at work."

Ewan was bouncing up and down by now. He reached over and pulled open the box.

"A kitten!"

"She's from a family of criminals, so we're going to have to keep a close eye on her. The others went to an animal shelter, but I thought she might like it here. Oh, and her name is Witch. No arguments."

"I love her!" Ewan pulled the soft furry meowing thing into his neck and held it tight.

Finn's eyebrows were climbing off the top of his head. "That's an awfully furry goldfish."

"Well, she needed to be rescued," Bernie said, not adding her other thought which was 'maybe we do too'. She watched Finn scratch the kitten under its chin until it started to purr. But we might just be all right.

Afterword and Acknowledgements

Thanks for reading the latest set of adventures from everyone's favourite group of mums. I'm having an absolute blast writing these stories. Maybe because the setting and characters are not a million miles away from my own life in a sleepy town in Central Scotland. I do not own a superhero onesie, but if someone were to buy me one I would definitely wear it on the school run!

A brief note on witches. The town of Paisley – which I have called Invergryff in the book, so that no one sues me! – had several famous witch trials. You can find out all about them if you search online for the 'Paisley witch trials'. The one in 1697 was particularly gruesome with seven people killed as 'witches'. The real story, I'm afraid, is much more depressing than the fictional one I have used in this book. Difficult women, loud women and women who are not prepared to bow to authority have always existed in Scotland, and I like to think that the WWC are carrying on that proud tradition.

Thanks as ever to my family who put up with me hiding away with the laptop whenever I can. This time around I wrote a large section of the book in the 'Shut up and Write' sessions run by the very lovely Jackie, so extra thanks go to her.

To everyone who reads my books, you're a bunch of superstars! Cheers! If you want to continue reading this series then the third book in the Wronged Women's Co-operative series, *Romance is Dead*, is available to order now from Amazon.

Printed in Great Britain
by Amazon